# *CATAPULT*

*A Timetable of Rail, Sea, and Air Ways to Paradise*

## By Vladimír Páral

translated from the Czech and
critical introduction by William Harkins

CATBIRD PRESS * *A Garrigue Book*

Translation of *Katapult* © 1967 Vladimír Páral.

The translator acknowledges his indebtedness to the late Dr. Miroslav Renský, who helped him greatly in matters of contemporary colloquial language, slang, and technical jargon. The publisher acknowledges the help of Ellen McGoldrick in developing the concept of the bookmark.

Library of Congress Cataloging-in-Publication Data

Páral, Vladimír, 1932-
   Catapult: a timetable of rail, sea, and air ways
to paradise.

   Translation of: Katapult.
   "A Garrigue book."
   I. Title.
PG5039.26.A7K313 1989   891.8'635   88-34053
ISBN 0-945774-04-4

## Characters and Pronunciation

**JACEK JOST** *Yahts'-ek Yohsht* (hero, lives in Usti nad Labem *Oos'-tee nahd Lahb'-aim*, or Usti on the Elbe)
**Jaromir** *Yahrr'-oh-meer* (formal name)
**Jacinek** *Yahts'-ee-nek* (Lenka's special name for him)
**Jastrun** *Yahs'-trroon* (Hanicka's name for him)

**LENKA JOSTOVA** *Lain'-kah Yohsht'-oh-vah* (Jacek's wife)
**Lenunka** *Lain'-oon-kah* (Jacek's special name for her)

**LENICKA** *Lain'-each-kah* (Jacek and Lenka's daughter)

**TROST** *Trrohsht* (Jacek's across-the-way neighbor and alter ego)

**NADA HOUSKOVA** *Nah'-dah Hohs'-koh-vah* (Jacek's first lover, lives in Decin *Dyeh'-cheen*)
**Nadenka** *Nah'-dain-kah* (nickname)
**Nadezda** *Nah'-dehzh-dah* (nickname)
**Speranza** (an Italian word with same meaning as her name—hope—and name of Yugoslav hotel)

**VLASTA** *Vlahs'-tah* (Nada's friend)

**PETRIK HURT** *Payt'-rzheek Hort* (Jacek's boss)

**VERKA HURTOVA** *Vyairr'-kah Hort'-oh-vah* (Petrik's wife)

**VITENKA BALVIN** *Veet'-ain-kah Bahl'-veen* (Jacek's co-worker, originator of the Balvin experiment)
**Vitezslav** *Veet'-ehz-slahv* (his formal name)
**Vitak** *Veet'-ahk* (another nickname)

**MILADA BALVINOVA** *Meel'-ah-dah Bahl'-vee-noh-vah* (Vitenka's wife and Jacek's doctor)

**JAROMIR MESTEK** *Yahrr'-oh-meer Myehs'-tehk* (Jacek's across-the-hall neighbor)
**Jarda** *Yahrr'-dah* (nickname)

**ALOIS KLECANDA** *Ahl'-oh-ees Klets'-ahn-dah*
(Jacek's old co-worker who's now a rock
star; **Candy**)

**FRANTA DOCEKAL** *Frahn'-tah Doh'-check-ahl*
(Jacek's old co-worker who's now the boss
in Brno *Bare'-noh*, Czechoslovakia's second
largest city)

**BENEDIKT SMRCEK** *Behn'-eh-deekt Smairr'-check*
(Jacek's old co-worker who's now head of
the research institute in Brno)

**ANNA BROMOVA** *Ahn'-nah Brrohm'-oh-vah*
(Jacek's woman in Prague, scientist)
**Anci** *Ahn'-tsi* (nickname)

**HANICKA KOHOUTKOVA** *Hahn'-each-kah Koh-
hote'-koh-vah* (Jacek's woman in Pardubice
*Pahr'-doo-beets-ah*, teacher)

**LIDA ADALSKA** *Leed'-ah Ahd'-ahl-skah* (Jacek's
woman in Ceska Trebova *Chess'-kah
Trzhay'-boh-vah*, forest ranger's widow)

**JANICKA** *Yahn'-each-kah* and **ARNOSTEK** *Ahrn'-
oh-shtek* (Lida's children)

**TANICKA RAMBOUSKOVA** *Tahn'-each-kah Rahm-
bohs'-koh-vah* (Jacek's woman in Svitavy
*Sveet'-ah-vee*, bookkeeper and poet)

**MOJMIRA STRATILOVA** *Moy'-meer-ah Strraht'-ee-
loh-vah* (Jacek's woman in Brno, translator)
**Mojenda** *Moy'-ehn-dah* (nickname)

**TINA VLACHOVA** *Teen'-ah Vlak'-oh-vah* (Jacek's
woman in Bohosudov *Bow'-hoh-soo-dohv*,
barmaid; **Tina de Modigliani**)

**MR. STEFACEK** *Shtaif'-ah-check* (runs the storage
room at Jacek's plant)

**NORBERT HRADNIK** *Nohr'-bairt Hrrahd'-neek*
(Jacek's first attempt at replacing himself;
*nahradnik* means replacement)
**Nora** *Nor'-a* (nickname)

**TOMAS ROLL** *Toe'-mahsh Rrohl* (Jacek's second
attempt at replacing himself; **Tom**)

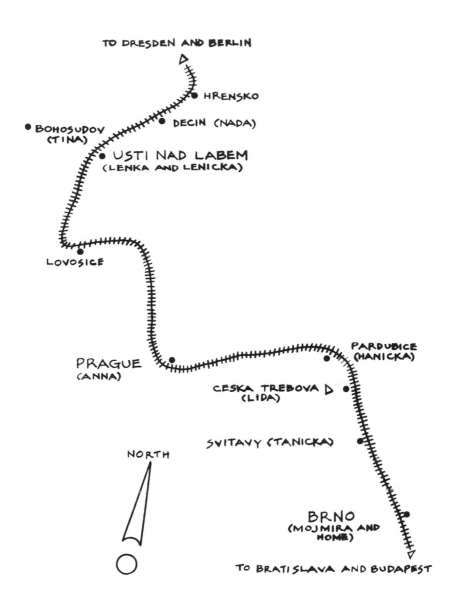

TO DRESDEN AND BERLIN

HRENSKO

DECIN (NADA)

BOHOSUDOV
(TINA)

USTI NAD LABEM
(LENKA AND LENICKA)

LOVOSICE

PARDUBICE
(HANICKA)

PRAGUE
(ANNA)

CESKA TREBOVA
(LIDA)

SVITAVY (TANICKA)

NORTH

BRNO
(MOJMIRA AND
HOME)

TO BRATISLAVA AND BUDAPEST

## JACEK'S TRAIN ROUTE

© 1989 James H. Kwalwasser

# INTRODUCTION

Vladimír Páral came to literature in the mid-1960s, a time of great promise and development in Czechoslovak culture, early in the Prague Spring that would end in 1968. It was a time when a whole generation of young Czech writers were reaching maturity: Milan Kundera, Josef Škvorecký, Ludvík Vaculík, and Ladislav Fuks. Páral's finest novel, *Catapult*, published in 1967, was greeted by both the critics and his fellow countrymen as a masterpiece, one in certain ways emblematic of the Prague Spring itself.

*Catapult* is a parodic exposé of Eastern European socialism, of wasted economic potential, of a lazy and self-indulgent managerial class to which the novel's hero belongs, and of indifference to Marxist ideology. But Jacek Jost, the book's central figure, is much more than just a "drop-out" from socialism. His literary roots go back to mythic figures such as Don Juan, the bored lover whose desires can never be sated, and Faust, the man of science whose thirst for knowledge and experience can never be slaked. Jacek, however, lacks the spiritual stamina of his two prototypes; it is this failure—a comic failure born of inadequacy—that makes him a true child of our century.

Jacek Jost is neurotic, a man who can conceive goals and quests without number yet cannot fulfill a single one. But Jacek the neurotic competes with another, a fantastic Jacek, a paragon of smoothness and competence, who gives the appearance of surmounting every difficulty without effort, often even against his own wishes. This latter quality makes him a picaresque hero and this story of a journey to nowhere and back and forth again, a picaresque novel. In the end, however, the delicate balance produced by Jacek's central conflict breaks down and the neurotic, not the prodigy of success, takes over.

Jacek is a hero comic in the extravagance of his dreams. Thus, he requires not one woman but seven (Don Juan) in addition to the wife he already possesses; not one career but another seven prospective ones (Faust). His madly comic flights of fantasy are inspired both by the gulf between his dreams and the dreariness of reality and by the gulf between his would-be abilities and the triviality of his real achievement.

*Catapult* is, in a unique way, identified with its single protagonist: its entire content is an extension of Jacek. Although the narrative persona is not Jacek himself, still he is never once absent, even for a moment, in the flux of the novel. The other characters are scarcely true characters— and this is deliberate on the author's part—they are extensions or reflections of the protagonist. His wife and child, called by variations of the same name (Lenka and Lenicka), are presented largely as incumbrances responding to Jacek's antics. His wife acquires a completely independent existence only toward the end of the novel, when she tells Jacek to leave. His two best friends at the office mirror opposite poles of his own fatal ambivalence in love: one lives harmoniously in a cunningly divided apartment which prevents him and his wife from ever meeting or speaking; the other enjoys an idyllic relationship but completely sacrifices his intellectual and even spiritual integrity to that idyll. Most clearly reflective is Jacek's alter ego in the apartment opposite his windows, who mimics his every action and speech, but in a parodic, vulgarized manner.

Behind Jacek's comic aspect there is pathos and even tragedy. He is a romantic dreamer who longs to exceed himself; this uncontrollable striving is his tragic flaw. He is a romantic—and so is Páral himself, no doubt—in spite of all his apparent cynicism. But our age is no time for romantic dreams, which now figure chiefly as symptoms of our neuroses. The disparity between these dreams and the material reality of our age is central both to the comedy and to the pathetic tragedy of *Catapult*.

The conflicts out of which Jacek Jost's personality is constructed are reflected in the novel's style and imagery. *Catapult* is a uniquely modern blend of disparate literary elements and devices: of satire and parody, of alternating black humor and delicate pathos, of imagery that turns away from the humanized metaphor that animates the world about us to a dehumanized system of images that surround the novel's hero with a whole world of bleak, despiritualized material objects. Most of all, the novel is characterized by irony of many kinds and shadings. Much of the irony derives from the quick shifts between black humor and pathos and between images that are living and human and those that are lifeless and materialistic.

The black humor in *Catapult* is typical of much of our century's literature, but as in Jacek's character, it is offset by a pathos often foreign to such works. Black humor depends in part on the release of taboos concerning sex, violence, disease, and death. It does not heed canons of taste—in *Catapult* one target is a dwarf—yet its purpose is not to ridicule the unfortunate, but to ridicule everything, as did Rabelais and Swift. Jacek's inane love affairs, his repeated efforts to get fired from his job and to get his wife to divorce him—these are the real targets of the author's black humor. What makes this novel unique is Páral's ability to shift rapidly back and forth between his black humor and the pathos of all his characters, so that they come to appear as opposite sides of the same coin.

The novel's style is equally original. The author experiments with the use of separate sentences connected by commas; this may take some getting used to, but it pays off, providing a fluid stylistic medium by which the author can make his rapid moves back and forth between humor and pathos. Páral's style is one of free association rather than logic, a style appropriate to his story of neurotically unfulfilled desire.

*Catapult* is characterized by pervasive irony, by a philosophical view of life and the world lacking in any commitment. Jacek is comic, in part, because he can conceive of self-dedication but cannot bring himself to make it. Irony is typical of much of modern Czech literature (we need mention only Jaroslav Hašek and Karel Čapek); in our day, Páral shares it—along with his sexual subject matter—with his contemporary Milan Kundera.

For nineteenth-century writers, the metaphor and, in particular, the animizing metaphor (e.g., Keats's Grecian urn) was a favored device. It seemed to endow inanimate matter with life and thus attested to the organic character of a universe animated by positive spiritual values. The twentieth century has gone another way, as the philosopher Ortega observed, toward the abstraction and dehumanization of living characters. Some modern writers (e.g., Joyce and Hemingway) have cultivated an imagery of inanimate objects; by doing so they fill the void of the world surrounding their characters, but give no illusion of life or spirituality to that void. Materialized images suggest our world of industrial technology, but even more than that, they displace spiritual images. Páral has gone very far along this road. His hero, who could exist equally in a communist or a capitalist society, dwells in a world of timetables, advertisements, and the contents of various apartments, offices, and refrigerators. As much as it is the story of Jacek Jost's comic futility, *Catapult* is also the story of the creature comforts and material toys with which twentieth-century humans try in vain to distract themselves.

# THE FIRST HALF OF THE GAME

*Not to dare is fatal.* —*René Crevel*

## Part I — Chances and Dreams — one

With its usual delay, Express No. 7 from Bucharest, Budapest, and Bratislava was just pulling into Platform One at Brno Main Station. It was Wednesday, April 1, and there was the usual confused rush of travelers who lacked reservations but were trying, as a matter of principle, to board the middle cars of the train, even though these cars were intended (likewise as a matter of principle) for those who had reservations. In the midst of this rush Jacek Jost (33/5'9", oval face, brown eyes and hair, no special markings) took in the always unexpected sequence of numbers on the middle cars until, sufficiently amused, he finally caught sight of his own car, No. 52, hooked up between Nos. 34 and 38.

In compartment E two unpleasant surprises: First, Jacek's seat, No. 63, the second from the window, was just being occupied. Second, and even more unpleasant, its occupant was that loathsome Trost, like himself from Usti, in fact, from the apartment house opposite his own. In the window seats, Nos. 61 and 62, two women stopped talking, as if scandalized by the two newcomers actually venturing to sit down—in an otherwise empty compartment—right next to them.

"I've got No. 63," Jacek Jost declared, his ticket in his hand as a justification to the women and a challenge to Trost. "I'd like to sleep and I don't want to be awakened by somebody trying to claim my seat."

"So just sit across from me on No. 64," said Trost. "It's mine. No one'll disturb you."

Jacek shrugged his shoulders, carefully placed his large black satchel with brass fittings into the baggage net above seat No. 64, hung up his raincoat, and the train pulled quietly out.

"Twenty-two minutes late," said Jacek.

"We'll have to look lively in Prague to catch the 4:45 to Berlin," said Trost.

"I've never missed it yet."

"You make the trip often, don't you?"

"Quite often. And you?"

"Not so much. The weather's nice, isn't it?"

"It is now."

The women by the window began to talk again, they leaned so close together they hid the view, the compartment was overheated as always, and already Trost had taken shelter behind his dangling coat. Jacek spread his own out in front of him and, in the darkness behind it, he closed his eyes.

It was getting harder and harder to reach an agreement with the higher-ups in Brno, three days of exhausting negotiations and we still won't get any ethyl acetate this year either—better not to think about next year—where have the days gone when you could save something from your travel expenses, Lenka will be pleased with the Dutch cocoa, we can sprinkle it onto our hot cereal, milk dishes sit best in a stomach queasy from six hours on a train, that's what Lenka says, they're the cheapest too and they take the least time to make, if I don't miss the 4:45 to Berlin we'll find Lenicka still awake and the water pistol will amuse her, but for how long?—ten minutes, no more, the blow-up squirrel would have been better, of course she'll spray the water pistol all over the place, when she gets fed up with it we'll build a playhouse out of mattresses and then an obstacle course, but that might be too much jumping around and she won't feel like going to sleep and she'll keep calling from her crib, our sweet little beastie, Daddy come and tell the story again about the enchanted prince, you know, the one who had to ride the train through eleven black tunnels until the golden aurochs taught him which one the princess had been walled up in—aurochs, my sweetie, you're saying auwochs, yes, it's a great big hairy cow, this big.

"...and when Joe told her about the bidet, she bought him a bathroom brush."

"What?!"

"A pink one, made of nylon—" the women next to the window were making each other laugh and to Jacek's distaste his neighbor pushed her hip farther and farther across the border between seats Nos. 62 and 64 and into Jacek's territory. From the expropriated No. 63 across from him, Trost's pig-like snoring could already be heard.

So far, first class was still authorized for trips over 150 miles, the seats had armrests, and you could still save something out of your travel expenses, but what would it be like five years from now or ten? Lenka probably had some Dutch cocoa left from last time, Lenicka would probably have taken a dislike to the squirrel too, if only the girl were older, no, if only she could be a two-year-old again, how she's growing, soon she'd be coming home just to eat and sleep as if to a hotel, what would it be like ten years from now or twenty?—only on a train it seemed could a man get at Gauguin's WHERE DO WE COME FROM—WHO ARE WE—WHERE ARE WE GOING, once Lenka and I used to go through it almost every evening, but surprisingly the answer was always harder to come by—better not to think about some things—but Lenka's a good wife and we do have a lovely, clever little girl, we both earn good salaries and we've got a first-category apartment, the first year each of us in different dorms, the second year each of us in different rooms, the third year at last a little attic room together, but Lenicka had already come by then, entire nights by her bed, carrying water from the cellar and heating it on our hotplate in the sink, if only it could be settled all at once, the fourth year a comfortable co-op at last, but another down payment to make, a loan to negotiate, furniture, rugs, a refrigerator, television, enough cares, if only it could be settled all at once, the best five years of your life suddenly gone, not very happy years at that, but now it was all settled and fulfilled, even that final wish, THE SEA—

—crowded on his right by his intrusive neighbor, baked from below by the uncontrollable heating system, tossed rhythmically and knocked on the head by the stiff imitation leather of the backrest, struck on his left by the draft from the door, and tickled on his face by his hanging coat, to the snoring of Trost, the slob, and the prattle of those women by the window, in the tension of the ever narrowing time span linking the delay of the Bucharest express to the departure of the 4:45 to Berlin—

—alone with the sun in a blue, blue hemisphere, outside time, naked, free, only desire, will, body, sex—all that makes a man a man—blissful, Jacek was swimming toward Africa.

Half an hour must have passed already, hurriedly he turned, quickly back toward the shark net, he tore his trunks free of the wire (Lenka had knitted them from an old sweater), swiftly back toward the rocky coast of Istria with its dozens of tiny terraced beaches separated by rocks, up to ours, the highest above the sea (and farthest from it), swiftly into his red beach chair alongside Lenka's red one: "You're always going off someplace," Lenka says, and Lenicka wants him to play bunny-rabbit.

From the highest section of the tiered beaches of our hotel, the Residence, beach is visible to the south as far as the narrow channel on the horizon—a day's sail off in that direction is the coast of Africa. Right behind Lenicka's little white knees, one level down, lies Mrs. Vanda (she kisses in the elevator), she keeps drawing into her mouth and then letting slide from her lips a huge, dark red, swollen oval grape. On the tiny concrete square by the Pension Jeannette the freckled artist presses his chin to his knees (he had offered to paint Jacek in the nude). On the rocks at the Belvedere handsome Yugoslav boys open black mussels with a knife, swallowing the contents and rubbing the remnants on their chests and thighs. On the tiny beach of the Hotel Palma lies that magnificent black-haired Frenchwoman (before breakfast she too went swimming without a suit) and with her palm she slowly wipes her moist, shiny hip. High up on a cliff, gazing toward the horizon, sits the bearded Swedish pastor (he keeps trying, in his absolutely incomprehensible language, to attract Jacek's attention to something or the other). Lenicka's gone to sleep in our arms. "Where are you flying off to again?" Lenka asks.

Jacek swam southward toward the freckled painter at the Jeannette and got a piece of chocolate from him, but what were Lenka and Lenicka up to—in order to see, Jacek made his way through the bushes up to the rail of the promenade—everything's fine, Lenicka's asleep and Lenka's talking to the Mareceks, Jacek swam off toward the beach of the Hotel Palma, the dark Frenchwoman spoke fluent German with a husky laugh, suddenly he noticed her watch, he jumped up and ran out to the rail of the promenade—everything's fine, Lenka's talking to the Janeceks and Lenicka's still asleep, and Jacek swam around the beach of the Stefanie (where they make those fried sardines) and the Kvarner (where the redhead is lying) toward the cliff with the bearded Swede, his childish, trusting blue eyes and the warmth of his unknown language, suddenly Jacek started and now he was leaping over the stones and up to the rail of the promenade—everything's fine, Lenicka's splashing with some kids and Lenka's talking to the Mareceks again, and greedily Jacek swam along the beaches of the Naiad, the Speranza, and the Miramar toward the south, suddenly, in order to see, he struck out toward the east—his empty beach chair between Lenka and Lenicka, a red trapezoid like an insistent outcry, and nervously Jacek turned and swam quickly back, through the warm green waves that washed the welcoming stairs of the Miramar, the Speranza, the Naiad, the Kvarner, the Stefanie, the Palma, the Jeannette, and the Belvedere, to the stairs of our Residence and straight back to his place, with Lenicka's head propped against his shoulder and Lenka's fingers clasping his wrist.

Mrs. Vanda had struck up a conversation with the bald butcher from Chomutov, and before long her leg was lying across his fat hip. The freckled artist swam over, on the rocks of the Belvedere he handed out chocolate and soon he was posing a skinny boy. The waiter from Lovosice lay down near the dark Frenchwoman and soon they were kissing under her parasol. The Swede on his cliff was saying something to two children and pointing to something on the horizon.

But on the stones at the Kvarner the redhead is still alone, she's lying on her stomach again and untying the back of her top, floating onto the warm green waves are rafts with girls stretched out on them as if for lovemaking, on the bottom of a metal boat a half-naked sunbrowned blonde, and calling out along the shore toward the south a strip of radiant sea stretching all the way to Africa.

"Time to go," says Lenka, never with anyone else but her, she had a touch of sunstroke, Lenicka throws up on a rock, she must have a fever, it's all from the sun, my darlings, tomorrow we'll spend a nice long day at home and pull down the blinds, with a smile Lenka clasps one handle of our enormous bag full of towels, bits of uneaten food, rags, baby oil, talcum powder, and a thermos, she takes the other handle in one hand and the exhausted Lenicka by the other, "Time to go—" the strip calls to the south, never with anyone else but Lenka, an open road of green waves all the way to Africa, at an unheard command the higher-ups take their positions on the cliffs by their mine throwers, singing Lenka sprinkles Dutch cocoa on the sidewalk in front of the apartment house, this week we're on clean-up duty, and from bed, with a screech, Lenicka fires a pistol full of burning ethyl acetate, the blow-up squirrel would definitely have been better, pull off Lenka's constraining shorts and swim with a frantic crawl from the stairs of the Residence, warm green waves to the stairs of the Belvedere, the Jeannette, the Palma, the Stefanie, the Kvarner, the Naiad, the Speranza, and the Miramar, to Africa—

Thrown violently out of his seat, Jacek Jost flew across the space between the odd and even numbers and fell full force between Trost and his neighbor by the window, with a screech Trost pushed him roughly away with his shoulders and his knee, with his arms thrown out in desperation Jacek grabbed the shoulders and breasts of woman No. 61, fell kneeling to the floor, his face in her lap, and then, when he set his right cheek on her thigh and looked up, he saw the girl smile and saw his pale hands on her black sweater. The train had stopped.

No. 61 might be a bit over twenty, blonde and good-looking. Jacek's neighbor, No. 62, some ten years older, grinned and rubbed her stomach, which had struck against the small folding table under the window. It might have been the emergency brake—we lost something or ran over someone. The express soon started up again, on the main east-west line a train passes every four minutes and each delay must be held to a minimum. Irritably Trost hid himself behind his coat and Jacek spread his own out over himself, the theater last night had cut the irreducible minimum of eight hours of sleep to a mere six, they still hadn't reached Ceska Trebova and we always sleep as far as Pardubice.

No. 61 happened to be pretty and not at all disagreeable, how charmingly she had protested that he didn't need to apologize, Trost had bleated something or other and crawled behind his coat, she was wonderfully well developed, Lenka should start exercising again.

"...and then I didn't take it from him."

"But Nada, really..." the voices of the women next to the window.

No. 61 is called Nada, Nadenka, Nadezda, she's really very pretty, we hadn't even noticed whether she was wearing a ring or not—of course she is. We've still got half a tin of Dutch cocoa at home and a whole one, too, we bought it when the general director came on board, what things he said then and what he's doing now.

"I haven't met a man like that so far," Nada said.

"How about Jirka?" said No. 62.

"He was very kind, pleasant, and an absolute zero."

"You used to talk differently about him."

To put that water pistol into Lenicka's hand would mean an immediate call to workmen to repaint the apartment, that's what happens when you buy gifts on the way to the station, what year was it when we interrupted a trip so that Lenka could have an umbrella right from Ceska Trebova, a local specialty, then she left it behind somewhere.

"I wanted to believe it... I would again, too, but about someone quite different...," Nada was saying.

"Do I know him?" No. 62 whispered.

"I don't yet myself. I may run an ad for him: 'Slim 23-year-old blonde with her own apartment looking for a man. Key word: MAN!'"

"Speak softer, or those two..."

"They're snoring again. Do you think I'd catch anybody that way?"

"Sure, mostly with that bit about—her own apartment—"

"I'd take him home for the night, for a test run in bed!"

"Don't shout so, Nada..."

"Seriously, if he liked me... But if I didn't like him, then I wouldn't chase after him so. You know, the way you did that time with Milan Renc."

"Yeah, that was almost it..."

"But it was wonderful, wasn't it—" Nada said loudly. No. 62 only giggled.

Lenka is on her way home from work now, she hasn't forgotten the milk for his hot cereal or to stop by the school for Lenicka, this week we have clean-up duty in front of the apartment house, it's a lot for her, Lenka is a good wife, and if he's going to make up those two lost hours—eight hours a day keeps neurosis away—he has to go to sleep at once, counting off the order of the hotels on the Adriatic: the Residence, the Belvedere, the Jeannette, the Palma, the Stefanie, the Kvarner, the Naiad, the Speranza, Speranza in Italian is the same as Nadezda in Russian: *hope*—

"It was wonderful, wasn't it—" Nada said loudly, she almost shouted it, she's beautiful, with a smile she had bent over the face in her lap and had tolerated the touch of his pale hands on her black sweater, she almost called it out as a challenge, yet he stayed under his coat, he ought to ask her where she was going...

"I stay under this coat," Trost's beery voice suddenly thundered forth, "and I don't even know where we're at. Was that Ceska Trebova? Good God! We're really making time, aren't we? And where are you ladies going?" He was trying to make an ordinary and quite vulgar pickup.

Jacek was suffocating under his wrinkled old raincoat, why didn't we take the new iridescent, it was just like that pot-bellied Trost, the idiot, the way he sticks his muzzle out of the window every day, with our windows right opposite, 100% visibility, as soon as he gets home he strips to his shorts and sniffs in the pantry and the oven (the two apartments are identical in their lay-out and appliances), gobbles down a roll fresh from the pan and follows it with a slug of beer straight from the bottle, then he brings a pillow to the windowsill and starts to gape from window to window until TV comes on for the evening, then he gapes at that, pisses and snores, and that's the entire zoological profile of Mr. Trost.

"You don't say, really? Then we're practically from the same town!" Trost was master of the whole compartment, he wooed and pursued the poor women by the window, Nada of course soon stopped answering, but No. 62— "why don't you call me Vlasta"—had taken the bait and was giggling more and more, Trost wooed and pursued her, and Vlasta, already taking up half of Jacek's No. 64, twisted her backside, Jacek, rubbed and shoved by her hip, was rhythmically gyrated, slapped on the back of his head by the backrest, rubbed and burned by the artificial leather underneath him, annoyed to the point of pain, and then tenacious efforts to fall asleep, to sleep, back to the warm green waves and the stairs of the Belvedere, the Jeannette, the Palma, the dark Frenchwoman stroking her moist hip under the parasol, the Stefanie, the redhead is descending the stairs of the Kvarner and raising her hands to the shoulder straps of her bathing suit, at the Naiad the girls are rocking, stretched out on their rafts for love-making, and floating out from the Speranza is the sun-browned blonde spread out in the bottom of a glass-bottomed boat, Speranza is Italian for hope and the Miramar is already a dream, Mrs. Vanda kisses the huge swollen red grape, and on the rocks the handsome Yugoslav boys with their smeared chests and thighs, a seaside amphitheater of clamoring naked spectators and the rhythmic beat of the waves insistently pressing against the rocky cliffs.

Jacek Jost pushed his raincoat aside and stood up, stared at Nada's inquisitive face, and went out of the compartment into the corridor, where, badly shaken, he staggered and clutched at doors and walls, locked himself in the little room at the end of the car, and looked at himself in a quivering mirror.

Lenka is on her way to school now to pick up Lenicka, in her bag a bottle of milk and on her palm calluses from that eternal bag, even on Sundays she doesn't get enough sleep, she never leaves anything undone, a wife a hundred times better than we deserve, so loving, never with anyone else but You, and she's a perfect mother to our clever, pretty little daughter, on Sunday morning we take her into bed with us and after dinner we go to the zoo. It's true, in our civilized age the life of the father of a family doesn't offer many experiences that are particularly exciting, in fact it doesn't offer any, but then, instead of that—but five years of married life without the least shadow of infidelity aren't worth spoiling now for the sake of that.

Jacek Jost washed his hands and face with cold water and went back along the vibrating corridor to compartment E, he stopped short in the door—Trost was lounging on his seat, No. 64, alongside Vlasta on No. 62, he had even dared to take his coat with him and to hang Jacek's opposite, above No. 63, "Excuse me," he blared with his hand already resting on the shoulder of his new neighbor, Vlasta, "but in Brno you said that you wanted to sit there and anyway that's the seat you've got a reservation for!"

"We worked it out this way," Vlasta giggled.

"Of course, only if you don't mind...," Nada added sweetly from the window, Jacek shrugged his shoulders and settled down very close to her on the green imitation leather seat. To be thrown out of your seat three times is obviously good luck on purpose, all the more when all flights have the same direction—when catapulted, you've nothing left to do but fly.

The train sped smoothly over the remaining hundred kilometers, no one else would come in now. Opposite the mutual and constantly growing admiration of Trost and his already "darling" Vlasta, Jacek and Nada sat together on the settee designated for them, Nos. 61/63, and in the rocking rhythm of the warm green waves of the imitation leather seats they swam out toward the sun. The eleventh and final tunnel came just before Prague. Even before, Trost was panting heavily on darling Vlasta's neck, the golden aurochs had already fulfilled its fairy-tale destiny, and in the glowing eleventh tunnel the happy prince, no longer bewitched, kissed his laughing princess, now at last released from her wall.

When they got out at Prague the other two disappeared and Jacek and Nada easily caught the 4:45 to Berlin.

"All my life I've never gone any farther on this train...," Jacek whispered as it pulled into the station at

Usti, and Nada grinned. Fine nylon lines twitched painfully on his wrists and knuckles and around his body the sensation of tugging straps with felt lining, like a horse's harness, and the train pulled silently out along the shore and down the springtime river, but then Decin is only twenty minutes from Usti and the next stop on the express.

## 1 — two

A feeling of vertigo on leaving the Decin station, the stream of passengers quickly poured into buses and streetcars, all going by the shortest route to their Lenickas and Lenkas.... Jacek Jost was suddenly left alone on the empty sidewalk with Nada.

"What sort of program do you propose, my lord?" she said.

"Dinner with champagne, dancing, two cognacs, and the longest way home to your place...."

"Mmm, I've read that somewhere. How about a swim?"

"Now?!—"

"Why not? I don't have hot water at home and the baths are only a few steps away. But we've got to hurry."

"But I don't have any trunks and...."

"Leave it to me."

At the baths they seemed to be closing up already, but Nada arranged it easily, laughing she picked out a large pair of canvas trunks for Jacek. As for Nada, she had her own, the warm glow of golden brown flesh in stiff white nylon, "How do you like me?"

"Very much," said Jacek, self-consciously drawing together the excess folds of his bathing suit, "you don't have to give your opinion of me."

"Except for the fabric you'll do," laughed Nada, she pushed Jacek off the edge into the pool, he swallowed a lot of chlorinated water and as soon as, sputtering, he could see again, he grabbed her legs and pulled her in with him, they dunked and pushed each other around, she taught him the proper way to dunk and he taught her how to make a star, and in the glow of floodlights they swam together in the warm green waves.

"And now for dinner!" Nada cried on the dark, now silent street illuminated by the flickering light of TV sets in the homes they passed.

"What's the best you've got here?"

"The Grand, I suppose, but you can't smoke there and there's a lot of unnecessary hoity-toity. I know a great place, even if it is third-category."

"Whatever you want, but..."

Nada's third-category didn't look too bad, no more than ten tables with checkered tablecloths, bright landscapes in thick frames of stained wood, and above a copper counter a stag's antlers with fourteen points, Jacek sat with his back to it, wondering whether the place would have champagne.

"Boy am I thirsty," said Nada. "Two beers, Mrs. Vasata."

On the menu the only stand-out was some sort of Belgrade cutlet, otherwise just some humdrum dishes, and chocolate semolina pudding.

"Two Belgrades—" was the order Jacek gave to Mrs. Vasata.

"Jacek, I'd much rather have the Slovak sausage... Don't you like it?"

"Very much, but after all..."

"So, two helpings of the Slovak with bacon... And a heap of peppers in oil!"

It was a wonderful meal, the beer was smooth and light, in the corner by the cast-iron stove sat a group of boys singing along with a guitar, their heads turned up toward the low ceiling:

> Blue mists on the lake
> Vanished like far-off desire

"You're wonderful, Nada, really, and I..."

"Oh shush! Listen to those kids instead."

"No, really... I only wanted to tell you... You know, I'm really not used to... There are circumstances which... which..."

"You want to tell me something about yourself?"

"Look, Nada, I don't have to tell you that again, surely... that... well... Of course..."

"Will you tell me without lying?"

"No, Nada, look, I only thought..."

"You won't. Then don't tell me anything."

*Oo, oo, the song of the Manitou.*

"You're really such a special girl, that really..."

"Oh shush with that, I know when it's April Fools' Day. Tell me something more about Opatije in Yugoslavia. I may go there this summer."

"You tell something, you do it better..."

Jacek ran his fingers along the ridge of his palm and, really quite involuntarily, he looked at his watch: 10:07. Lenicka has been asleep for a long time with her thumb in her mouth, while Lenka, worried, has put the bottle of milk away in the refrigerator and she'll stay up until the arrival of the night express, he ran his fingers along his wrist and looked straight into Nada's expectant face.

*There the redskins stood,*
*Wild horses flew,*
*Oo, oo, the song of the Manitou.*

Suddenly he stood up. "Let's go—" Nada was already on her feet.

The restless grey of TV screens flickered out onto the dark, empty street. "I live over there," Nada pointed, it was hardly more than a hundred and fifty feet, and: "We really stuffed ourselves, didn't we?" she said and then she stopped. She wasn't making it any too easy, what could you talk about in the course of a hundred and fifty feet, and to kiss in front of a restaurant—

"Isn't there a park over there?" Jacek pointed at random.

"In the opposite direction. Why?"

"Nothing, I just thought... You know what, we could have those two cognacs now."

"I'd prefer Egyptian brandy... But that's awfully expensive."

"So let's have six of them!"

"OK, Jacek dear, I've already come to realize that you're the rich señor from Rio, but—"

"From Usti nad Labem, and I make 1,800 a month, but—"

"—but what do you really care for most? No pretending."

"Nadenka..."

"You see. So come on."

Quickly they traversed those hundred and fifty feet in silence, and inside the lobby Jacek tried to at least pinch her, but Nada pushed him away: "I smell sauerkraut, phooey—" she laughed silently and pushed him toward the stairs.

Nada's room wasn't very big, a couple of pieces of light-colored furniture and a cream-colored kitchen chair, a large bay window looking out on the harbor and beside it a drafting board on a stand. Jacek played with the jointed weight-beam, tried out the T square, and managed to recall a couple of drafting techniques.

"You look as if you knew something about that sort of thing."

"At vocational school, I majored in construction."

"I thought you said you were a chemist."

"After high school I wanted to study architecture, but that was the year they transferred the school away from Brno, so I had to take chemistry instead."

"Which they'd just transferred to Brno."

"No, they had it there already."

"Then why didn't you start with it?"

"Because I wanted to be an architect."

"But why didn't you become one?"

"Because they transferred the... For whom does everything turn out the way he wants..."

"For me, for instance. And how did you get from Brno to Usti?"

"Laugh if you must, but they transferred me."

"That *is* something to laugh about. And what, really, do you do in the chemical factory there?"

"It's actually a textile factory, you know, for cotton... But I don't have much to do with it, I travel mostly, we've got our main office in Brno."

"That's not something to laugh about—Jacek, Jacek, you can build houses and concoct explosives, and you're a traveling man in textiles..."

"You know, I didn't have things easy and there was the pressure of circumstances which... which..."

"...which kept pushing you somewhere, or there was a vacuum which kept sucking you somewhere— Like me from the train here."

"But I really did want to come with you..."

"So you only had to wait for the pushing and the sucking to work."

"Life often..."

"Don't be silly."

OK, sure, laugh all you want, but why really?, and then in an animated tone carry on your pre-rutting conversation, why really?, still Jacek stubbornly tried to talk, but in silence Nada looked into his eyes with ever growing derision, finally she yawned without even putting her hand over her mouth and heedlessly interrupted Jacek in the middle of a sentence: "I think you're sleepy too."

"Nadenka..."

"Wouldn't you rather get some sleep... before...?"

Jacek got up quickly and embraced her, no easy task since she remained seated in her chair, still he tried, he hunched his shoulders, bent over, attempted different approaches, knelt down, sat on the floor for a moment and then got up again, just cooperate a little for God's sake—

how could one cope with the difference in height, bend one leg at the knee and spread the other far out in back, that might do it, a little more, on the edge of the sole and now on tiptoe—but everything suddenly gave way with thunder and the crack of wood, everything landed on the floor, and behind the overturned chair Nada was shrieking with laughter.

He'd had it up to here with these April Fools' jokes, he stepped over the legs and seat of the chair and as if storming a trench he attacked Nada from behind, an open cuff link cut him on the wrist, let's hope it isn't an artery, on, on with hand-to-hand combat, but hell, how does that unbutton, how many years has it been now since Lenka and I, Nada was laughing again, they make them without buttons now, sure, but how actually do you—

"I haven't got the stamina for this," Nada finally said, she got up and went to the door. "But never fear, I'll be back."

Sure, enough reasons to clear out for good, but when wasted opportunities pain you so much later on, and then comes depression and neurosis—if it weren't for fear of them, we'd have long ago been at home in bed—what a joy to find out how little is left when forbidden pleasures have been realized and then we'll be glad to get home again, sure, meanwhile why not make the bed, and Jacek, as he was accustomed to do at home, spread out the sheet, tucked it in neatly at the corners and smoothed it out, put the plumped-up pillow at the head, and carefully turned down the blanket, then he stood a while admiring his decorating efforts. "You don't want coffee now, do you?" came from behind the door, "No," he called, as was expected of him, he turned off the light, undressed, and climbed into bed.

Nada came back in a black bathrobe and turned the light back on. "I knew you wanted to sleep."

"No, no I..."

"So let's get some sleep, all right? Do you have anything against making love in the morning?"

"OK, Nadenka, I've come to realize that you're the un-conventional girl in a Swedish movie, but—"

"Look at him, he's almost turned into a man in that bed. OK, I'll take charge now. Get up—oh, I see..." Nada took a nightgown out of a drawer, threw it to Jacek, and again went out, while Jacek put on the gown Nada pushed the other kitchen chair into the room, placed the two chairs opposite each other, sat down on one of them and said, "Come and sit across from me."

"Still the Swedish film?"

"No, it's a game now."

"What's it called?"

"Train. Let's start at the beginning. Come here."

Before Jacek could sit down, she'd brought in his coat over her arm, a hammer under her arm, and a nail in her teeth, she pounded the nail into the wall above his chair and sat down on her own across from him.

"Your ticket says seat No. 63, but you're sitting in No. 64," she said. "You'd like to sleep and you don't want to be awakened by somebody trying to claim your seat. Oo—oo—we're pulling out of Brno, ch-ch-ch-ch—so far you've never missed the 4:45 to Berlin. By six you'll be home in Usti. Now throw the coat over yourself and close your eyes. Ch-ch-ch-ch—"

Jacek shrugged his shoulders under the open-work nightgown with a bow, still April Fools', but at least the masquerade would come to an end now, he hung his wrinkled old raincoat on the nail and threw it over him-self, why didn't we take the new iridescent, he closed his eyes.

"Repeat after me: ch-ch-ch-ch," Nada whispered.

"Ch-ch-ch-ch," Jacek whispered diligently under his coat.

"Ch-ch-ch—I liked you the first time I saw you—ch-ch-ch-ch—I wanted to get to know you—ch-ch-ch-ch—you didn't pay any attention to me—ch-ch-ch-ch—so I'll wait until you get a little sleep—ch-ch—repeat after me: ch-ch."

"Ch-ch-ch-ch."

"Ch-ch-ch-ch—now you've been sleeping for an hour—
ch-ch-ch-ch—if you'd only go to the dining car to eat—
ch-ch-ch-ch—but what to do with that stupid Vlasta—ch-
ch-ch-ch—let's wait till Trebova and by then we'll think
of something—ch-ch. And here we are at last, bang—
smash! The trains crash and Jacek is flying toward me—"

Nada stamped her foot, Jacek jumped up from his chair
and came to rest on Nada, then he grasped her shoulders
and breasts, fell kneeling to the floor, his face in her lap,
and then, when he set his right cheek on her thigh and
looked up, he saw the girl smile and saw his pale hands
on her black bathrobe.

"Dear Jacek...," Nada said tenderly and with warm
hands she pressed his hands to her, the magic of the
eleventh tunnel returned and quickly grew.

"I like you, Nadenka..."

"Don't tell lies and go back and sit down again. Crawl
under your coat, sleep some more and repeat after me: ch-
ch-ch-ch."

"Ch-ch—but I didn't go to sleep after that—ch-ch-ch-
ch."

"Ch-ch—I'm glad of that—ch-ch—but what were you
doing behind that coat—ch-ch-ch-ch."

"I was thinking of you—ch-ch-ch-ch—I was remember-
ing what you looked like—ch-ch-ch-ch—I was longing for
you—"

"And you didn't even open your eyes, my sleepy
man—ch-ch-ch-ch—I always wanted a man like you—ch-
ch-ch-ch—slim 23-year-old blonde looking for a man—"

"Ch-ch—number sixty one is called Nada, Nadezda—
ch-ch-ch-ch."

"I never knew a man like you—ch-ch-ch-ch—I always
wanted to have one—ch-ch-ch-ch."

"Ch-ch-ch-ch—the Residence, the Belvedere, the Jeannette, the Palma, the Stefanie, the Kvarner, the Naiad, the
Speranza, and Speranza is the same as Nadezda! Nada, I
love you—"

"Don't tell lies, you've hardly known me two hours and of that you slept a hundred minutes—ch-ch-ch-ch—and it'll be wonderful—"

"Ch-ch-ch-ch—with you on the warm green waves—ch-ch-ch-ch—kissing you under a parasol—"

"It'll be wonderful—"

"Your moist hip lying on a raft ready for love-making—"

"I want you, Jacek, so much—"

"Stretched out in a glass-bottomed boat, a swollen red grape, well-smeared boys on the rocks, and the roar of the amphitheater—"

"So much—Terribly much!—" Nada screamed, her arms around his neck, pick her up, she isn't laughing anymore, and carry her a couple of steps.

With the sun on his face, at the sound of a siren from the harbor, Jacek slowly awoke and still half asleep he turned toward Nada, lightly placed her hand over his shoulder, and tenderly let his hand run over her other one, that's the way it's done, and the tousled Nada wriggled, turned over, and finally sat up, she rubbed her eyes with her fists and then an enormous yawn, which is always contagious, Jacek too opened his mouth like a hippo.

"But you're still asleep," laughed Nada and she yawned again. "It doesn't matter, I am too." And she rapped Jacek across the knuckles.

"Do you have anything against making love in the morning?" he quoted her with a grin.

"OK, Jacek, I've already come to realize that you're an athletic boy. But how about stretching a bit first? And then a cold shower!"

She went to open the window, in the current of fresh air the two gymnasts stood opposite one another by the drafting table, "Follow my lead," she commanded. Jacek made a few timid movements and stood with his arms modestly crossed on his chest. "I used to do exercises every day by the window, but then—"

"Then they transferred the window on you!" Nada burst out as she did a remarkable toestand.

"Lenka—she's a girl I used to know, you see, she always made fun of me... And in my new apartment, a prefab, it would wake up the neighbors and their children..."

"You, my boy, are so considerate, not to mention house-broken, and then there's that act of yours—" Nada opined as she did a push-up, and Jacek, feverishly recalling his military exercises, stubbornly kept up his efforts. Two people can get under a shower, Lenka is too modest, only cold water in the morning gives you that feeling of the world at your feet, and how many lost mornings have there been now without it...

"What can I make for breakfast?" asked Jacek.

"What do you eat for breakfast?" asked Nada.

"Cookies and instant coffee."

"You like that?"

"Not so much, but... There just isn't any time."

"I always make time for breakfast."

"OK. So what have you got?"

"Kippers, honey, bitter chocolate, pickled mushrooms, and—cookies!"

"How about some of those pickled mushrooms."

"All right. But you know what I'd really like? Imagine hot tripe soup with sharp pepper, two crackling fresh rolls with poppy seeds..."

"And herring with onions..."

"So let's go."

At Nada's third category they had everything, even the herring, Jacek's favorite dish.

"Then why didn't you order it last night?" Nada said in surprise.

"I didn't consider it a suitable prelude to... You know, the onions..."

"That's just what I expected you to say. But at home you could have it every day."

"There's no time in the morning..."

"You could buy a whole can."

"I hadn't thought of that."

"And so for years you've been eating cookies and instant coffee."

"Sometimes a person— But you're right. I'll buy a can."

Outside it was a magnificent morning. "It's a magnificent morning," said Jacek and: "How about an outing somewhere...," he suggested timidly.

"I'd go, but even Swedish girls have to work sometimes. You know that drawing I have on the board, I've got to finish it by Friday."

"So go finish it, I'll disappear..."

"So disappear if you want to. Am I keeping you on a leash?"

"No, I mean I wouldn't bother you if I could only..."

"Then don't disappear if you don't want to! It's clear that you'll bother me, but if you want to—or don't want to—good God, who can tell, forchristssakegoodgoddamncarambahombredediosshimmelherrgott!"

"You're *recht*. I love you."

The sun was drawing golden trapezoids in the room overlooking the harbor, Jacek looked over Nada's shoulder, she stuck out her tongue and flashed her hand back and forth, she rolled up her tracing paper and sat down to her calculations. "What are you up to, fella?"

"I could figure it out for you on a slide rule..."

"No, you're too good at that. Wait—" and Nada stretched a clean sheet of tracing paper out on the board, explained what he had to do, and sat down at her papers again. "Now, not a peep out of you for an hour."

Jacek took off his coat, rolled up his sleeves, and took his position at the board, he lit a cigarette, crushed it, and went to wash his hands, he lit a cigarette and took his position at the board, he crushed it and went to the john, he took his position at the board, went to wash his hands, took his position at the board, and excitedly began his assignment, my God, fifteen years, fifteen years vanished like a cloud, Jacek executed Nada's simple assignment, we're eighteen again, the September heat beats down on the asphalt roof and outside there's the buzz of a bench saw, underneath the draft of a sewage project the secret sketch of a new opera house for Brno, on the back of a motorcycle to a chalet set in a bend of our "Forest Freeway," the strong scent of felled pines in the noon heat and the wild whirling of a brook tumbling down "Jost Falls," on the warm grass tanned, half-naked men and the barefoot Libunka carrying a jug of goat's milk over the warm grass, guitars by the fire, songs reaching up to the dark treetops, Libunka in the grass that warms one far into the night, and in the morning diamonds on the grass sparkling by the sparkling river, what had happened then and why had what he'd wanted so much not come to pass, was there anything—

"When are you going home?" asked Nada, standing behind him. "For God's sake don't ask me if I want you to stay or I don't want you not to stay, I mean, whether I don't want you to stay or I want you not to stay..."

—and was it only an oppressive fiction, the erosion and the landslides of the last few years, here, all of a sudden, he felt himself again, happy, why should he ever leave here, was it the last day that was the dream or was it the last fifteen years—

## I — three

"How do you get long distance here? And what's your phone number?" said Jacek, lifting the receiver up from its cradle with his right hand and reading the time off the wrist of his left: 9:14.

"Long distance is ten, my number is four-two-one-eight. But what..."

"Four-two-one-eight," Jacek said into the receiver, "I'm calling Brno three-nine-two-oh-three, urgent, snap to it, pronto!—Thanks, I'll wait."

"I've got a brother in Brno, he's a great guy," he explained to Nada before the call came through. "Brother? Hi! Yep, it's me. Look, let's keep this brief, it's costing me a bundle. Send two telegrams right away, both express—instead of wasting talk, let me dictate—Cottex, Usti. Ethyl acetate still uncertain, stop. Will make unofficial efforts. Jost. And the other to Lenka at home: Arrive Friday usual train, no later—no, that's not necessary. Arrive Friday usual train. Jacek. What's that? No... Who knows... Maybe we'll be spending more time together and maybe... Seriously, send them off right away and some time we'll celebrate with a few Egyptians... It's a kind of brandy, you yokel. So long."

"You seem awfully concerned about that Lenka you used to know," Nada said softly. "Not that I give a damn about her. But perhaps you didn't realize in your sudden rush that today's only Thursday?"

"I've decided to stay one more day."

"Oh—he's decided. My lord grants me twenty-four hours."

"It's for me, too. One more day."

"OK. So let's start out with a good dinner. I'll let this work go for now, darling Jacek, and—"

"I don't like to see you do that, Nadenka."

"But it's already two o'clock."

"Why couldn't we dine at five, at nine in the morning, or just after midnight?"

"Whew!" Nada exclaimed, she shook her head and went back to her calculations. Not for long, however; Jacek picked her up along with her chair, carried her off, and simply dumped her, "Wow!" she cried, "your technique's sure improving!"

At exactly a quarter to five Jacek decided that a quarter to five was the ideal time for dinner, Nada repeated that it would be a bore to go three times in twenty-four hours to the same restaurant, even if it was wonderful and so close to home, in bed in unison they gulped down kippers, honey, and bitter chocolate, and for dessert Nada ate cookies while Jacek had pickled mushrooms, without a word of discussion they both got up at almost the same moment and met by the window, they both dressed quickly and went out into the springtime streets of Decin, walking along the harbor and seeing a boat they boarded it and, for four crowns, sailed all the way to the last stop on the excursion steamer Moravia, to Hrensko.

From the harbor jetty, on a concrete ramp, they climbed up to the highway, "I won't check the return time," Jacek said as he passed the timetable for boats and buses.

"The last bus leaves at nine-thirty," Nada informed him.

To the left, below the railing, the Elbe rolled on toward the rum and banana docks of the Hanseatic city of Hamburg and on, now salty, past the dunes and sands of Cuxhaven and under the piles of Alte Liebe out to the sea toward Helgoland and Sylt, all that from his school reader, and to the right, over the highway, twigs and bushes still naked and dark-brown but snow-strewn with tips, kernels, tendrils, and wicks of bursting green.

The red-and-white barrier of the border station reached across the highway, and Jacek went right up to it. "Don't go over there," Lenka once said, "Why not?" "They'll want to see our IDs." "Well, haven't we got them?" "But what do you want to see there?" "I just want to..." "Let's go back to the bus!" Jacek shoved his foot as far as he could under the barrier, its tip out into the wide world, of course that other country was actually still some distance away, but even so... "Have you got a cramp in your leg?" Nada asked.

Alone in the twilight they walked through the canyon of the River Kamenice to the caves, galleries, and tunnels of the fanciful Duke Leopold Valley, in summer an endless procession made its way there, "Resorts are always better out of season," said Nada. "That's just what I expected you to say," Jacek parroted her and they had a tussle on the little bridge over the rapids.

"I'd like—" said Nada looking at the menu of the Elbe Chalet.

"Today I'm doing the ordering," said Jacek and the champagne dinner suited him just fine. "Well, I suppose," Nada remarked, "you haven't spent very much on me."

"But," she warned him ten minutes before nine-thirty, as Jacek came back to the table, "that bus at half-past nine is really our last chance, to call a taxi from Decin would hardly be of any..."

The bus was already waiting on the embankment, Jacek lit a cigarette and smoked with relish, "Put it out!" "No hurry." "But the door's closing—" "I don't feel like putting it out!" Jacek took Nada by the shoulders and, as if uncertain, the bus started off.

"OK, so what now?"

"Leave it to me," he parroted. "Look how the water sparkles..."

"There's ten miles of that sparkle back to Decin."

"No more than eight."

"They might have a vacant room at the Chalet..."

"Resorts are always better out of season."

"But they close at ten."

"So we'll knock."

"They'll sure be glad to see us!"

Shortly after ten Jacek knocked at the door of the Elbe Chalet, "Good evening," the manager said politely and he went away without another word. Jacek went straight upstairs, on the stairway he took a key out of his pocket, unlocked the door, and walked through the room to the balcony.

"Hmmm...," said Nada, she sat down in a huge old-fashioned easy chair and when, after a long time, Jacek returned she said amiably, "So what game are we going to play tonight?"

"We've had nothing but games lately."

"OK," she said, she grasped the carved lion heads on the easy chair and locked her legs around its machinelathed legs. "This old antique is a good deal heavier than my kitchen chair, so you'd better try to remember your simple machines: pulley, lever, screw, inclined plane... I've taken your breath away, huh?"

"I no longer wish to ask what you care for most. And no pretending."

Nada was silent, she gradually relaxed her comedian's grip on the shedding easy chair as hands slowly slid along her arms and up to her shoulders, "Jacek darling...," she whispered.

"Let's start again from the beginning. Come here."

He reached for her and slowly clasped her hands, she slowly slowly rose toward him from her jester's throne until she was standing beside him, "Jacek—" she said and her voice broke into sobbing.

The next morning, now almost with expertise, Jacek led the exercise drill, more military in character than Nada's had been, then a cold shower, two quarts of milk, and the commuters' bus back to Decin.

"And what if I handed it in on Saturday," said Nada as slap-dash she finished her calculations. "Though last time the boss was hinting..."

"So do you want to hand it in today or don't you?"

"And if it were up to you?"

"I've copped out many times in my life, but I've always handed work in on time."

"So long," said Nada, thrusting her papers into her bag. "I'll come back as soon as I can."

Slowly Jacek walked back and forth through the room and involuntarily he began to pace it off, about 175 sq. ft., the tiny foyer with a john and an improvised shower in the corner, in the room itself a daybed with a small chest for bed linen, a two-section wardrobe, a table, the drafting table, a bookcase, a little radio, and two kitchen chairs, no more than 5,000 crowns' worth in all, but everything that's needed to live, just what we had then, it seemed so little, but how much of that original state was left now with all the growth, today we've got over 500 sq.

ft., pile carpets, a refrigerator, a TV, the sequence would further dictate a car, then a cottage—all of it well-furnished with cares and more crowded than this poor 175 sq. ft., with Nadezda we could have lived here the entire time, with her one would like to live here forever—

Jacek walked back and forth through the room, the morning sun lowered its golden trapezoids from the wall into the room itself, he shook his head and grinned grotesquely, it was a tragicomedy to contemplate one's own life-story, one's *curriculum vitae*, as a gradual growth of the fiction from which the *vita* had evaporated with time and all that was left was the *curriculum* and its transcription, was it a horrible delusion or simply a pile of facts, the sun had reached the floor and Jacek looked out the window toward the harbor, on their ramps cranes were reloading from rail cars to barges and from barges to rail cars, the sinking of the loaded boats to the cargo line and the rising of the unloaded ones above the water's surface, until, completely full or completely empty, they are untied and given permission to sail off, and so on again from the beginning.

"You gave me the right advice," Nada said in the doorway, "Things very nearly went bust. Do you advise that we go to dinner now or later?"

"Later. If we do it this way," said Jacek kissing her and unbuttoning his shirt, "we can save ourselves a trip back here after dinner."

"After dinner you plan to go— When's the very latest we can eat?" and Jacek and Nada, wildly and tenderly, out loud and in silence, while the sun made its trip across the floor to the opposite wall, cruelly and with laughter, almost to the point of fainting.

"I couldn't make it to the station," Nada whispered, not getting up, "hardly even to the restaurant across the street... You've matured immensely here with me, but you must have had some talent... Buried for years..."

"Thursday, April 2, just after nine," said Jacek, tying his tie at the window, "is when my re-excavation began."

"Come soon—"

Cross the ends, he could move here, make a loop, and make a fresh start with Nada, pull the other end through the loop, have a second family and a second life, tighten it, or a second fiction, and pull it tight around his neck. That was how it had been with Lenka at the beginning, that's the way things always begin...

"I love you, Nadezda..."

The sun had already climbed the wall and left the room, but it was making its way through other rooms, a single human life and a single fiction are definitely too few... perhaps even two... Nadezda is Speranza, of course, but the Miramar is no more than a dream now and beyond it the call of the strip leading to the south, the open path of green waves shining toward Africa, into the twilight of other rooms, for thirty-three plus fifteen is only forty-eight—

"It's almost terrifying to look at you when you grin in the mirror like that...," Nada said, but there was no more time, Jacek received one more kiss on the forehead, she crammed some tattered architecture textbooks into his black satchel, and the train pulled out of Decin precisely at 5:29, right on schedule.

On the bank of the Elbe, back upstream along the springtime river, on the green waves of the warm imitation leather, how curiously those two girls looked us over when we came into the compartment, and with what meaningful affability the one on the left returned our greeting, but how elegantly too we made our entrance, how fluently we put our satchel into the baggage net, trains are full of women and how many more times will we set out, and we won't sleep now either, an electron fired out of orbit has so many chances, so many possibilities—hell, the satchel!

Awkwardly Jacek pulled down his large black traveling satchel with brass fittings and hastily searched through its numerous compartments and pockets to see where Nada had crammed the architecture books, Lenka unpacked his dirty clothes and what would she have said about those textbooks signed Nadezda Houskova, Jacek hid the books among some official papers and up went the satchel fluently as before, why should he be a draftsman in some construction cooperative when he had a degree in chemical engineering and business experience from numerous deals and trips, hurray for trips when we've got a brother who's such a great guy—

With growing excitement Jacek went out into the corridor and leaned against the frame of an open window. "When are you coming home again?" his brother had asked on the telephone, and by "home" he'd meant Brno, "Maybe we'll be spending more time together and maybe—" we were on the verge of saying "permanently," as if with sudden conviction, but I've always insisted to Lenka that we're permanently settled in Usti and that's why Lenka's been planting apple trees, we've got a first-category apartment there, we both have well-paid jobs, of course mine's not so good, but then it's convenient and peaceful, but how quickly such self-conviction can arise, in a second even, but that could only mean—as if in horror Jacek pressed his hands to his throat, to pierce a dam can be the same as to break it and what else might we learn about ourselves—this time truly in horror Jacek pressed his hands to his throat, a good thing that Usti is only twenty minutes from Decin and the first stop on the express.

## I — four

A feeling of vertigo on alighting at our own Usti station, but which station is really ours now—with his large traveling satchel Jacek tottered along the platform in the stream of those getting off, from a fairy-tale pop-up book back to the daily paper and, in his throat, anxiety, new streams getting off newly arrived trains from Most, Uporiny, and Lovosice, all hurrying home to their Lenickas and Lenkas; my darlings, it was only sunstroke, we'll stay at home now as we should and pull down the blinds, Lenka's a good wife and we have a clever, pretty little daughter, but Daddy can't come just yet, my sweet, until his train comes out of its eleven tunnels, that's for Mommy's sake, you see, so she won't cry if people tell her Daddy came home today on a strange, bad train.

Jacek tottered along the platform and in the gathering dusk he raised his watch to his eyes every so often, the 4:45 to Berlin was late today, God forbid that anything should have happened to it—the platforms emptied quickly, Jacek dragged his satchel from the platform down the steps and up the steps onto the platform, WHERE DO WE COME FROM—WHO ARE WE—WHERE ARE WE GOING, but I live here with my wife and we have a child, a hundred times better than I deserve, my love, I have soiled you... Jacek with his satchel on the steps, going up and going down.

"Express from Prague, to Decin, Dresden, and Berlin, arriving on Platform Two—" the loudspeakers sounded, Jacek ran up the steps to Platform Two, the train was already thundering in with its usual insignificant delay, and already the crowd was streaming out of its cars, Jacek in its midst, quickly out of the station and home by the shortest route, Jacek in the middle of the current streaming quickly into buses and streetcars, all by the shortest route, Jacek too, to his Lenicka and Lenka on streetcar No. 5 to Vseborice.

To reach our part of the housing development you ride to the end of the line, today after the next-to-the-last stop there's only one person left, on the rear platform, Jacek entered the car from the front, it's a man, two daddies coming home from the 4:45 to Berlin, Jacek hurried to the rear platform, but in the doorway he stopped suddenly—the man leaning on the brake was Trost.

"Hey, this is a coincidence, isn't it—" Trost bellowed, under his chin a band-aid big as a large coin, "—it's a good thing we caught the Berlin express in Prague, isn't it?"

"It sure is, that's right. I've never missed it yet."

"You make the trip often, don't you?"

"...Quite often. But you do too, I see."

"Oh, no, not at all. The weather's nice, isn't it?"

"It is now."

At the corner the daddies separated and Jacek hurried past the children's playground, the carefully swept sidewalk was still damp from having been sprinkled, this week we have clean-up duty in front of the apartment house, and Jacek raced up the stairs, on his door a nameplate JAROMIR JOST, ENGINEER, I live here, and already as the door opens Lenicka calls, "Daddy—" and Lenka comes to greet him with a smile.

"Daddy—" our darling cries with her chin on the brass pole of the net that surrounds her crib, down at once with the net and his rough chin against her sweet little tummy, Lenicka cries out with pleasure, nothing's so sweet to kiss as our little one, "Daddy gwab me—" cries our pretty little girl, take her in his arms and swing her.

"Daddy don't go way—"

"I'm just going to give Mommy a kiss."

"Daddy come back again—"

"You know I'll come back right away."

"Daddy tell stowies—"

"You know he will!"

Lenka had already taken a bottle of milk out of the refrigerator, it was warming up, and already she was up to her elbows in our traveling satchel, the official papers she leaves untouched, only bothering with the dirty clothes, "Look what I brought you— "  "That's wonderful, you're very kind and thanks—but you forgot that white plush again, didn't you—"

"Like breathing, but I won't next time, you can count on it... And Daddy forgot his little darling too—"

"Daddy din't fwoget—"

"You know he didn't, and look what he brought you," show our little one what this strange thing's for, Lenicka went into ecstasy over the water pistol and again the net came down, trampling her nightshirt underfoot she staggered through the kitchen and covered the walls with water, "Putting that thing in her hand," said Lenka, "means an immediate call to workmen to repaint the apartment," but after all, it's only water, my love.

On kitchen chairs Jacek and Lenka sat across from one another and, in unison, gulped down hot cereal sprinkled with cocoa, "And why actually did you come back two days late?"

"But Daddy must tell stowies—" Lenicka called from her crib.

"Once again Chema made up its mind it wouldn't raise the OMZ's balance-sheet allotment over the limit for the second quarter, and KZZCHT wouldn't approve the last quarter's drop in material, whereupon our PZO—"

"Just a minute, I have to go and put the key back in the cellar..." said Lenka and she was back again soon, "...well, so—"

"Well, so I got home two days late. And what's new with you?"

"The OS inspectors are asking again for periodic reports on all MS- and TK-data measured against the plan norms, while USMP insists—"

"Daddy tell stowies—"

"Just a minute, please let me go and take care of her— So which story shall we tell, my darling?"

"The sad pwince!"

"Once upon a time there was a prince and he was very sad..."

"...becwause he had to wide the twain so much..."

"...and his little girl at home made yum-yum so little that Mommy got angry..."

"...Thwough many many bwack tunnels..."

"...and since the prince wanted to have a strong, pretty little girl..."

"...he always wode that twain and cwied and the pwincess cwied too, because the tunnel had no wight..."

"...light, darling. Light. And so the prince kept riding on the train and because it was dark he didn't see the princess..."

"...and out of the woods cwop-cwop-cwop came the auwochs..."

"...aurochs, darling, you're saying auwochs—aurrochs..."

"...and he was all gold, a cow this big with a gweat big meen..."

"Mane, maaane. A buffalo..."

"...and the auwochs said, pwince, here is your dear pwincess and don't cwy, and the pwince went boom! And it wasn't dark anymore in the tunnel and the pwincess gave the pwince a gweat gweat big kiss like this—"

"—a great great big one like this. And now beddie-bye, darling."

"But Daddy don't go way—" and he had to stay with her till she fell asleep with her thumb in her mouth, he felt the chafing of the tepid nylon on his wrists and the warming felt of the harness around his entire body.

Clean all his shoes in the foyer and take a hot bath, "You're not going to bed yet, Lenka?"

"How can I, it's Friday!"

"Can I help with anything?"

"Just go to bed, you've had enough with your trip."

"That's true. OK then, beddie-bye now."

Every day the morning theme song of motorcycles tuning up and the rattle of Lenka's alarmclock, Lenka turns it off and goes to get Lenicka dressed, but Lenicka doesn't want to get up, tears, objects falling and cries.

"Daddy cwome today?"

"But he came back last night."

"Daddy din't come!"

"But you have the pistol he gave you—you think you just dreamed that, don't you? Hop into your pants!"

"Daddy put on pants!"

"Shh—Daddy's still beddie-bye, we mustn't wake him..."

"...we mustn't wake him...," Lenicka whispered and screamed, "I want to see Daddy!" and Jacek crawled out of bed, my darlings, and still half asleep he staggered in to help pull on Lenicka's tights and to kiss Lenka, Lenicka sprayed his side with her pistol and Lenka was very nervous, he climbed back into bed to get some more sleep, another fifty minutes, and he was asleep before the two of them had left.

The roar of trucks starting up and then stomping on the ceiling always preceded the rattle of Jacek's alarmclock, Jacek raised the clock face toward his eyes, another eighteen minutes, and he turned over onto his other side, think of something pleasant, suddenly he got up, dumbfounded, and walked to the door to the balcony—it wasn't a dream, it had actually occurred—and now he was naked, upstairs they were stomping around, a sprightly army drill, over there across the river Speranza was exercising too, only now did the alarmclock ring, in the tub, to his surprise, he could take a fine shower, after a cold shower the world is at your feet.

The kitchen floor was strewn with all sorts of things, in a mug on the sideboard the instant coffee was already mixed (all you add is hot water) and three ceramic crackers, why this dieting all the time, and already Jacek was locking the apartment door, but then he unlocked it again, went back to the kitchen, and flushed the coffee mix down the drain—but in cold water it didn't go down too easily.

"...it really was out of the question. And so I made an effort to arrange it through friends," Jacek slowly told the deputy director of Cottex, he was happy, stuffed with tripe soup, herring, and a stein of beer, and pleasantly surprised by his own suddenly deep and serious tone of voice. "As you no doubt are aware, I studied engineering in Brno and my classmates there represent a significant..."

"Of course I'm aware of that and I'm very glad that, at last...," the deputy said with zeal, "you've finally hit on the proper technique, today unfortunately one can't do without it and..."

"However, there's no ethyl acetate."

"One couldn't expect it, but we would be very grateful if next time... Do you understand... If you could keep it up..."

"These things are difficult to arrange, of course, and I wouldn't want to press too hard..."

"Of course, I abide by what you're saying, obviously... If you would only keep trying... By the way, I'm reviewing the quarterly bonuses, in your case there must have been an oversight and..."

"That hundred crowns really did bug me. If only—"

"...I've already approved it, you'll get four hundred and ten crowns in all, we were saving the increase for Danek, but now— Besides, I intend to propose to the director that he give you the top pay in your grade."

"Top pay, but that's really terribly— Really, it comes just at the right time. After all these years—"

"The director will certainly okay it if I ask him. Cigarette?"

"Thanks— No, I don't like filters."

"Actually, I just smoke filters... Well, and so on Wednesday you should go to see KZZCHT..."

"I'd prefer to go on Tuesday."

Jacek leaped through the ridged mud of the courtyard toward the wooden annex to the technical division, whistling the March from *Aïda*, four hundred plus two hundred a month extra, trips to Brno at his own whim, why not stop off somewhere in the forest on the other side of the dam, or even at Pernstejn Castle, we haven't been to Telc yet or to Bratislava—

In Jacek's office the chief colorist Petrik Hurt and the technician Vitenka Balvin were already waiting—shouts, laughter, and some new anecdotes from Brno, Petrik signed a red issue slip for the 300 grams of Saturday's absolute alcohol and Vitenka diluted it expertly: sixty-forty would hit the spot just before dinner, and on Saturday we always get a bit plastered.

When they finally got on Jacek's nerves he kicked them out, it's strange to imagine that Petrik's actually our boss, and Jacek sat down to his typewriter to make his travel report: 3/30-4/1, shit! and a new sheet of paper, 3/30-4/3. I continued my earlier efforts at the main office in Brno..., suddenly he felt again the oppressive sensation of those long corridors in that grey palace, the uneasy backward glances and the whispered reports, "The general director is ready to throw him to the prosecutor... The whole place is to be disbanded immediately... They're hanging that sixteen million around his neck... Hartung broke him sooner than anyone could have expected...," the anxiety and agitation, here one didn't turn one's superiors out the door, Vitenka and I would have fought for a hint of a smile from Petrik, how happy we'd been when they'd had us transferred—

Quickly Jacek finished his report, filed it, and breathed a sigh, he reached for the newspaper and read it through from A to Z, then the arts review, and after lunch a short novel, he opened Armand Lanoux's *When the Ebb Tide Comes* to where the bookmark was:

> *Apple trees rose from the dense grass,*
> *wringing their twisted, crippled twigs. The*
> *sap wept. Jacques slept with his face buried*
> *in the hay. They had fallen from exhaus-*
> *tion... Abel looked at his watch... Three*
> *hours passed. They had come from the other*
> *village, from the one near the coast, the lit-*
> *tle valley, the fortified farmhouse, the sleep-*
> *ing bridge, and the yellowish brook. From*
> *the south roared the sound of war, indif-*

*ferent to them. The sea was no longer in
view... With an effort they tried to move
their feet. Each boot weighed at least fifty
pounds. Jacques took off his boots. When he
put them back on, they would hurt him.*

At 1:59 P.M. Jacek banged Lanoux shut, got up, and
stretched, this year summer would be magnificent, those
four hundred and ten crowns for current expenses and
those two hundred extra regularly for his secret hoard—
again, suddenly, that feeling of horror he'd felt in the corridor of the Decin train, when would he first touch our
secret hoard, for what had it been established, and Good
God, how awfully soon—2:00, the siren screamed, and he
was literally dragged outside by a long-conditioned
reflex.

"Suppose we go have a swim."

"Now?!"—Lenka and Grandma shocked.

"Why not? Better than rooting around in the ashes of
this apartment house."

"Wherever did you get that idea from? And where
would we go?"

"There won't be much hot water today anywhere, we
can take the streetcar to the baths. My little darling, want
to swimmie?"

"I want swimmie!"

"Well, go along, then, Good Heavens," Grandma said,
"I can take care of things!" "I have to iron," Lenka said.
"But it's nothing for me, I can do it..." "You didn't come
to visit for that..." "But I like to..." "How many times
have I told you, Mama..."

"I want swimmie!"

"Come along with us, Lenka. Remember how you used
to... Come on."

"I'd like to... But I've got to iron."

"Lenunka..."

"So go on, then, but be home by five!"

In the glow of floodlights reflecting off the warm green
waves, Lenicka shouted for joy and Jacek laughed, twelve

minutes till closing, he could still do two laps, but how could he leave the little one alone even for a second, seven minutes left, at least one lap, "I want a wow-wypop—" at least five strokes of freestyle, "I want a wowwypop!" just two minutes left, "Daddy'll buy one, but his darling can wait a bit..." "Daddy don't go way—" she squealed and grabbed him by the leg, but just then someone came by with an orange rubber ducky and Lenicka was off after it, he had to catch her and she squealed that she didn't want her Daddy, desperately she tried to escape toward the duck, but the blow-up bird had already been thrown into the deep end and a bunch of laughing girls was jumping after it, Jacek picked Lenicka up in his arms and with his body he warmed her already chilled little body, with her fists his daughter struck her daddy on the face, once again her desire was left unsatisfied, because of one another we don't get what we want, away at once from that golden fairy-tale bird and the sparkling naiads in the green waves around it, we must go to the streetcar, back home to the Residence.

A familiar figure in a green windbreaker with a hood strode nimbly along the broad roadway—their neighbor Mr. Mestek was going to the mountains, tapping his carved stick disdainfully on the concrete.

"I'd like to go somewhere where there's lots of grass," said Jacek glancing out at him from the kitchen window. "My little darling, will you come with Daddy? And you, Lenka?"

"His little darling" definitely wanted to go with Grandma to the movies, Lenka had to make dinner.

"So go alone, at least you won't be in the way."

The development on Sunday morning—featherbeds hung out of the windows exuding the collective dampness left from Saturday's fulfillment of marital duties, last night's satisfied lazily shaking standardized white pails out into trashcans, gnawed bones, molding halves of lemons, dripping garbage wrapped in pieces of newspaper, and the hard heels of loaves of bread, still unwashed children grudgingly dragged shopping nets crammed with clinking empty bottles to the self-service store, while last night's participants with pale veiny legs and droplets of hardened grease in the corners of their eyes, hit by the rotating house duty, torpidly pushed along the common brooms of rice-straw purchased only after repeated, often evening-long meetings of the co-op members, a hundred speakers blared out the same stupid hit, and in the windows a thousand Trosts—Jacek fled as out of a tunnel onto the bus, shaken up amid the shaking throng until, after the fifth stop, he could feel in his legs that the bus was beginning to climb the mountains, so far no one had got out, at the final stop they all got out, Jacek last, with downcast eyes he crossed the highway, stepped into some bushes, crouched, and with his face in his palms waited a while until the last voice had faded into the distance and vanished.

The grass was green again, perhaps it had been so even beneath the snow, from the twigs a billion green micro-explosions—Jacek struck out on one of his guaranteed un-frequented paths, but to be safe he soon deserted it and made his way upward through the underbrush and over the rocks, here you could drink right out of the brook, he tried to walk on all fours, on all fours backwards and somersaults forwards and backwards and sideways, out from under some pine needles he dug up a slightly rotted stick and rapped with it and knocked things down and leaped with the stick across the brook and with the stick he made a short, deep furrow at a right angle to the brook, then he pushed together a dam of stones, clay, and wood, and when he pulled away a barrier on the bank, the water streamed in the new direction, drove leaves along with it and, aided by the stick, bit powerfully into the soil, tore up pieces of turf, and washed them quickly along—increase the declivity and finish choking off the old channel and the liberated cascades could rush onto the hard, sleeping earth, tear pieces from it, and strike and resound against the very rock of the mountain.

Naked, with his stick over his head, Jacek lay on the warm grass and through the silence the sun penetrated his entire body.

Suddenly it was late, Jacek rose as if he'd been struck on the head, he gathered up grass with the sun-warmed pieces of his clothing, which itched now on his sweaty body, and dazed by the harsh glare he staggered in his heavy, warmed-up boots through the underbrush and over the rocks down to the path and the waiting bus. The Hurts, in their matching homemade jackets cut folk-style, hardly noticed Jacek, they whispered as they rocked on the plate-metal steps, holding hands in a whitening clasp.

The development on Sunday afternoon—surrounded by young greenery, blocks of buildings with delicate pastel hues, behind the windows vases of pussy willows and lively music, on the clean-swept concrete road a children's carnival, little girls with toy baby carriages and parasols, a gang of little boys on a surrealistic wagon made from an ironing board, their neighbors the Tosnars with their six-tiered pipe organ of girls, daddies with children on their shoulders sitting on sandbox rims.

Grandma, Lenka, and Lenicka were about to leave for the garden plot, but Lenicka wouldn't let them, she'd rather make yum-yum, in perfect unison her Daddy and she put away a huge cutlet apiece, one potato for Daddy and one for Lenicka, "That girl only eats her food when you're around—" and they left for the garden plot, Jacek took the ecstatic Lenicka on his shoulders and carried her across the road to the field, set her up in a tree, and acted like a bear, Lenicka was afraid and ecstasic, her hands around his neck, and wet, great great big kisses.

After unremitting digging, watering, and fertilizing, the tiny square of clay soil had at last sent up its first green shoots. Kneeling, Grandma and Lenka fondled the diminutive beds, Lenicka with them on her knees, in the soil on the bodies of these three generations something eternal and eternally fresh, WHERE DO WE COME FROM, here on each bit of earth a young woman and a half-naked man against the tepid undulation of the reddening horizon. And in the twilight across the broad roadway in a slow chain of duos and trios with tools on their shoulders, silent, covered with stigmata of clay in the flickering of the fluorescent lamps. Behind the crowd, sadly dragging along, a solitary figure in a green windbreaker with a hood, his neighbor Mestek was coming back from the mountains, his carved cane tapped out its lonely beat.

Outside their window, in the network of the eighty windows of the building across the way, in the open four-sided grottos of gradated shades of gold, young women leaving bathrooms and half-naked men with their cigarettes lit, the unheard trampling back and forth and the springs of tones mixing in the lake of music that rose over the buildings.

"Jacinek, my darling...," Lenka whispered, my wife, we know each other as no one else, a perfect interplay of limbs, love-making simple as milk, a wife with whom I live and with whom I have a child, WHO ARE WE, there is no peace outside existence in an order, never with anyone else but you, my love, I must tell you that—

"Lenunka..."

She was asleep already.

On Tuesday we are going away again. And then again and again.

WHERE ARE WE GOING—and where would we want to go—

## Part II — Games — five

Jacek had put on his sunglasses before he got off the streetcar, and as he got off he read the time on his wristwatch: 3:28. So the trip from Cottex to the main square takes 13 minutes.

He walked past the column with its enormous painted poster of Candy's jazz orchestra, over to the office of the notice agency: SERVICE TO THE PUBLIC. The notice was still there.

646
ROOM with balc. in Vanov. Beautiful view.
For rent or for sale.

In the PERSONALS column below, the outcries of a 48-yr-old bach. farmer and several healthy pensioners a 27-year-old intel. no childr., looking for intel. husb. up to 35, and a college graduate of the same age a 25-year-old refined wom. of girl. appear. offered herself, and she even had her own furn. apart. For less sensitive tastes there was a 30-year-old div. woman, native of Usti likes the woods, for whom Child is no obsticle.

In the crammed columns of POSITIONS AVAILABLE dozens of appeals blared out for all kinds of people, for anyone who might be willing to work anywhere, whatever might come into his head.

Jacek drew in his breath and went through the swinging door. In front of the counter stood a line of five persons, all buying tickets for the *The Red Gentleman*.

"Six forty-six," Jacek said in a barely audible voice.

Behind the counter a disturbingly beautiful girl typed out the address on a card and, smiling, asked him for twenty hellers.

At the bus stop it was 3:44; according to the timetable, the bus to Vanov leaves every twenty minutes, every 10,

30, and 50 until 11:00 P.M., after that every hour. Since the streetcar arrived at the square at 3:28, it was possible to catch the bus at 3:30, a perfect connection.

The red 3:50 bus arrived at 3:49, it's true, but loading held it up till 3:51. During the ride Jacek took off his dark glasses and memorized the address: J. Krivinka, 71 Dock Street, Vanov. Getting off the bus he made it out to be 4:07, and after two minutes of brisk walking he stood before No. 71, so that—subtracting the time he had taken at the notice agency—it was 34 minutes in all from Cottex.

On the whole, J. Krivinka made a solid impression, right away he laid his cards on the table: he already had six prospective tenants, but he needed money and would sell the separate room on the second floor to whoever would buy a quarter share in the house for 2,760 crowns and thus become a co-owner, the price was so low because the house had been confiscated, all the papers were in perfect order.

On the second floor there was a separate electric meter, running water, a toilet and, besides the bedroom, a small storeroom was available. The room measured some 200 sq. ft., dry, well-maintained, a light switch and two outlets, a washbasin, a varnished floor, two alcoves, glass doors onto the balcony and a large double window, two shutters, as for the furniture we'll come to terms, my daughter will be glad to do your laundry, the grocery store is right down the street, and there's a tavern around the corner, it's a five-minute walk to the pool and there's the dock, it has stairs and you can tie up a boat there, in winter you can go skiing just above the garden, we're rarely home, never in summer, it's the real outdoors, you don't need any curtains here, you can heat with coal or with gas, or with oil if you'd rather have oil, it's really nice, it's rare that one finds something so nice and it would really be yours exclusively, "Just look here—" said J. Krivinka and he went over to the window.

"Thanks so much, but if I could just have a moment
here... alone..."

"Stop by on your way down."

With his palm pressed against his lips Jacek waited
until the steps on the staircase had ceased, then he spread
out his arms as if to embrace all the things needed to
live—

Breathless with exhilaration he found the perforated
door of a small food cupboard under the window, its two
shelves were more than enough for a bottle of milk, a
quarter-loaf of bread, a can of herring, a couple of eggs,
some cheese, and a bottle of wine, one pot and one
saucepan, the one alcove for his dirty laundry and the
other for developing photographs, on the floor there
could be a brown shag rug and on the wall a carmine-
colored hanging, for the corner a wing chair and a floor
lamp, for the wall a bookcase and a small radio, for the
opposite one an arrangement of nude photos clipped
from magazines and sprayed with shellac, or one of bottle
labels, or a globe? No, a guitar and a corner couch, the
bed linen in one alcove, the dirty laundry in the
storeroom on the corridor, there he could keep his skis
and his off-season clothing, a paddle, a tent, and a kettle,
a corner couch and on it a black leather cushion, and beside it a little table for a bottle, two glasses, and an ashtray, a large mirror, a low ottoman so she wouldn't have
to throw things on the floor and so they could see the sky
while making love.

With his eyes half closed he silently approached the
window, gently opened the door to the balcony, and one
step over the threshold: the tops of the trees flowed in a
trembling glitter all the way down to the river, through
the unbelievable tranquillity and the transparent, gleaming air a barge passed downstream, the open path of sparkling waves to the Decin docks, under Speranza's windows, and on to the docks of Hamburg, the beaches of
Cuxhaven, and out to the sea—the moist green of the opposite bank stretched up through the tiers of deserted

vineyards to the shaggy masses of the woods and between the grey, stiffened cascades of rock, straight up the
sharp curve of the mountain's crest.

The dial of his watch shouted 4:42, and Jacek bit his
lower lip violently, gently but hurriedly he closed the balcony door and rushed down the stairs. "I'll bring the
money in a week!" he called to Krivinka in the doorway
and ran to the bus stop and the bus drove rapidly away
out of the valley.

Jacek changed at the main square and took the streetcar
through the canyon of familiar facades, none of which
could be skipped, endlessly to the end of the line at Vseborice, quickly between the solid concrete enclosing
strips of long-since dead grass, trampled day after day,
past dozens of ironically identical copies of the four-story
apartment house unit model T 03 to his own T 03, No.
511/13, straight up the stairs to the third story, and already from behind the door that bears our name cries of
laughter can be heard.

Grandma and Lenka were putting on a puppet show,
on the back of a kitchen chair their hands, holding the
wires, on the seat the action of the fairy tale was reaching
a climax, and on a cushion on the floor the spectator, Lenicka, was biting her little fist in excitement.

"Did you bring the money?" Lenka whispered and then
again, slowly, with dignity, moving the figure of the
water-goblin a little, "...whoo whoo whoo, whoo whoo
whoo... I've swum across nine brooks and nine ponds
and the princess isn't anywhere, whoo whoo whoo,
where is she?"

Gripped by the story Grandma scarcely nodded, hiding
the princess behind the chair leg she lisped, "I'm hiding
here, I'm afraaid of the water-goblin—"

"Where is she, whoo whoo whoo, where is she? Lenicka, tell me, where is that wretched little girl hiding?"

"I don't know—" Lenicka lied, choking with excitement, "She isn't here—"

"But she was here just a little while ago—whoo whoo whoo!"

"No she wasn't, watagwobwin, oh no—"

"It's water-goblin," Jacek whispered, "and you mustn't tell fibs, my darling—," but no one paid any attention to him, only Lenicka cried, "Daddy, go way!" over her shoulder and right back with her eyes fixed on the kitchen chair, what was the hurry anyway—

The performance dragged on considerably, and Jacek's efforts to enter the action successively as a king, a wicked witch, a bandit, and a giraffe were rejected three times over, "Go way, Daddy—" Lenicka repeated louder and louder until she screamed it, after the performance she and Grandma cut out paper stars, then with Lenka she made necklaces out of bits of folded newspaper, Daddy in disfavor, and she threw the water pistol at his feet, then trampled it, the celluloid cracked and it was all over with the toy from Brno.

On the table and the sideboard a pile of plates and dishes with the uneaten remains of five different courses, "I left you some buns on the tray—" but the cottage cheese in the buns had been picked out by a child's fingers, obviously unwashed, "Well then, find something in the pantry—," but the eggs were for Lenicka, the ham for Grandma for tomorrow, don't cut into the bacon, the cheese is for your snack tomorrow, the sardines are for sandwiches, they didn't deliver the beer.

"And don't turn on the cold water!"

"Do you have to stand right here?"

"Turn off the radio!"

"Out of the way, please."

"Don't smoke here— And not in the bedroom either!"

"You're in the way."

Jacek went out onto the balcony among the lines of laundry and lit a cigarette, in the kitchen the entertainment had started right up again, as if some unwanted visitors had just left, we're in the way here—he inhaled deeply as he cautiously paced the narrow concrete floor between boxes, cases, and empty flower pots and gazed at the darkening sky, suddenly an oppressive sense of someone looking—right across the way Trost was spread out in the window.

Trost was pouring out clouds of smoke, behind his elbow on the table a charred baking pan could be seen, a bottle of beer right on the sill, fists under his chin, and a shamelessly fixed stare—Jacek drew back quickly, stumbled over the laundry tub, and rushed inside, he turned on the light and immediately turned it off again, the blind in this room doesn't work, and in a fever he walked up and down in the darkness of the room, violently put out his cigarette, its light could be seen, and what else was there here anyway—

The simplest thing would be to leave without a word—Jacek went out to the foyer, took the key to the cellar off the nail, and went downstairs, the black suitcase would do, he locked the cellar and put the key back on its nail, ten shirts—no, three colored sport shirts and four polyesters, those we can wash ourself, twelve pairs of nylon socks is enough to have to wash socks just twice a month, the black leather tie's enough and six pocket handkerchiefs, three pairs of shorts, three towels, wear the grey suit, and then the suede jacket, a pair of dacron slacks, and the black sweater into the suitcase, there's a razor at the office, our toothbrush and comb from the bathroom, two pairs of pyjamas, a dagger, and the secret hoard.

Jacek walked through the foyer, from behind the kitchen door whooping and exultation, silently he closed the door, down the stairs and off across the wide roadway, the shortcut across the dead grass, and finally the last stop on the streetcar line, from over the curve of the mountain range a glow and from the city the streetcar is already coming for us...

...already it was moving into the turn-around, it brought a worn-out family, the mommy with two shopping bags crammed full, behind her the daddy with a child, the little girl had fallen asleep on Daddy's arm and now the family was hurrying home— It wouldn't work, we could never make up our mind to do it, not yet, not this way, not today—

Jacek turned his back to the streetcar, from the yellow windows of the restaurant the lament of an accordion and near the door the sad figure of neighbor Mestek in his green windbreaker with a hood sitting over a melancholy kipper and a glass of stale beer, Jacek downed two double slivovitzes, tripe soup, herring and onions, ten ounces of sausage, and three beers, and quietly returned home.

From behind the kitchen door shrieks and loud laughter, they were putting Lenicka to bed and Jacek went to lie down himself, to sleep, tomorrow Lenka's alarmclock will wake us and we'll go pet Lenicka, and then a second time we'll sleep and the second time we'll wake up without them.

## II — six

The simplest of the other possibilities is to give each other freedom—the famous "improvement" of the Balvins began right off at the front door with its double mailbox, double bell, and double visiting cards

DR. MILADA BALVINOVA    VITEZSLAV BALVIN

and in a rigorously binary spirit it covered the entire floor-plan of their conveniently symmetrical apartment: on the left Mija's room, white with a white square yard of foyer, on the right Vitenka's purple room with a purple square yard of foyer. Common ground—the kitchen, the john, the bathroom, and the center square yard of foyer— was known as "no man's land," and it was azure blue with white and purple enclaves in the two shelves under the mirror, two towel racks, two wings of the food cupboard, and two metal holders for toilet paper.

"I couldn't get along without the gang," said Vitenka as he entered his purple wing, "and Mija couldn't do with it, so why force ourselves on one another—"

On the enormous square dark-red couch in the middle of the purple room a kneeling girl in a men's nylon shirt was combing the golden locks of a handsome long-haired boy, on a horsehair mattress below them right on the floor slept a girl in a nylon raincoat, and a mirror hanging askew from the ceiling showed a segment of two uninhibited lovers hidden behind a column of four suitcases stacked one on top of another, "Today it's kind of dead," said Vitenka and he clapped his hands.

The girl in the raincoat sat up, looked at her watch, kissed Vitenka and Jacek quickly and, leaving, held the door open for girl twins in attractive Norwegian sweaters.

"Sweet cherrries have rripened—" sang the twins as they sat down on the horsehair mattress, and before they got to the refrain a slim Congolese with a bluish tint put in an appearance and poured out of his briefcase several bottles of byrrh, the lovers climbed out of their retreat behind the suitcases, and the refrain sounded from all nine throats: "—and how it happennned thennn."

"He had to have a soundproof wall put in for me—" in her white wing Mija pointed out an equally white porous wall, "and I had to promise that I wouldn't encroach on his side even if there was shooting there."

Jacek was given an imitation silver cup containing a milk cocktail, and with the tip of his tongue he fished out the floating strawberries. Mija sat down in a wing chair and, stretching, clutched the two wings of the chair, yawning peacefully. For ten minutes they sat in silence.

Jacek put the cup down on the table, picked up an illustrated Swiss magazine, and looked at pictures of a Soviet air force review at Tushino, we should study German again sometime, "What does *Fahrgestell* mean?"

"There's a dictionary over there. I'd like to sleep."

"As you like, I only wanted to get away for a moment from that caterwauling."

"What's that on your neck—"

Mija got up and sat down on Jacek's lap, ran her fingers over his neck, and then unbuttoned his shirt, she ran her warm palm over his chest and finally untucked his shirt, he embraced her gently and she tapped him on the nose.

"Do you see those white spots? You've got a skin fungus..."

"I never even noticed..."

"There are dyes that kill that, I can write you a prescription. What color would you like? Red, blue, green..."

"Is it anything serious?"

"No. You've just got a fungus."

"Sometimes I think I'm rotting away. But then again..."

"I'd like to talk to you some other time, now I'd rather sleep... Go sit down again, please, button up your shirt and don't be ridiculous... Those things don't amuse me."

Mija quietly dropped off to sleep in her chair and her white slipper fell from her foot, through the soundproof wall and the central wall of the apartment the singing of Vitenka's gang, further dampened by the music from Mija's record player, sounded as if at a great distance. "That female has no use for anything—" her husband Vitenka vented his resentment when he divided the apartment into its white and purple wings, "Neither for people, nor children, nor a dog, nor a canary, nor food, not even drink, not even for a goddamn boyfriend—"

"For me the sun is enough, plus two thousand a month net," said Mija, from January to May she drives out in her white two-seater to the southern slopes of the Krusne Mountains and reads and falls asleep in her beach chair or even in the car, at the municipal swimming pool she rents a cabana for the whole year, from June on she drives there straight from her office, pulls a white canvas beach chair out of the cabana, reads in it, and falls asleep in the sun, in November she goes to the Adriatic and in December to Egypt, always the same light, neutral color, the type that never burns—

In the purple room Vitenka had drawn very close to one of the Norwegian sweater twins and had pushed the other one, who seemed willing enough, off onto Jacek, but the gang had made up its mind to head off, "—but someone has to wait here for Milena Cerna!"

"So wait for Milena Cerna," Vitenka told Jacek, "she's a wonder, you must know her from the swimming pool, she's real dark, would you like to see her in the raw? When she rings four times, go into the bathroom and call through the door, "Hi, Milca, take it off!"

Jacek was left alone in the now silent room and involuntarily he began to clean it up: the discarded men's shirt and a black sock into the top suitcase, empty the ashtrays and smooth out the red couch so you'll like it here with me, lying on his back on the couch he gazed at himself in the mirror hung askew from the ceiling, waiting for his beloved, come here to me in my room—

Four short rings and Jacek ran to the bathroom, already a key was rattling in the lock, pointlessly Jacek turned on the shower, "Hi, Vitak—" a girl's voice resounded from the other side of the door, "Hi, Milca," Jacek called as he'd been schooled, "take it off!"

Breathlessly, silently, he advanced to the door and opened it a crack, his glance ran to the mirror on the ceiling, in it was Milenka Cerna like Goya's *Maja desnuda* on the red fabric, your beloved waits for you in your room—

Quietly Jacek closed the purple door and walked through the foyer to the white one, now locked, where the sound of soft music could be heard, Mija would go tomorrow to the southern slopes of the mountains and would place herself in the sun, which is needed to live—

With a child you couldn't divide your apartment that way, of course, and when in the foyer she shouted, "Daddy gwab me—" how many miles of soundproof wall would he need... perhaps the fifteen between Usti and Decin would suffice.

"Tomorrow I'm going to Brno," Jacek said to Lenka, "please put two white shirts in my bag, and no lunch."

"Lie this way... and put your hand under your head...," Jacek whispered to Nada in the room overlooking the Decin harbor, "I'll go to the door now and quietly steal back...," for a while he stood in the dark foyer, Good Lord, all this should have died out in us long ago—

The next morning Jacek sent Nada off to work, threw back the bedcovers, fetched himself a bottle of milk and some stale rye bread, extraordinary expenditures await us, then he made the bed, swept, and with a cigarette in hand leaned out of the window, from under his fingers a bluish ribbon floated up to the clouds; the cool wet breeze from the harbor, on the docks men leaned on steel cables and one of them all by himself pulled in toward the jetty the prow of a 700-ton barge, the cry of gulls and multi-colored flags on poles.

Sell this two-section chest and buy a three-section one secondhand, it would do for two, buy a folding bed at the thrift shop and these two blankets would fit into Nada's chest, a mattress—or just find a canvas army cot, we never slept as well as we did on that, and in the daytime you can stand it up in the foyer—only inexpensive things secondhand and from the thrift shop, but in the new apartment everything of good quality and new, so a cot then and instead of a three-section chest a lean-to beside the two-section one: two suitcases on top of one another and a metal coat tree in the corner.

"Wellll—" Nada dragged it out like an expert as she inspected Jacek's drawing on the board, "you can see the third year of vocational school in that and even something of the fourth year—Ouch! you're wrenching my— no, seriously, you could earn a living with that. I've got a surprise for you, but I'll tell you later, because now... I can't... concen—" and so on to the end of our twenty-four hours.

"And now for your surprise," she said, lying on the cushion, he went to the window to tie his tie. "I've got a job for you—and it's right around the corner, it's called Wood-Pak."

"What do they make?"

"All kinds of shipping containers and so forth. They'll take you on at once as a draftsman and in time they'll have an opening for a supervisor, you know, when you haven't had any experience yet... I know a Mr. Dvorak who has designs on Sternfeldova, the manager of our cafeteria, and it'll definitely work out."

Cross the ends, Wood-Pak would hardly be the acme of technology, make a loop, shipping containers are actually crates, pull the other end through the loop, is it really for the birds that he holds a degree in chemistry from Brno, tighten it, a career as box maker arranged by Mr. Dvorak and the cafeteria manager, pull it tight around his neck. Time has become an express train making up its time now that it's running on level ground, should he get off at thirty-three and start all over again as a student...

"You're awfully kind, Nadenka."

The convoy had entered the harbor, the men had run to their stations on the docks, the steel cables from the barges whistled through the air, and now they were being tied to metal posts, and Jacek shivered.

"So bye-bye and good night, darling—" he whispered.

Holding a cigarette he leaned out of the window of the train, hygienic ceramic ware in slat boxes was being quickly unloaded in a pile right onto the slag, on the other track a car full of girls on an outing, the boxing material cracked, and the train pulled quietly out, hi there girls, and a couple of them waved, look here, Mr. Jost, what has the railroad done with those boxes, sort it all out again, OK?, and Jacek waved at the girls' car, he sat down on the warm green imitation leather, but it was too hot, in the corridor he leaned out of the open window, the April river rushed on, flooding beaches and meadows, this is its high point, ta-ta-ta-dum, that's how time drips from the calibrated bottle with our business card on it, Nadezda is wonderful, I'll come with my suitcase and we'll start a new life, ta-ta-ta-dum, or a new fiction, ta-ta-ta-dum, or keep both and cultivate an isosceles triangle, water it regularly, and shudder at the thought that one of its two sides will break—and which one will that be—but is that all life allots to a man who's thirty-three, where has that sketch of the Brno Opera gotten to, the grass and the sea, when will this train dump us out, is this the overture ta-ta-ta-dum, or is it our NEVERMORE—

## II — seven

Jacek was the first to step off the crowded local, he read the time off his wristwatch: the trip here takes 52 minutes.

From a poor, once conceivably blacktop road a good half-mile of magnificent, four-lane divided highway shot out to the right, and a row of fluorescent streetlights towered above plowed fields. From a distance, Interchem looked just like an atomic reactor. The employees' concrete-and-glass bus stop would have been an ornament to any second-class airfield, the laminated-glass entrance an ornament to any first-class one. Projecting ten stories out of the runway-like concrete strip was the silver fairy tale of a freestanding apparatus. Ex-classmate Bachtik was master of it all—two and-a-half acres worth a hundred million crowns.

The highest level of the hydrogenation tower like the captain's bridge of a carrier, and the job of first lieutenant open. Captain Bachtik had never been in any way distinguished—save that he'd made his decision to leave Cottex at just the right moment.

With a damp hand Jacek grasped the quivering rail, here one could accomplish things, so come on, never fear, we send our leading technicians to be trained first in the Soviet Union and in England, I know both those languages well enough, of course you do, and you can fool around here to your heart's content, I'd introduce a central computer and monitors, that wouldn't be bad at all, in the meantime there are all kinds of people here, but I've already commanded a squad in which half the men were convicts, I remember you could be a stickler for discipline, just give me a free hand and things here will go as at a launching-pad— "And now come down," said Bachtik and he began to descend the stairs.

"Just let me fool around here a moment longer..."

A surrealistic domain of silver and from the mountains a moist wind blew, Jacek climbed down the winding metal stairs, once more around the tower and then once more around.

"So what, then?" said Bachtik down below.

"It's wonderful...," Jacek sighed.

"Better than your two-bit plant at Cottex?"

Jacek sighed deeply.

"I can hold the job for you till the first."

"I'll... I'll give you a ring."

"You're yellow."

Jacek trailed across the runway behind a futuristic, bright-orange electric-powered truck, toward a glassed-in pavilion which could have taken off without much modification. With a familiar, guilty smile, Pharmacologist Karel Zacek led Jacek between banks of philodendrons and club chairs.

"Come on," he whispered, "no more of this sitting in the corner."

"Here you'll have the whole floor—" Year before last Pharmacologist Zacek was master of half a desk and half a Rumanian lab assistant, a girl he'd knocked up. Here he has a palm tree, a *Phoenix canariensis*, right by his door.

"On this floor I've got part of the physical chem lab. The rest of it and the organic are downstairs, the inorganic upstairs, and the qualitative in the pavilion."

In front of a row of illusory machines, under plastic covers, a row of empty chrome chairs sparkled, while lost in the corner a girl in a surgical smock cringed.

"You've even got a real Beckmann thermometer here...," Jacek whispered.

"Two of them and an infrared spectrophotometer," Pharmacologist Zacek smiled wanly.

"Can I sit down with this for a moment?" tenderly Jacek pulled off the rustling cover and piously touched the switchboard. "If I were to come here—would you give me this machine?"

"I'd be awfully happy to give you all of this."

"The whole floor?"

"The whole building and the pavilion over there. I'm going to Prague."

"I'll give you a ring on Monday—"

"On Monday I'm flying to London," Pharmacologist Zacek smiled guiltily.

"Living quarters are available for singles the day they come in," the manager of the living quarters said as he led Jacek through a vast opaque glass corridor right out of a spy or sci-fi film, "family apartments in nine months." Glass bricks went all the way back to the showers and naked men with wet hair promenaded with towels thrown over their arms like overcoats, behind a white door a hotel-style room for three and everywhere green upholstery, "I might be able to put you in here—," a grey-haired roommate was in bed reading a thin volume of James Bond 007 with the help of the thick tomes of a three-volume dictionary, and under a propped-open window a fellow was whispering Russian words, "—or upstairs on the second floor, where the upholstery is blue."

"Engineer Jost? Comrade Bachtik has ordered me to drive you to Usti—" a well-tanned swell in a grey-blue uniform said as he opened the door of a large silver-grey limousine for Jacek, "—you say you've got your factory here between these house lots?" he marveled later when he couldn't find the entrance to Cottex in the gap between wooden fences.

In the just beginning drizzle Jacek jumped over puddles across the ridged mud of the courtyard to the
wooden annex of the technical division and he sank down
into his wicker chair. Nine-by-twelve feet of creaky
boards and a roughed-up desk of soft wood from the days
of the Germans, promoted by the painter's brush to
"stained oak," on a plant stand a half-century-old Urania
typewriter and, behind a curtain of local manufacture,
five bookshelves, six-by-fifteen feet of files full of letters
that had come in and copies of nonsense that had gone
out, a chemical engineer ten years later—

Outside the window it was raining hard and under the
overhang of the roof of the electric plant opposite two
men had run to take cover, a seventy-year-old fireman
(also a chemical engineer, before the war the manager of
sugar factories: "How much a year do you make here,
Mr. Jost? Twenty thousand? Well see here, I made two
hundred and twenty thousand in Louny, then in Kralupy
two hundred and seventy thousand, in Roudnice only a
hundred and ninety thousand, it's true, but in Lovosice I
made four hundred and thirty thousand plus—") and a
fifty-year-old guard (after the war a high functionary: "I
had all those directors called together and I told that
crowd, goddamn it, gentlemen..."), they crouched
together and pressed their backs against the wall, at that
moment through the gate a heavyset tattooed man rolled
a reel of cable three yards high and pushed it heavily forward, it got stuck in the mud, the fellow roared at the two
has-beens under the overhang, the pair rushed out, and
all three together rolled the enormous reel out into the
cloudburst.

Slowly Jacek lit a cigarette, by degrees he leaned with
his entire weight against the right side of the back of the
chair, gradually he hardened the whole side of his body
from that point of concentrated pressure down to his
knees, and very slowly he moved that whole side left a
couple of inches, so that his buttocks rested on the seat in

a new position, cool and newly pleasurable, as when in bed one lets his cheek slide down on the pillow.

Vitenka Balvin looked in the door and a short while later Petrik Hurt, the boss, to ask about the big limo Jacek had just pulled up in, but he had only to press his fists to his temples twice and look tormented: this pantomime signaled the state known as "Jacek's got neurosis" and the fact that it was necessary to spare him for the rest of the shift.

We too will spare ourselves, Jacek lit another cigarette, stretched the left side of his back and then shifted to the right, twenty-seven more years till our pension and we'll have our whole life saved up, so that then we can mourn it all in one piece—Jacek leapt up from his chair, kicked it, and paced back and forth for the remainder of the shift.

Petrik Hurt jumped off the streetcar at the main square just before the stop and from behind the column that carried the huge painted poster advertising Candy's orchestra Verka Hurtova ran to meet him, Petrik's third wife and his "true love," as Petrik unashamedly claimed, but that third marriage had cost him two furnished apartments for the preceding wives and eleven hundred a month support for their five children, costly enough if one succeeds only the third time, but Petrik didn't complain, "My first wife and I understood one another sometimes, with my second we were both content, but only with Verka did I find out what true happiness is—," and for seven years it had been uninterrupted, he wouldn't have found it if he'd only switched once...

There was still a lot of spare time, Jacek went to the window of the notice agency, SERVICE TO THE PUBLIC, and read the PERSONALS column, the 25-year-old refined wom. of girl. appear. with own furn. apart. was still available, also the native of Usti likes the woods; Child is no obstacle!, it must require a very special taste to make a spectacle of oneself in the main square.

To kill time, Jacek stopped in at the barber shop, let's wait till Kamilka is free, he picked up the only newspaper on the table, the day before yesterday's *Prace*, and ran through the already familiar news, under different headlines and less of it, we're used to *Rude pravo*—but look, they even publish personals here, nearly two full columns, and it's more tasteful than a spectacle in the main square, it's a real horror how many people there are dying to switch—

"Next, please—"

"As usual?" Kamilka smiled at Jacek in the chair.

"No clippers," he nodded.

"You have such thick hair..."

"And yours is as lovely as Egyptian cotton... It must be a pleasure to comb it..."

She giggled and stroked him, perhaps she pressed a bit harder than she need have, but we've known one another for two years now, only so far we never dared try anything, and he kissed her on the elbow.

"That isn't done here," she was pleasantly angry.

"Because I don't get to meet you anywhere else."

"Because you don't go out."

"Because no one ever invites me anywhere..."

"Shall I trim your hairs?"

"I'll do the same to you... and it'll scratch."

She tore the towel away from under his chin and pressed it over his mouth.

"Kamila!—" said the manager into the mirror.

"Check for No. 5!" cried Kamilka and she began to dig in the drawer. "Come here tonight at ten...," she whispered.

"But the last train leaves at half-past nine," Jacek whispered, "and then in the morning..."

Kamilka's neck reddened.

"...at five-thirty...," Jacek lied, grinning meanwhile at the manager in the mirror, "That's why I never go anywhere..."

"Come here tonight at ten," she whispered.

Horrible, how easy it would be, Jacek inhaled the scent of his cologne and stopped in front of the travel agency window, with smiles two pretty girls were inviting us to visit the Czech Paradise and a white ship was sailing to Tunisia across the vast green expanse of the Mediterranean, Nadezda was Speranza, should he trust the rest of his life to a chance meeting on a train, the Miramar was already a dream and the open road of green waves shone toward Africa, a superannuated cratemaker's apprentice spending the night in a stretcher for corpses—

As if catapulted Jacek rushed back to the barber shop and picked up the old newspaper from the table, it would contain the address for notices, and he carried it off in his pocket, the manager called out something, a crowd of people flowed out of the streetcar and dragged Jacek along in the direction of the main post office, quickly past the shop windows of the notice agency, the newspaper sends replies by mail, Petrik Hurt succeeded only the third time, people said his neighbor Mr. Mestek had gotten as many as thirty offers and had cured his inferiority complex that way, we can have them mailed to the office—

In a sweat Jacek stood at a speckled counter in the huge hall of the main post office, over the writing paper and envelope he had purchased, on the envelope the stamp was already printed and Jacek glanced under his elbow into the purloined newspaper, 36 YEAR OLD divor. with child seeks wife if poss. with own apart., 42-YEAR-OLD divor. eng. seeks young intellect., what nonsense, 58-YEAR-OLD man with artif. leg seeks— and Jacek was already writing:

*33-YEAR-OLD eng., divor., seeks partner*

But what sort of partner, they all write something or other, but then this is only an attempt to relieve your mind, after all before making a permanent appointment you have to announce a competition, that way no one can be blamed for anything, they all include a key word, it has to be there, some sort of key word—

*Live!*

it's short, at least it won't cost much.

Jacek threw the letter into the slot, the newspaper into a wastebasket, and then he went out and back to the square, now sufficiently amused.

From the enormous poster a sun-bronzed Candy in a purple tux rolled his eyes at him FOLLOWING OUR SUCCESSFUL GERMAN TOUR, while five fabulously pretty heads gazed up at him ecstatically, you old swindler, you, at Cottex years ago Candy had been called Alois Klecanda, a miserable lab-assistant who played nights in a jazz band and came to the lab only to sleep, if he came at all, at Cottex they put up with a great deal, but for the theft of some tow-cloth and mercury Alois Klecanda got a year in prison and ever since he's been out he's done nothing but play in that band, he makes more in a month than the director of Cottex and his two deputies put together, and in his green sports car he carts around the most beautiful girls in the area.

Jacek stood beneath the clock and observed his own reflection in the black glass, 33-year-old divorced engineer of pleasant appearance—the simplest possibility was divorce.

Lenka and Lenicka were already coming down Revolution Avenue, we can see each other from a distance, but Lenka doesn't run to meet me the way Verka does with Petrik, perhaps she's never run, it's only my first, every fifth Czech is divorced and there are twenty thousand divorces a year, why on earth do we remember the statistics anyway, Lenka's caught sight of us, but she's more interested in that display of knitted goods, but then we might have gone to see it together, the little darling sees her Daddy but runs away, she's more inclined to go for Russian ice cream, Daddy would be more likely to buy her some than Mommy would, of course, but you like

Mommy better, "We had a wonderful time—" Lenka says when I come back from Brno, well so did we—

Lenka looks old for her twenty-eight years, soon she'll have as many wrinkles as her mother, she no longer likes to talk in bed, she'd rather sleep, how frightened she was yesterday—watching TV she suddenly gave a start and ran to the bathroom, it happens more and more often, she locks herself in for three-quarters of an hour and then that thief-like crawling into the next bed, as if begging for mercy—please don't—

"Did you bring the money?"

Let's admit that's all that matters to you and the court will determine precisely how much, it will take your side and I'll be glad to send it to you, for three hundred crowns a month a new life, twenty-four hours of freedom for ten crowns, pass by this indifferent wife and child who, in a year, won't even recognize us, and go back along Revolution Avenue in the opposite direction, toward the railroad station and the docks, under the burgeoning chestnut trees, free to take off—

"Daddy swing me like an angel—" Lenicka called, Lenka took her by one arm and Jacek by the other, they raised her up and swinging her feet the little girl soared into the sky.

## II — eight

The general director leaned back from the oval ebony table and laughed quietly. *Rien ne va plus*—Jacek, his lips in position to pronounce the word "cheese," observed the boss of a hundred and ten thousand employees and an annual turnover of nine billion, here direct attack alone promised any chance of success and already now the little ball was rolling around the roulette wheel, the big boss began to turn red in the face and to wheeze asthmatically, his fingers dark brown with nicotine and too much coffee, it's all too much for you, and a nice big desk would just fit into your anteroom. Let's say "cheese" and look into each other's eyes.

"This isn't badly thought out, in fact," the general director said at last. "And of course you'd want to be in charge of it all. But there isn't such a position on the chart."

"Let's put it down as a special deputy, Comrade Director. A good gardener needs a ferocious dog."

"The next few months will give us some indication..."

"There's no hurry..."

"But for the time being I haven't promised anything."

"For the time being I haven't asked for anything."

The general director grinned knowingly and pressed Jacek's hand just perceptibly harder than was customary, it was boringly simple, one more glance at those three tables, the oval one for conferences, the enormous executive desk, and the long table with its twenty-four leather-upholstered seats of knighthood, of course there were twenty-six factory directors, but you could squeeze in a pair of stools, or three if need be, and out through the padded door into the anteroom, under the palm tree *Trachycarpus excelsa* there's a free corner with good lighting from the left.

"You're to order a car for me—" Jacek said to the secretary, and "To the offices of the Regional Committee—" to the chauffeur. Through the springtime streets of the Brno of his sweet days as a student, since they've held the trade fair here things have been going up and up, "Have you got any children?" he asked the chauffeur and then: "That's fine. Stop here and I'll get out."

Through the long corridors of the grey palace the word had spread that Jacek Jost from Usti had lasted fifty minutes with the general director. Only at dinner upstairs at the Avion was it possible to find all the higher-ups together, and they had all come to greet Jacek at his table.

The grotesquely fat Franta Docekal had grown even fatter and was now serving as deputy, his classmate Libor was in charge of exports and was now living, after his third divorce, with a circus acrobat named Manuela, Venca had brought a Mercedes back from Germany and Kikin was the general representative in Cairo, they were all on top of things and none of them one bit smarter than we are, maybe less so, but now they're all big bosses and they look very serious when they fly back from France or Belgium and take off for Argentina or Zanzibar.

"Is Kindl still working in Moscow at COMECON?"

"He's at the embassy now."

"And Valasek... the shrimp who was so frightened all the time, the one who peed in his bed in the army..."

"Oh, he's in Addis Ababa, he sent us his picture taken with the emperor."

On the floor upstairs his classmate, the deputy Verosta, was at the billiard table looking for a weak opponent, Jacek made an effort to scale his game progressively down from fair to poor, "You've got real class," he said, inclining his cue like a knight his lance before his liege-lord, "Oh, yes, just so I don't forget it, the general direc-tor asked me today what kind of impression you made on people as a student. I covered you with silver and gold..."

"What can that old fart be trying to smell out," said Deputy Verosta, obviously pleased, "it must be on ac-count of the ministry. Many thanks, Jacek, and drop in to see me this evening, here's the address."

"I'd like to, but I'm in a real bind. Our director's raking me over the coals for not coming up with that ethyl ace-tate."

"How much do you need?"

"A carload?..."

"You've got it, and give me a call the next time you're in Brno."

Another floor up, the great Benedikt Smrcek, the future first member of the Academy from the field of textiles, was playing chess alone.

"You really clouted him, Bena...," Jacek whispered piously, and Benedikt the Great smiled a trifle, "What are you going to ask me for?"

"What does one ask from the head of a research institute?"

"If you're really interested, sign up for a graduate fellowship starting October 1, it wouldn't be a bad idea to have a factory man for a change."

"Bena, do you remember how we once played chess all night in the guardhouse at the Jaromer barracks and we promised one another—"

"I remember that you were black that night, you opened eleven times with a double fianchetto and you lost twenty-two times," Bena said as he set up the pieces, "that's what I call persistence. The secretary's office will send you the application forms."

His father (66) was just getting ready to go out and play cards, his mother (61) to see some friends, but they could stay and talk to Jacek for a while, what was new in Usti, not a thing, Mom, just as there hasn't been anything for ten years now, Dad, but here there were lots of new things, Mom was working in an apiary co-op and Dad was teaching languages to earn money to go to the seashore, then they'd cut out and make the rounds of the relatives—no, not to Usti, what would we do there, tell us—to Prague and Carlsbad, in autumn Dad will take foreigners on hunting trips and live with them in Castle Mikulov, Mom and her friends will take temporary jobs sorting apples, and at Christmas time we'll both work for a month at the chocolate factory, "And when are you planning to move back to Brno?"

"I'm working on it..."

"Why didn't you stay here—" his mother sighed again, "all your schoolmates..."

"A young man has to go out into the world," said Dad. "At ¬our age, let's see, that would be in thirty-two..."

"⸴ you were in Morocco."

"That's right, it was great there. Sure, a young man has to..."

"I've spent ten years now in Usti."

"So many?" Mom was frightened. "That's terrible!"

"I'm working on it. The general director will have something for me, and Bena Smrcek's promised me something at his institute."

"Of course, you could always come and live with us, but what would you do with Lenka and Lenicka?"

"I'm working on it."

Jacek's room seemed noticeably larger than the one in the Usti pre-fab, the window on the magnificent old park, the wooden saber on the wall, and in the corner the globe Dad had given him, oh Lord, nothing ever seems to die—

We used to go to school every day along Sand Street, between the rows of trees below the stadium, as a freshman in high school we hadn't the least doubt that the first Czechoslovak field marshal would be named Jost ("J.J. the Great") and he had already planned the reorganization of the army, up the hill along the wall of the seminary garden, as a sophomore the brilliant director of a revolutionary film: the camera looking through the hero's eyes so that his face wouldn't be visible, but it would show his hands when he drinks, as they pick up the glass it would come up in full detail across the entire width of the screen, when he walks the whole picture would sway rhythmically with his step, when kissing the whole audience would kiss with him and when shooting they would look down the rangefinder of his gun, along the asphalt of quietly elegant Masova Street, as a junior the famous spy, Flying Jacek—the terror of governments, with a wristwatch that shoots bullets, through the kiosk below the steps of the University Library, where not even a high-school senior ventured, until, thrilled, he was a freshman at the University, the winner of the first Czech Nobel Prize (that was before Heyrovsky) had come to look for a girl to serve as his assistant.

Jacek ascended those same steps, in the reading room beneath fluorescent lamps a fountain murmured, and at the tables a hundred girls of twenty-five nationalities, near the Chemistry Division a blonde girl stood with a thick copy of Gajdos's *Chromatography* in her hand.

"A truly awful book," Jacek said and he grinned.

"I wouldn't say so," the girl answered icily.

"You're not going to praise me!"

"Why should I praise... you? You're..."

"Dr. Gajdos," Jacek smiled, "and thanks for the tribute."

"Doctor— I'm Libuse Cveklova. And I'm really—"

"When you register for my course, I'll take you out to dinner."

Majestically Jacek walked out and then skipped down the stairs, on the door a notice to the effect that Dr. Benedikt Smrcek, CSc, National Awardwinner, would lecture in the Great Hall—Bena had had persistence and so things had worked out for him. In the streets of the big city, which were just lighting up for the evening, Jacek, the unattached research worker, was looking for his fellows.

And at the White Crocodile, the Bellevue, the Slavie, and the International Hotel they beckoned and waved from tables in the back, with new wives, girlfriends, and mistresses, this is Marcela, Kamila, Jana, Yvette, the girls smiled and shook hands, fresh-looking, sun-tanned, well-cared-for, with pointed breasts, flat stomachs—tennis instead of breast-feeding, sailing instead of pushing baby carriages—dazzling with make-up, perfect, they returned Jacek's prolonged handshakes. Pavel Vrbka had been working freelance for years, writing scenarios about Mendel, proteins, and the Battle of Austerlitz, and at the Black Bear drinking wine our old Professor Muzikar (58) with a marvelous girl from the Brno-at-Night Cabaret.

In the enormous park beneath his window strings of lights, laughter, and music from the dance floor, from below the black treetops up to the quivering halo of the city of three hundred thousand, and Jacek fell asleep in his childhood bed, out of the night starlets, sports stars, and upper-class co-eds, today Marcela, Kamila, Jana, Yvette, and we'll dwell with them again as we did before.

Jacek woke up before the sun entered the room, he exercised and took an ice-cold shower, at the lunch counter he had a roll and two glasses of warm milk, two crowns forty in all and that can be cut, a graduate fellow in science gets fifteen hundred, and of that three hundred gets sent to Usti, that leaves forty crowns a day, heh heh, four times as much as you had when you were a student, on the way back through Luzanky Park he met a girl with a violin, a music student, you'll never know your whole life long what a timeclock is.

In his room he twirled the globe Dad had given him, Dad had gone to Morocco at thirty-three and without a tourgroup, by himself, and with his finger Jacek traveled over the blue sea, from Rijeka on the Yugoslav coast down between Charybdis and Scylla, past Malta and Majorca through Gibraltar out to the open sea and to Africa, to the white city of Casablanca... nothing has died in us yet!

Excitedly Jacek waved his wooden saber and piously he hung it up again, from the bookshelf he took down his old *Physical Chemistry* by Brdicka, it would be best to start with that, greedily he began to read and the forgotten pages came to life again.

And Express No. 7 conscientiously tore along Line No 1, the main artery from east to west, from Bucharest, Budapest, Bratislava, and Brno to Ceska Trebova, Pardubice, and Prague, in Prague you change for Paris with connections for Le Havre, Calais, Marseille, or to Usti and Decin, our line, on which we've been riding now for ten years, we were leaving home then to go out into the world, but the emptiness of the passing years has maliciously tipped the scales, the world is always at the other end of the line—

"I didn't sleep at all last night," yawned the tousled Nada rubbing her eyes with her fists, "all night long you kept shouting something in your sleep about Africa, and then you kicked me right here. I'll sleep in the army cot when it comes... What's wrong? No exercises today?"

"I don't feel well, Nadezda."

"Why not?"

"Not well at all. I can't go on this way..."

"Lenka and Lenicka..."

"...and everything. I don't know how to pull myself out of it."

"So get a divorce."

"If that were all there was to it."

"Then go back to them, I told you already on the train that I wouldn't chase you. I really won't."

"So much the worse."

"You don't know what you want again?"

"The trouble is I know—precisely."

"And it's—"

"Everything."

"Then you're not so bad off. The opposite would be worse. So let's go, you can lead the exercises."

The sun imperturbably glided down over the wall and began to cross the floor, Jacek between the walls, the arms of the dock cranes unloaded from rail cars to barges and from barges to rail cars, to be everlastingly on a chain-rope-line-hook would drive one mad, use force to cut through and do it firmly, the barges sink almost to the cargo line, only death is the last possibility, the rising of the barges above the surface, but one does not wish to die so where should he aim, they raise anchor when completely full or completely empty, completely-completely-completely emptied, if only both of them died at the same time they could sail out, Lenicka and Lenka—and without chains, ropes, or nylon fibers, without straps, lines, or hooks, free to enter the world's splendor—in horror Jacek pressed his palm to his throat, by the window overlooking the harbor, in the windowglass the throttling fingers of my own, this my own right hand are buried almost to the point of vanishing.


## II — nine

It's already Lenicka's beddie-bye time, but we've had so little fun, so let's play just a tiny bit more, Jacek took apart the couch and from its cushions he built her a playhouse on the carpet, with the coverlet as the roof and a little balcony out of pillows, Lenicka was in ecstasy as she crawled through her hut, now she must go beddie-bye, and so quickly quickly once through the obstacle course, Jacek placed two cushions down flat on the floor and a third one perpendicular to them between, the little girl climbed over it, fell and again climbed up, shouted and cheered and had to be put to bed by force, "Daddy gwab me—"

"I'll grab you—where it hurts!"

"Gwab me, Daddy! Gwab—"

And down again with the net, nothing's so sweet to kiss as our little one, but you really must go beddie-bye, "Daddy won't go way—" Jacek bent over the brass pole, stroked his darling's hair and cheeks, tucked the coverlet under her chin, out of the damp twilight my dark hand cries out on her little white throat—flee, go away without a word or get divorced before something horrible happens... you'll never make up your mind to say that first word.

It was raining for the third day in a row, a cold, prolonged rain, and Jacek dozed on the streetcar in the heavy odor of damp clothing, Lenka was carrying a muddy Lenicka along the wide concrete road, Lenicka had fallen down and was crying a great deal, she's terribly heavy and Mommy can scarcely hold her, Jacek took the exhausted wet little girl into his arms and the family staggered home up the steps, Grandma had spent the whole day ironing and on all the chairs shirts were exhaling the warm odor of heated cotton, "I don't feel like doing much today either...," Lenka yawned, "I feel the flu coming on," yawned Jacek, Lenicka had her mouth wide open too and apologetically Grandma placed her wrinkled fist to her lips, "So let's have a sleep day," Jacek decided, "everyone lie down!" "But not in bed," Lenka added, "I'd never get up again..."

So Daddy and Mommy on the couch, Grandma in the armchair, but Lenicka screamed that she didn't want to be by herself and so they had to bring in her crib, Lenka fell asleep first and her heavy body warmed his side, Grandma nodded in the chair and Lenicka snored lightly in her crib, with sticky eyes Jacek looked over that happily sleeping little flock and then soothing, stupefying sleepiness came to his eyelids.

At two in the morning Jacek suddenly awoke and could not get up, in her sleep Lenka had embraced him and he was a long time freeing himself from her, there was a terrible sensation of hunger in his stomach, quietly he crept into the kitchen but he found nothing edible there, only kohlrabi and cookies, they'd even forgotten to buy bread, a ravenous Jacek greedily guzzled cold chlorinated water and he quivered with disgust, now we won't get back to sleep again, a pain seemed to be developing in his throat, in the bookcase we had some Swiss chocolate, but someone's already eaten it, the triple snoring in the living room and the sleepy Jacek shuffled in a rage through the nighttime apartment coughing experimentally, it could be the flu, in the refrigerator he found some frozen yogurt and vengefully swallowed it in the largest pieces he could get down, then water "on the rocks," an inflammation of the lungs, fine to neglect it, with a pack of cigarettes and a chair he went out on the balcony and sat down, a blanket thrown lightly over his shoulders and so till morning...

Although his temperature was only 99° the whole apartment was turned upside down, a struggling Jacek was quickly stripped, on the kitchen range Grandma's teas and decoctions were boiling, "Daddy is ticky and you must be quiet," Lenka whispered to Lenicka, to be "ticky" was one of our favorite childhood games, the pleasure of being manipulated—fingered, measured, picked up, carried from place to place, put in bed, covered up all the way to the eyes, and left to follow the bustle and excitement created, already Mommy was bringing a pint of cranberry jam, there weren't any seeds and you didn't have to cut it or even chew it very much, just the first bittersweet taste, and already Lenka was bringing a good two pounds of cranberry jam and spoon in hand she sat on the edge of the bed.

"You faker," Lenka threatened him with her finger when for two days now Jacek's temperature had failed to go above 97.9°, "you're just pretending, right?"

"But I kept saying there was nothing wrong with me..."

"It's OK, as long as you get to spend some time at home..."

"You shouldn't have gone to so much trouble..."

"That's all right, I'm glad to do what I can..."

My wife has the sincerest blue eyes in the world, and Jacek quickly drew her to himself.

"Lenunka..."

"Wait a moment, I'll just close the door—"

Like milk, my love, there is no peace except existence within an order, "Jacinek,,,," my wife whispers and presses her delirious lips against the ridge of my stroking palm: "Jacinek... I'd like one more little one..." On her white throat my black hand roared and there was a taste of bitter and of salt.

"This is the first time I've been here for two years," Pepik Tosnar said absentmindedly as he sat down at Jacek's table, he was the creator of the six-tiered pipe organ, daddy of six girls, and their neighbor from the apartment house, "let me have two beers right off, Mr. Innkeeper!"

"Once in two years to a tavern?"

"No-o, I'd be telling a fib, last Easter I went to The Five Arches."

"Then you're my guest, let's make it worthwhile—" impressed, Jacek looked at this balding man who spent most of his time in the children's playground below their window and who earned extra money fixing blinds delivered in a state beyond repair by the factory that had produced them, "—two more, let it be six in all, like your daughters, and I'll get the check!" A good man, but beyond daughters and blinds he didn't know too much.

Not taking no for an answer he dragged Jacek to his own place for "slivovitz twice distilled and three times passed through charcoal," well, let's have a look at that apartment underneath which we've been living for two years, where there's so much trampling every morning— right in the doorway an acrid mixture of smells hits the nose like a blow from frozen reins, the same apartment as ours but what have they done with it, six little beds like coffins in stacks, on the floor a foot-deep pop-art layer of a thousand unnameable things dragged in by the children, the wild romping of six filthy little devils, "I've made them all with clefts down below, nothing but rejects so far," roared the circus manager to outshout the wild beasts climbing all over him the way the chimpanzees at the zoo climb their tree, and he poured out into mustard glasses more lethal doses of wood alcohol incompletely distilled, which this innocent fool had evidently spiced with brown coal rather than filtering it through absorbent charcoal, "But the seventh time's in the bag, it'll be a boy," roared his cannonball of a wife while the slobbering monkeys clambered over Jacek's limbs as over tropical vines.

If Lenka were to have triplets, there'd be seven of us, including Grandma—the frightful alcohol flamed up inside Jacek and Lenicka rapped her head against the bathtub, terrible screams, if she rapped it harder she wouldn't scream anymore and from your slippery hands a child could easily slip and fall, "What are you up to in that

bathroom—," Lenka with gas, "We're almost done...,"
take them both up to Maria's Rock and push them out between the wires, the little one tore away from me and my
wife leaped after her, "Hey, you two, march to dinner—,"
from her ten containers of sleeping pills somehow
procure the right substance and then throw the ten empty
containers on her night table, work in gloves, perhaps
she'd find out about my girlfriend N. Houskova and
solve it all that way: Lenicka to Grandma's with two
hundred a month, everything immensely simple all of a
sudden, exchange the apartment for a room or a one-
bedroom co-op, also first-category, and take as much as
ten thousand under the table, sell the furniture, rugs, curtains, and then with his savings he could manage a
Hillman Minx, "—we're working on it!"

Jacek stuffed himself to the point of numbness, pass the
roast, with his fingers he tore crisp meat from the bones
and standing over the refrigerator he drank his fill
straight from the bottle—an imaginary line to the window right across the way, Trost with a piece of meat in
one hand and a bottle of beer in the other, that unbearable
alter ego, and Jacek ran off to the bedroom, Grandma and
Lenka had already tuned the TV to their favorite Dietl
soap opera, you bet Trost and his Mrs. were also watching Dietl.

On Sunday morning Jacek and Lenka took Lenicka into
their bed, the little darling crawled along Daddy's leg
and up to get a great great great big kiss and then a
second one, still sweeter, and with his knee under the
coverlet he once again played polar bear, Lenicka was
frightened and ecstatic, "Daddy don't go way— "

On a bus up into the hills Jacek fled under the windows
of the Tosnars and the Trosts as from a prison cell, at the
summit, on the vibrating metal floor, two pairs of
lovers—the two Hurts and Vitenka Balvin with his guitar
and Milena Cerna, away on the most secret of the secret
paths to the very top, under Kneziste the white spot of
Mija's two-seater and the smaller white spot of Mija in

her beach chair, he turned and fled through the waves of hard-gleaming emerald grass with a million gold dandelions like medals for bravery on green velvet, waiting to be awarded, now only to kill on a Maytime meadow with so many women and horses, Lenkas for the world or the world for Lenkas, now only killing was left—

After a Sunday cutlet with potato salad and a slice of crumbling cheesecake we, the Josts, and Grandma go to the zoo, and Lenicka in ecstasy in front of the monkey cage. "Come, darling, Daddy will hold you up—"

At the office his fists were now constantly pressed to his temples and his face looked tormented, "Jacek's got neurosis," he was depressed for the fifth day in a row, *alles ist schon egal,* "It's Jacek again, Mija, write me a prescription for three containers of those pills—I said three!" "And today will be another sleeping day! What's that—OK then, I'll do it myself."

On Sunday morning he and Lenka took Lenicka into their bed and before dinner out to the high Maytime meadows, the gleaming grass gleaming straight up to the gleaming sky calls like the shore to the sea, we will swim out, something will happen, SOMETHING WILL COME, the humble expect to be exalted and the masters are afraid of loss, all count on change and so it must come, SOMETHING WILL HAPPEN, faith is needed and an amused interest in how we'll be violated this time, SOMEONE WILL COME AND SHOW US WHERE TO GO, all that's left for us is to prepare for that coming, IT WILL BE RESOLVED AND IN GRATITUDE WE WILL SUBMIT, already the bolts of the catapult are being tightened and the flight path adjusted, LET US TAKE OFF SOON—we pray and we prepare.

## Part III — Preparations — ten

A flat green ceramic ashtray, two plain wineglasses made of lead glass, a pot, a saucepan, and a guitar pick, only three hundred from the secret hoard and we're all set—carefully, on his stomach, the way a woman might carry her child, Jacek carried his black traveling satchel onto the bus to Telnice, "Let's have that, Mr. Jost, I can hold it on my lap—" "Good day, Mrs. Klusakova, that's very kind, but I'll manage—" "Just give it here!"

The bus left the square at 3:55 sharp, Mrs. Klusakova is our new neighbor, her husband works for the police and she wants to sell us strawberries, he must not make very much, it's useful to seek out support from the local authorities and strawberries too in the bargain, you can eat them just as they are, with sugar or with cream, definitely try them with condensed milk, "You're so very kind, really—," the bus drove through the canyon of familiar facades infinitely faster than the streetcar on its way to the last stop at Vseborice, outside the window the model T 03 cinder-block buildings flashed by and then, as if demolished, they disappeared to the rear, right after them the garden colony unrolled, made up it seemed more of wire mesh than of commonplace young radishes and carrots sown from packets for a crown apiece, and we're on our way—

Between rows of old chestnuts covered with pontifical candle-blossoms, through unending fields of spring grain, a sharp turn around the chemical plant, and the enormous shallow crater of the strip mine with ramparts of transported bare earth, towards the monument with the green bronze lion and along a granite road straight into the mountains, through waves of meadows, tiny houses buried in the tops of trees, and now that linden tree with the sign, and we're home, "So don't forget, Mr.

Jost, they'll be ripe in a month and I'll let you have them for eight crowns a box."

Into the transparent air, intensity fifty thousand candlepower, and a blindingly lit dirt path leading upwards, down the slope a flock of butter-fat goslings rocked to and fro and by the trunk of a pink apple tree a snow-blue kid goat, as if posing for an Agfacolor, but the kid had three dimensions and could be petted in the bargain, "Good afternoon, Mr. Svitacek, I'm just..." "But we play with him too, he likes it best when you scratch him on the horns...," Mr. Svitacek delivered the mail in Ritin and his wife was chairwoman of the local town committee, he'd brought her the box of detergent that had stood around too long, a token tribute to their power, so that they might leave him in peace, "Here is some of that American laundry powder for your wife, you pour it into a little hot water and then shake it up till the tub is full of foam, then pour all the water in at once..." "But how can we thank you, Mr. Jost, really we can't take it for nothing..." "But I've had a good time playing with your kid." "Then we're very grateful to you... and some time you must stop by..."

Our main avenue here is a curved pasture with a little stream and marsh-marigolds, ours is the last yellow house, Mrs. Heymerova would come back from her daughter's in the fall, Jacek unlocked the door with a key that seemed made for a church and then impatiently up the wooden stairs to his "retreat."

The room measured a little over 200 sq. ft., on the brass bed an orange blanket made of merino wool, a dark oaken wardrobe big as a closet and four heavy chairs around an oval table, on its cover a scene of stags rutting and more deer hanging on the wall above the bed, made from the same antique woven material, an unbelievable sofa in the shape of a sitting bathtub, and outside the window a strip of shiny green grass all the way out to the horizon—all for fifty crowns a month.

Cautiously Jacek unpacked his satchel, an ashtray between the horns of the rutting stag, two glasses onto the shelf in the cupboard next to the bottle of Beaujolais, the pot and saucepan onto the shelf by the cooking stove, and the guitar pick behind the strings of the instrument, all the wrapping paper into the fireplace, in a sudden inspiration he brought an armful of fir brush in from the courtyard, he lit a match, and a fire roared in the fireplace, the crackle of dried wood and the sweet, pure scent of a real fire, and what was time—

"You've practically moved into that 'retreat' of yours...," Lenka mumbled, but she had no time for conversation, for outside there was laundry to take down, and decisively Lenicka preferred to go with her, it seemed that three times a week with Daddy was enough, "And do you really have to study so much for your work?" Grandma asked again, "Technology is moving forward with seven-league boots—" Jacek said firmly, "and what I learned ten years ago—" "I know, they were saying the same thing on TV the other day..." and she followed the two Lenkas out to get the wash.

It had gone easier than he had at first supposed, let's start getting ready, like an inventory taker Jacek strolled through the empty apartment, or more like a future heir through the apartment of someone who has not yet passed away, leave all the pictures here, we'll swipe a thermometer from Cottex, take the desk lamp to the retreat with him, leave the glazed plastic red hip popotamus at home, don't take any junk, as with cattle out on the range so on all his things Jacek saw one of two brands: TAKE or LEAVE—the polyester shirts, the sport shirts, the black leather tie, the suede sports jacket, the black sweater, the dagger, all glowed in the dusk of the vacated apartment like a neon sign TAKE, the undershirts, the worn-out shorts, the knitted vests, ten Christmas ties from Grandma, all the glass and porcelain, the slippers worn till they shone, and the gardening jacket labeled in black LEAVE, a bottle of Yugoslav Badel brandy TAKE, the

ficus LEAVE, in the kitchen there are perhaps hundreds of
things which we learn about only in a closing inventory,
for what in God's name are these funnels, mashers, glass
spoons, sieves, jugs, saucers, and slicers, the technologi-
cal furnishings of the industry that has gradually pushed
us out onto a corner of the balcony, allotting us just a slot
for depositing paychecks, a slot without a bottom.

The three women (how many of them did we actually
freely choose?) were returning from collecting the wash,
more excited by what was going on in the yard than
they'd been that time on the excursion to the Giant Mountains, and almost surprised that we were still at home—
surprise on both sides would have been appropriate—
and without delay two of them recommenced that bub-
bling, hissing, baking, and boiling, that costly sixteen-
hour chemistry on conveyor belts out of which there
emerges for us, most of the time, a warmed-over sausage
or cold toast and watery tea.

"Why do you always take those old socks when you've
never worn the red ones?"

"Why do you have to wear those black suede shoes in
this heat?"

"Why don't you ever wear your suede jacket?"

The old socks and the suede shoes are things on their
way to wearing out, thus LEAVE, but save the red socks,
thus TAKE, and the suede jacket is a component of the
Suitcase, worked out a hundred times in the finest detail
and packed as perfectly as the luggage of a cosmonaut.

"Daddy gwab me—" Lenicka says today for the first
time and in ninety seconds "Want down—" and right
back to Grandma's skirts, counting Lenka's question,
what is confectioner's yeast, together with the appropriate answer, plus bringing potatoes up from the cellar, we were needed today for only six minutes in all, of
that really needed for only a hundred seconds. To the
sound of triple snores Jacek selected a suitable knife from
among six candidates in the now silent kitchen, the one

selected was thoroughly put to the test by cutting into the sideboard: the knife TAKE, the sideboard LEAVE.

From Cottex he could now make it comfortably without haste, after 2:00, to the self-service store to buy a quarter-loaf of bread, a bottle of milk, and a piece of Swiss cheese, the bus to Telnice leaves at 2:28 and stops around the corner, "Good day, Mrs. Klusakova!" "How are you, Mr. Svitacek!" and at three we're already at home in the retreat. Jacek put the provisions away on the shelf and from his empty satchel into the waiting dark oaken wardrobe only one hanger for his cosmonaut's suede jacket, take off his wristwatch and lock it up in the wardrobe.

With the orange blanket slowly to the grassy strip at the edge of the forest, from the sparkling green clouds of the treetops the dark flashes of treetrunks down to the high grass, lying there seeing only the half-circle of grass against the ocean of sky. And then hour after hour by the window, until the grass turns grey and then black, from the ridges the night breeze of eternity and freedom, when did we last have time for the stars, I'm coming to see you, I'm here, your new neighbor, hello, Cassiopeia, how are you, Big Dipper—

## III — eleven

A large yellow envelope, METERED MAIL, a good half pound, another book, no doubt, Jacek tore open the paper and from the large yellow envelope a stream of dozens of variously colored smaller ones splattered onto his desk, on all of them written, in different hands and in different places, the same thing:

Key word: "Live!" 63064-v

Perhaps fifty of them and another fifty remained inside, in terror Jacek crammed the flood into his desk drawer, banged it shut, and locked it, horror—

From the desk to the window and to the curtain from the flower stand, at least one, Jacek unlocked the drawer and in the concealing frame of his chest and both his arms he tore open a small blue envelope:

Dear Sir!

I read your advertisement in the newspaper Prace, and because I have the same interests as you, I took the liberty of writing you.

I am 17 and I work as a salesgirl in a food store. Should you be interested in making my acquaintance, write to this address:

Milena Klimtova

Rorysova 28b

Litvinov.

Seventeen, aren't you ashamed, and Jacek again banged the drawer shut, then opened it again and greedily read on:

Dear Friend,

because I too seek an acquaintance and a new life, I am taking the liberty of introducing myself to you.

My name is Kvetoslava Mozna. I am a teacher in grades 6 to 9. I have dark chestnut hair. I am 5 ft. 5 with a good figure and nice features. I will soon be 27. I have varied interests, a serious character, and a sensitive temperament.

Address: Kvet. Mozna

Teacher, Secondary Public School, Pikhartova St.

Carlsbad

Best wishes, Kv. Mozna

Dear Sir,

I am taking the liberty of replying to your ad.

I am 31 divorced the innocent party medium-thin figure all sorts of interests.

I have a daughter five years old pretty and clever.

I live in Ceska Trebova where I have a furnished apartment in my own house and besides that my own car.

I am answering your ad because I want to find a good father for my child and a good husband for myself whose strong and not to tall—Im 4 ft. 8 1/2.

I am answering your ad for a friend, whom I am very fond of and who doesn't know anything about it.

She is 27, an office worker, a pretty and intelligent girl She has a little boy by him She has a new model car. She does badly, because she avoids all action ever since that bad thing happened to her. That's why I'd like to help her. If her good points suit you

I have a mild, sensitive nature. I am 5 ft. 5, I have light brown hair, blue eyes and a sincere heart Surely you are full of ideals and you believe that at least some of them will find fulfillment. I believe that too and if it isn't too much trouble for you, please write to me at this address

I don't know what your further requirements might be. My hobbies are culture and nature. I've been in a number of countries on agency tours, and I take pictures sometimes

If you haven't found your partner yet, write to this address

you too are divorced, I believe, as a matter of fact, that a divorced man has a better basis for understanding and friendship and then marriage and also that he can steer clear of unpleasant experiences from the former marriage you won't be sorry and you won't be disappointed When the hand of Fate has cheated us so

Dear Sir! I am a civil servant, born 1939, and I am looking for a man who doesn't acquire anything too easily or without effort and who is familiar with losses and difficulties. Eliska Rejckova, Cheb, Obrancu miru 1182.

I haven't the least idea how to answer an ad and so I haven't any idea how to go about this, but I am very interested. I am an architect (4 yrs. professional school), twenty-three years old, a slender blonde they call me Dada.

By chance I was attracted to your ad today of course I really would like to meet you I have an active interest in literature and culture a charming little boy culture and nature 25 years old I have a daughter who doesn't know anything 5 ft. 8 for the purpose of negotiating conditions with a daughter for each one to pour strength into the other Dear Unknown still the highest form of love the slogan we share is LIVE! single lively 5 ft. 5 slender figure When a dear one dies culture and nature 29 years old be everything for one's husband 26 yrs. 5 ft. 6 29 yrs. 5 ft. 3 5 ft. 5 so he would love me dark chestnut 22 yrs. fine figure 24 yrs. 5 ft. 5 We live in a gamekeeper's lodge 26 yrs. really pretty 5 ft. 6 nature blonde 23 yrs. true love 26 yrs. 5 ft. 4 slender figure 33 years 22 yrs. 21 27 27 23

"I'll be late today," Jacek telephoned Lenka, "No, I'm not going to the retreat, a mountain of work's piled up here all of a sudden..."

A total of 114 female readers of *Prace*, from 17 to 38 years of age, were willing to begin, practically right away, a new life with a 33-year-old divorced engineer. After throwing out the ballast, there remained 22 potentially interesting cases, 10 as a reserve, and the rest to be disposed of along with all the envelopes.

On a metal shovel Jacek fed letter after letter into the fire, and he carried off the black heaps of ash to flush away, he drank strong coffee and with a cigarette he sat down to his old Urania, prepared 22 requests for further specifications, as detailed as possible please, and dropped 22 letters into the mailbox.

Within a week a second large yellow envelope with 19 additional offers, one of them for the interesting and two more for the reserve—and 22 replies, 16 of them within two days' time, i.e., immediately:

When from a distance I saw your blue envelope, I have a mailbox with holes in it and no letters ever come for me

terribly happy, of course don't make anything of it, but I'm awfully happy that you answered. Maybe you can understand how a person feels when he's terribly happy, and that's me today. I really mean it honest.

please forgive my answering so late. But it wasn't my fault. The letter came to my home and from the typed envelope Mother thought

I am an entirely normal girl, maybe a little above average. Of course, that's just my say-so. Many people at school say I'm pretty

I really don't know where to begin. You ask me to tell you everything that can be told in a letter, so I will try as hard as I can to

well, as for my head (I mean the hair), that's worse. I wear it red. So much for the head.

I graduated from college in Brno, a copy of my diploma may not be necessary. It would be nice if by chance you were a chemist too, but of course be assured

I'm a blonde, not so pretty, perhaps rather striking, from time to time people turn around and stare at me, but I hope it's not because I look like a freak. Modern dancing can really arouse me

I'm happy when lilacs are in bloom, especially white ones, and I'm terribly fond of jasmine.
You know, behind our garden

I spend my free days at home, we have a large
house. For me it's bridge, which under all circumstances

I love the sun, we could go sunbathing
together

especially in German and I can't resist—suddenly you seem so close to me—

I like the wind, the rain, Armenian cognac, I
don't like rice, noodles, or long intermissions

for five years now in the chemistry of fats
and I tell you it's an extremely interesting
field. I don't know what you do, but the
chemistry of fats

and so I began to study Italian. It would be
wonderful if you could go to Florence with me in
September. All formalities including liras
would be taken care of by my brother, who has an
important position

I too was disillusioned, but believe me, life
is wonderful. Sometimes strange, but always
wonderful. Imagine that all talent, experience, longing and dreams are possible,
that it is truly possible to live. I will wait.

Jacek wrote 19 answers, this time with a carbon for the
files. "This is Jacek again. No, Mija, not for sleeping,
rather the opposite—to keep me from sleeping... Five
containers or so. Oh, yes, and what you said that time,
that I was getting grey, that fungus infection on my skin,
well— You said that you could give me a prescription for
a dye... Yes? Well then, make it red!"

Naked, Jacek stood in the bathroom in front of the mirror and rubbed a solution of Tinct. Castellani onto his
skin, you only needed a little and even that would stain

his clothing, but then these pajamas are LEAVE, the healed and attractive skin TAKE, and people would look when we go sunbathing together—straight from the bottle he poured the red ink onto his body and rubbed it into his skin, Lenicka ran away in terror at the sight of her daddy bleeding horribly, Grandma crossed herself, and Jacek laughed softly as he lay down in bed beside a dumbfounded Lenka, not even an executioner could have produced such an effect.

## III — twelve

He left his new iridescent raincoat unbuttoned so that the suede of his jacket could be seen and the narrow strip of his black leather tie could stand out against the dazzling white of his nylon shirt, Jacek clicked his tongue in the mirror, walked slowly down the stairs to Platform Two at Usti Main Station, and at 6:20 sharp set out on express train R 12 to Prague.

Sitting by the window and facing forward, Jacek glanced at the newspaper headlines and tossed the paper into the net above his head, the chocolate-colored Elbe sparkled out of the milky vapor and the milky gauze hanging above the green fur of the opposite bank, in Lovosice at 6:41 according to the timetable, by Vranany an hour of refreshing second sleep, in Vranany Jacek pleasantly awoke, now quite himself, a Carmen cigarette and from his black traveling satchel an azure blue spiral notebook.

The first two engagements were in Prague, sheets I and II.

*I. Engineer Jarka Vesela (27), chief analyst at Foodcorp, natl. enterpr.*
*Grad. of Chem. Dept., Brno*
*Passion: chem. of fats*

*Erot: uncryst.*
*Other: tennis before work, camping*
*Charact: enthusiastic about chem. of fats*
*8:02 on arrival of R 12 CAUTION: II at 8:30 at the*
*Palace Hotel, 2nd fl.*

*II. Engineer Anna Bromova (37), dep. dir.* VUGMT
*Grad. of the College of Eng. of the* VST, *Prague*
*Likes wind, rain, Armenian cognac (remember when order-*
*ing!), dislikes rice, noodles, and long intermissions.*
*Erot: ironic. Divor.*
*Other: Russ., Eng., Ger. Terribly erudite*
*Charact: high intellect, high style!*
*8:30 Palace, 2nd fl. CAUTION: train leaves Main Sta. at*
*9:11 R 30*

R 12 drew into Prague Central one minute after 8:01, nervous Jacek got out last and was the last to leave the platform, at the exit gate a rather short powerfully built blonde with a white box (the obligatory identification sign for all of them) held timidly under her arm, Jarka Vesela—the fats chemist—erot. uncryst.—doesn't like rice, noodles—no, that's II, this is I, Jarka Vesela—the fats chemist—what else, quick—8:30 at the Palace—

"It looks like you're waiting for me—"

"Yes, that is... Hello, I'm Jarka Vesela..."

Calmed by the nervous way she played with the white box, Jacek offered her his arm, they threw the box into a trashcan and smiled at one another.

"You see, and I thought it was done by heat—" Jacek said at the soiled table in the station cafeteria.

"Oh, no, that would burn it! I tried countercurrent extraction, but the middle layer contained enough biological crap to puke, seriously, I felt like throwing up, even though I don't mind chewing frozen spinal cord and I love a bite of raw pork gall bladder now and then."

"So you went to school in Brno too...," said Jacek, pushing away the untouched bouillon imperceptibly but hurriedly, and quickly gulping down air.

"Yes, and I recall the slaughterhouse there with pleasure. Once they brought in three animals dead of hoof-and-mouth disease, and my colleague Kousal and I first cut out the guts—"

"It's a terrible shame I've got to run," said Jacek sweating, unable to down even a spoonful of the bilberry compote, "but I really have to..."

"I'm awfully glad I got to know you. Next time I'll take you to the lab, now I'm busy with bones from the salvage collection, and if there weren't so many flies on them—"

"I'm on my way to Poland for four months and then I'll definitely write you!"

"Just wait, I'll make a fats chemist out of you yet!"

"...except for the fact that I'm a wee bit old for you," said Engineer Anna Bromova (37, dep. dir. of VU) in the 2nd fl. café of the Palace Hotel, playing with a white box of Kent Micronite Filters (a crown per cigarette, remember when ordering!), "but I've already scored my first point."

"I can assure you...," Jacek said with an effort, over a bottle of mineral water.

"You could have turned around in the door and disappeared. You're reassuring, I like that..."

"...and you like the wind and the rain and—I'm awfully fond of taking walks in the rain."

"Rudolf—two Armenian cognacs. If you'll permit—"

"I was just about to say the same thing."

"Only five minutes left. I've been thinking it over, but I haven't thought of any job for you in Prague."

"But I wouldn't think of bothering..."

"Not a thing. No prospect even."

"Please don't think it depends on..."

"In any case you couldn't live with me. I can't do anything for you. Shall we go? Rudolf, I'll pay for the gentleman as well."

"Waiter, we're going! —Two more double Armenian cognacs and I'll pay for everything on one check, for the lady's Kents as well!"

"Those I brought with me from home..."

"That doesn't matter, you can divvy up with Rudolf. I'm glad to pay for your taxi in the bargain, and for the postage on your letters. The stationery looked very official, in any case."

"So did yours— That'll do, Jacek. If you're pretending, you're doing a marvelous job of it— No, you have two more minutes, don't be ridiculous... that was only to filter out.... Do you really think you could bear having me beside you—with your eyes open?"

"Yes, but first I'd have to stuff a towel in your mouth."

"I'm glad you didn't turn around in the doorway and disappear...," she whispered to Jacek when he got out of her black official limousine at the Main Station, ugly but very interesting, brown and skinny, her eyes sparkled and her slender fingers were warm. Jacek kissed them and left Prague on express R 30 precisely according to the timetable.

*III. Hanicka Kohoutkova (22), elem. teacher*
*Teachers Inst. with honor*
*Passion:   children and animals*
*Erot:   undevel.*
*Other:   lilacs, esp. white, jasmine*
*Charact:   a kid, naïve, sinc.*
*10:34 on arrival of R 30. 192 minutes. Depart 1:46 R 28*

A large white box with a pale blue ribbon, held like a baby, appeared on the platform of the Pardubice station—it belonged to a tall (5 ft. 7) girl with light chestnut hair.

"It looks like you're waiting for me—"

"Yes."

"I recognized you by the box."

"Yes."

"Should we go for a little walk?"

"Yes."

From the station to the tiny park in front of the chemistry school and then to the main street, "Wouldn't it be better to turn off somewhere?" said Jacek, "Why?" she retorted and down the main street to the square with its Green Gate, fortunately Pardubice soon comes to an end and from the square there are stairs leading to a large park, on the bench between the two lovers the barrier of the black satchel and the white box with the ribbon.

"We should have a little talk, Hanicka."

"Yes, Jacek."

White clusters of lilac burst forth from the tops of bushes, Jacek crossed the lawn and with repeated jumps gathered some of the flowers, Hanicka ran out after him onto the meadow, clapped her hands, suddenly took off her shoes and hop hop we've got a beautiful bouquet, flushed Hanicka laughed and Jacek tried to kiss her, "What are you up to?" and she patiently offered him her tender forehead.

"You taste like condensed milk..."

"Hey, I like that, and the best thing is eating it with strawberries!"

"And what else do you like?"

"Are we going to be so familiar right off?"

"Yes."

"First of all I like children. That's why I teach. Children are terribly sweet. I like them very much... And then white lilacs and jasmine... I like all white flowers very much, especially white lilacs and also—"

"And animals?"

"I like animals very much. At home we have lots of animals. We have chickens, rabbits, ducks—"

"And your Mother?"

"I like Mom and Dad best of all."

"Could you like me too?"

"That's why we're meeting—"

A Maytime fairy tale on the succulent meadows of Pardubice, where everything asks for caressing and where there is only a single mountain far and wide, Kuneticka, a green angelfood cake on a warm green plate.

On the train now, Jacek placed the white box with the ribbon in the baggage net over his seat, Hanicka herself had baked him that poppyseed coffee cake, she smiled at him from below the window, "I'm so happy that I have my own boyfriend now—" and R 28 left at 1:46.

*IV. Lida Adalska (25), forest ranger's widow*
*Schooling: scarcely*
*Erot: sincere*
*Other: lives in a forest rang. lodge*
*Charact: ?*
*2:48 in the car, 14 mins. DO NOT GET OFF! Depart 3:02*

On the platform at Ceska Trebova a woman with a white box, Jacek leaned out and waved, the woman came to the window—just 14 mins!—with a placid smile.

"I'm Jost."

"I'm Adalska."

"Unfortunately, I can't get out, because I have to—"

"That doesn't matter. I just wanted to see you."

"I'm terribly sorry, but in a couple of minutes—"

"That's enough. Don't say anything more, please."

She looked up at the window and smiled silently, a beautiful woman at life's summit, all around her the flow of those transferring for Ostrava, Krnov, and Zilina, they bumped into her but with dignity she held her place all fourteen of those minutes, one after another, as if embedded in the stone of the platform and finally now the whistle, "Mrs. Adalska, next time I'll come for longer..."

"It really was kind of you. This is from me—" and she handed Jacek her white box, already the train was getting under way, "—it's what I always gave my husband when he went away."

"Lida, I... I thank you and definitely—"

"It's me who should thank you."

R 28 continued on its way east through meadows and woods, in Lida's box there was bread, meat, salt, and a large dry apple in a dazzlingly white napkin, Jacek bit his lips, what else in God's name do you want, and with horror he opened the blue spiral notebook.

*V. Tanicka Rambouskova (20), wages bookkeeper at a flax mill.*
*Business school graduate*
*Passion: Tanicka Rambouskova*
*Erot: novels for girls*
*Other: terr. chaos*
*Charact: an incred. ambit. brat*
*3:23 on arrival of R 28. 115 mins. Depart 5:18 R 8*

"...and we'll leave this place for good. Some time in Prague and then out into the world—" Tanicka danced far ahead of Jacek and only from time to time glanced back at him, from the platform of the Svitavy station, in addition to his satchel, he had to carry her enormous empty white box, most likely visible even to jets seven miles up, "I know men too well already—" she asserted at one corner of the station building, "—never has one of them had me and none ever will—" at the other.

"That of course makes our further correspondence dubious," said Jacek.

"No, just the opposite, you'll fall in love with me and I'll flirt with you and that will attract you most!"

"How old are you really, Tanicka? Show me your ID card."

"And suppose I'm only eighteen? What does it matter—"

"In the letter you said twenty."

"A little white lie, so as not to discourage you from the beginning. Next time I'd like to meet in Prague or at least in Ceska Trebova. What kind of car do you have?"

"A white eighteen-cylinder Cadillac with a trailer."

"Why did you come by train then?"

"My left carburetor exploded and I had to wait for a repairman from Washington. They won't give him a passport..."

"I wish I had my own passport..."

"The foreign minister himself would provide one for my wife."

"Why did you get divorced— oh, that's a stupid question! You felt hemmed in, you longed for freedom, air, the sea, distant lands... and women. Your wife became indifferent soon after marriage, only for the sake of the child you kept up the appearance of a happy marriage, until one day a woman crossed your path like a ray of light in the darkness and the garden of singing roses opened for the mournful knight... Come, let's sit at the station, I like the tracks and the smoke... We'll have a fine love affair."

Tanicka's white box didn't fit into the net above his seat, Jacek carefully placed it on the seat beside him and for the last time he leaned out of the window.

"You see—" whispered Tanicka below him on the platform, "no, you don't see in the slightest how beautiful life is, how terribly beautiful—" and R 8 pulled out of Svitavy at 5:20, two minutes late according to the timetable.

*VI. Dr. Mojmira Stratilova (29), translator*
*Studied at the Fac. of Phil., a year in Paris*
*Long sents. w/o commas or content*
*Pure flame of soul w/o body, pure abstraction*
*Charact:  delicate, subt., ether., immater. angel*
*6:35 by the sta. clock*

By 6:50 according to the sta. clock six women had come and gone, one after another on someone's arm, at 6:52 a seventh rushed up, grotesquely tousled, straight toward Jacek who, leaning against the wall in a semi-recumbent position, already drowsing with his satchel, was now as ransacked and empty as the white boxes traveling by express to the east, "You're the one, yes—Jacek? All happiness, hi! Listen, weren't you supposed to have a rolled-up magazine in your right hand? What's that—me and a white box? Ha-ha, that's a good one! I'm frightfully hungry and if you haven't got any money let's go dine at a stupid couple's I know, you don't have to pay any attention to them... You've got money? Do you feel like investing in me?" Distracted, Jacek only nodded apathetically.

Two vodkas, two eggs with horseradish, two Rumford soups, two Moravian skewers flambée, two bottles of red Moravian wine, "What else?"

Two portions of kidneys en papillote, two portions of carp à la Moulin, and two bottles of white Tramin, "What else?"

Two orders of fried Swiss cheese and, worn out, Jacek gave in, it'd been a long day and tomorrow we want to get up at half-past five, two double cognacs "Armenian, and salvage me two portions of bones besides—" Jacek ordered for Mojmira, and he asked the head waiter to find him a place to room and board in Prague, preferably in the forest ranger's lodge, then all of a sudden a car of some sort and on the back seat he clapped shut like a pocket knife.

A terrifying clatter like a tank in a scrapyard, a monstrously beautiful alarmclock from the days of the Austrian Empire set for half-past five, on the floor slept a woman in a sweatsuit, Jacek stepped over her, the walls lined with books high as his chest, above them on all four walls a connected strip of reproductions of the Impressionists (here reality has been tranformed into spots of color) without frames, even the white margins had been cut away and all the pictures exulted together, above on the molding a display of empty bottles, So long, angel, and thanks a bonch! Jacek typed on the paper sticking out of the typewriter, below some French verses, and he ran down the stairs, the house gate was locked, he burst into the courtyard, hop onto the garbage can and skip over the fence, the scent of fresh asphalt and with it lilacs in full bloom, from the shrubbery four legs projected, and Jacek skipped across the lawns mowed English style, suddenly a familiar giant plane tree and behind it a small pink palace, at seventeen, behind that bench, he'd been initiated by Mrs. Sbiralova from Medlanky, the second circle of the spiral was beginning to unwind—

On express train R 21 he could sleep his rosy fill from 6:38 to 10:53, there was no need for sudden stops, in Prague baked lamb with spinach and a good local beer, at 1:59 R 55 leaves, up along the current of the springtime river, but why home so soon, what else have we got on the menu:

VII. *Tina Vlachova (27), occupation?*
*Address evident. false*
*Letters very brief, techn. matter-of-fact*
*Erot:   snapshot in bathing suit, like a Modigl.*
*Charact:    ?  WATCH OUT!*
*Bus:  CSAD from Usti at 4:00, stops Bohosudov Fun. 4:31*
*63 mins. Dep. 5:34, arr. Usti 6:05, as from Berl. expr. R*
*151*

At the Bohosudov Funicular, on the corner, a golden-orange Tina de Modigliani was unaffectedly smoking, "Looks like you're waiting for me—" no white box, a type you can't help but speak to and in half an hour you're talking to as if you'd known her for years, "...and then they made Prague off-limits for me. But it's OK here as a waitress. I can make out anywhere."

"I thought you were giving me a fake address..."

"I've been here for three months—" and she gestured with her chin toward the vista beyond the funicular, in the pervasive fragrance the numbered metal pylons ran up through the forest to the peak of Vulture Mountain, five hundred years ago, it was said, Archbishop Jan came here to sin, then meadows and further on above the precipice of Mt. Kneziste, on its peak the Mosquito Tower chalet, and at the tip of the tower Tina's room.

"Take me up there sometime... soon..."

"So come back."

"I've traveled five hundred miles to find you... And from my retreat it's only an hour's walk through the woods."

The bus back was already pulling into the turnaround, "Come whenever you want to—" Tina de Modigliani whispered, "but you must always call first!"

Depart 5:34, arr. Usti 6:05 as from the Berl. expr. R 151, streetcar No. 5 to Vseborice, from the door's opening Lenicka's voice, "Daddy—" and Lenka was coming to welcome him with a smile, "You forgot the white plush again, didn't you—"

## III — thirteen

Daddy, don't go way—" so stay with her until she goes to sleep, in a couple of years she'd be coming home only to eat and sleep, Daddy the cashier and hotelier, in any case he'd be good for little else by then and this eager child of the electronic age would only be bored by an aging man who had never achieved anything and who himself had never lived, I can only advise you, daughter, not to take after your father—the art of leaving in time—but since they've tied us here, the wrists bloodied by sharp nylon cords and the arms weakening with vain twisting, dragged in harness to one's pension and then to one's death, a man who once was able to live but who didn't come up with the courage needed to live, who started to die at the age of thirty-three on a cross of his own construction.

Clean all the shoes in the foyer and bathe in hot water, "You're not coming to bed yet, Lenka?"

"How can I, it's Thursday!"

"Can I help with anything?"

"Just go to bed, you've had enough with your trip."

Go to bed after your trip and get some sleep before another one, the rest of the night is spent ironing, sewing, or bathing, during the day we don't see each other and if we do it's only for a new verification of the fact that we get in each other's way, what's left of you, my love—

"Daddy come home today?"

"But he came home last night... So hop into your pants!"

"Daddy put on pants!"

"Shhh—Daddy's still beddie-bye and we mustn't..."

"I want to see Daddy!—"

And Jacek crawled out of bed, my darlings, and pulled on Lenicka's tights, she played, she was affectionate, flirtatious, she showed her belly-button and again so many many great big kisses, nothing's so sweet to kiss as my little one, "Daddy, take me to school!" "Daddy has to go beddie-bye some more!" fifty minutes more and then wake up again to the horror of desertion—

On the bright June morning Mommy and Daddy cross the lawn and the little girl flies up between them swinging on their arms, Lenka's happy laugh and her hair in the wind, "We can still run, Jacek—" up to the bronze gate of the institution for discarding children.

"When you're wittle, Daddy, and I'm all gwowed up, I won't send you to school."

"And where will you put me during the day, my darling?"

"I'll take you by the hand and take you to the pond and the movies and the swings—"

"So give me your hand and we'll go—" "But Jacek, how about your work?—," a couple of work days have already gone for experiments, so today we'll try a negative one, the little one and Daddy both had to be shown that it would bore them very quickly, Jacek took Lenicka by the hand and systematically led her through the child's vision, first to the pond to pick posies and bathe her tootsies, a pond in June is not so bad, actually—well, she's not bored so far, but what next, at ten to the movies to see a silly film in which a little boy and a little girl engage in a moralistic discussion on how to rehabilitate their drunken Daddy, but Lenicka's spoken subtitles transformed it into a larger-than-life story, half grotesque and half myth, the experiment went aground but, touched, Jacek swung his little girl in the swing for his sixth crown's worth, "Fwy wif me, Daddy, into the sky—"

In front of the gate of Lenka's factory a young man waiting with a motorcycle, when was the last time we stood that way, so impatient, of the crowd of exiting women Lenka is still the prettiest, happily the little family makes its way homeward.

Water our strawberry vines, why buy berries from the policeman's wife in Ritin, all three of us sit down on the grass in the sun and from both sides we smell the scent of a loved one, on our own land, WHERE DO WE COME FROM, our daughter gets her beauty sleep and on the other side of the wall we come together, our longing contained within an order, WHO ARE WE, my wife and I— half-naked, Jacek leaned out of the window with a cigarette in his mouth and inhaled deeply, directly opposite was Trost, leaning equally far out of his window and equally half-naked, he inhaled deeply too, and behind him the same dull glow of the lamp placed in the same spot as ours, over our beds.

"So yesterday I sank a German steamer," during Saturday's sixty-forty Vitenka ecstatically described an international collision of river boats on the frontier at Hrensko, we were lying in the garden in back of the house, WHERE WILL WE LAND, the afternoon before, Mija had flown off to Tunis.

Mr. Stefacek came out of the tow-cloth storeroom with a new toy for men, a sort of tiny TV set but when you turned the switch you saw color photos of film Venuses, "My Verka's better—" Petrik Hurt said with conviction, in his voice so much sated happiness had the sound of conviction.

On the ridged mud of the courtyard a large black limousine with a Brno license plate swayed magnificently, and out of its door, held majestically open for him, floated the general director's deputy himself, Franta Docekal (the director of Cottex suddenly grew smaller and his two deputies shriveled up completely), in the front part of the director's office the stout marshal of the courtyard was fanning himself with a handkerchief from those two precious sets we'd been having engraved for months, like gems, one for the Czechoslovak exhibit at the Montreal World Exposition, the other for the Shah of Iran.

Jacek was praised by His Majesty and rose, he grinned mockingly, don't bother, one possible way to start a career is to clear out, as you know so well yourself—an undistinguished planning expert, Franta Docekal had fallen ill here some years ago with an inflammation of the lungs, the "Usti syndrome," and the doctors had recommended a healthier climate, the Brno one for instance, here in unhealthy Usti Franta left behind a miserable apartment with a hateful wife and a lame malicious brat, there he married a pretty doctor with her own house and went rapidly to the top, a dizzying career built on an inflammation of the lungs, why not inhale some hydrochloric acid—

On the column in the main square a new color poster, Candy in a white tux BACK FROM HIS TRIUMPHANT YUGOSLAV TOUR, he had it thanks to some stolen mercury and tow-cloth, if it hadn't been for their mishaps, today we'd still have lab assistant Klecanda and planning expert Docekal at Cottex. And Vitenka, with his inferiority complex, came to life only when Mija stabbed him with scissors in a fight and thus provided grounds for the start of the highly successful Balvin Improvement, only through the alcoholism of his first wife and the infidelity of his second, through two misfortunes, had Petrik Hurt found happiness with his Verka, from the depth of failure one bounces back—

The flagellant Saturday ritual of order was going full blast, Lenka with five things at once and already grey with exhaustion, "If only you wouldn't keep getting in the way—"

A 28-year-old pretty intell. off. worker with an interest in culture and nature and with own 1st-cat. apart., forget that pudding, which we won't eat anyway, come and stab me instead with the scissors, it'll give both of us infinite relief, don't buy me new shirts I don't feel like wearing but buy yourself a case of that cheap Georgian cognac you like so much and invite over all your friends it wouldn't occur to you to invite without some reason, give me a pretext, bring someone you'd like to have home for the night, neglect me, get drunk, deck me out with horns, beat me, lose your mind, desert me or kick me out, and if you still love me then out of love be the cause of what I must commit, I WANT IT TO BE AGAINST MY WILL, the inability to make an end, to change, to begin, and the desperate desire for an end, a change, a beginning, we do everything for change except change itself and only out of failure can we rise to the top, SOMEONE HURL A BOMB, we thirst for the sweetness of the whip of necessity, at least throw a firecracker, let me then begin to throttle you, I HAVE PUT EVERYTHING IN A STATE OF READINESS, I ONLY AWAIT THE SIGNAL, on the catapult the last bolts are being tightened and the flight path is being tuned, I am taking my seat in the flight chair, WHICH CAPTAIN FAILURE WILL NOW FIRE OFF—send him a car and driver.

# THE SECOND HALF OF THE GAME

*All roads lead to paradise if we follow
them long enough. —Henry Miller*

## Part IV — Beginnings — fourteen

*T*he driver braked hard and turned to the left, the
springs of the limousine undulated, through an open
bronze gate they drove into the château park, Jacek let go
of Anna Bromova's warm fingers and gravel drummed
against the bottom of the car.

Outside their windows stretched a row of grey statues
of saints and on the court behind it a rather tan young
man dressed only in white shorts was playing tennis with
a charming black girl, "Now the backhand, look—" he
called to her, laughing, and the ball flew past the golden
arrows projecting from St. Sebastian's body.

Behind twelve-foot glass doors a red runner went up
marble stairs to the second floor and on a white tablecloth
a forest of bottles, "Have some Campari," Anna advised
Jacek in a whisper, "and some of that red caviar before
they gobble it up—," and on the way to the table Jacek
was introduced to twenty-three big shots, any of whose
visits to Cottex would have forced them to interrupt
production and press whole work shifts into clean-up
and decorating activities.

The young tennis player came to lunch promptly at one
in a consummate suit of dark-grey natural silk, he shook
his head no to the aperitif and gave Jacek a friendly smile:

"Physicist?"

"Chemist," Jacek said with a friendly smile.

"Isotopes?"

"Cotton."

"Please excuse me," said the young man (as if Jacek were suddenly dead as far as he was concerned), and while a waitress served sirloin steak (real sirloin in real cream) and poured out some white Melnik wine, the young man silently, carefully, and rapidly ate his bouillon with raw egg, cold smoked mackerel with three carrots, and a pint of warm milk ("He's on a high-protein diet—" Anna whispered as she heaped on Jacek's plate a second helping of dumplings Esterhazy with bits of bacon, boiled in a napkin, sprinkled with sautéed breadcrumbs and chopped parsley, and drowned in butter), he looked at his watch and left at once ("Now he'll sleep for ninety minutes—he wants to keep up full efficiency for another fifty years..." "But who is he?" "An atomic physicist. A leading one." "No, no more dumplings, please.").

Jacek followed Anna down the path between the hazel bushes and toward a vine-covered wall, Anna leaned her back against it and drew him to her, "I love you because you don't close your eyes when you kiss...," and she stepped onto a rock in order to be closer to his level. From behind a giant treetrunk in the middle of almost a half-mile of lawn a black-and-red figure emerged, skipping strangely and jerking its arms and head it aimed straight toward the lovers, suddenly it performed a series of somersaults and again that crazy rhythm, "Anci—" Jacek whispered uneasily, "there's something coming this way..." "But that's only Jozef... the atomic physicist."

The atomic physicist Jozef, in a black sweatsuit with red pleats, danced the *letkis* across the lawn snapping his fingers, when he reached the wall he looked at his watch and trotted back, disappearing into the hazel bushes.

"Clown," Jacek gave vent to his feelings.

"Not really. He pulled off a couple of terrific thermonuclear stunts."

"But they only do that in Russia and America..."

"He just flew back from America and now he's going to spend half a year in Dubno, outside Moscow."

"Is he really that good?"

"He is."

"Good God, how old can that kid be?"

"Thirty-three."

"Ouch... That's the age when you've got to do something. Or else die."

In the sitting and the assembly rooms of Academy House the furniture looked like something out of a museum, Anna explained to Jacek what Empire, Baroque, and Rococo were, "...but that's all rubbish compared with a Florentine chest in the little Yellow Salon, come—" The "little" Yellow Salon was big enough for a proper bleaching-room with a kettle for pressure boiling the skeins, along the back wall were two billiard tables, one the usual barroom size and a giant one for experts, between them, against a background of gold brocade, Jozef in a striped T-shirt and blue jeans making caroms at both tables in turn (Anna was trying to drag Jacek off to one of the windows), on the ordinary one with powerful blows of the cue the quick movement of individual balls over the whole table, on the big one with fine pecks pushing all three balls close together along the cushion, which he was using to advantage, so they play in country inns and so in championship matches, a carom every time, Jozef never even waited for them, he shot a ball on one table and then started toward the other, behind his back a carom every time, "Look at this workmanship—" Anna said, now kneeling, and piously she touched the medieval bands and bolts.

"Excuse me," said Jozef as he bent over the small table, "but do you know if there's a cellulose yet with Carbon 14?"

"I believe... they're working on it somewhere..."

The crack of balls on the small table and a carom, "Please excuse me, in five minutes I'll score three hundred and give up both tables." A fine peck on the big one, behind Jozef's back the balls caromed and assumed position for another one.

"But you aren't even looking at it—" said Anna, and she rose.

"Yes, it's very beautiful—" said Jacek, crawling around the chest on his knees.

Along the row of saints wrought-iron lamps lit up and Anna led Jacek further, behind the slender junipers a sheet of water sparkled like the one behind the cypresses, "It's like an evening at the seashore...," he whispered, "Let's go to the seashore together...," she whispered. On the facade of the château dark windows yawned, in the game room only the TV flickering, in the dining room the light of the chandeliers, and on the top floor a desk lamp by a window. "Of course," said Anna, "that's his room. I wish I could start life again at thirty-three—"

Jacek stroked the head on his shoulder and suddenly felt a fine pricking, he touched Anna's hairpin, passed his fingers over it, and then pulled it out, "Give it to me, Anci—I'll keep it in my wallet..." "And give me in exchange...," and Jacek gave, took, took and gave in that gift of a château park.

Later, on the 4:45 to Berlin, he carefully stuck Anna's hairpin into the dirty clothes in his satchel so that Lenka would find it, and in silence he looked at the river along the track, rising beyond Lovosice are the wavy hills of Stredohori, Varhost, then Ostry, then the thermal swimming pool, then the locks and the castle of Strekov, the Germans call it Schreckenstein, but the name doesn't imply any sort of horror, the final time it will all go by in reverse order—

"It's thoughtful of you to bring me back my hairpin," said Lenka over the open black satchel, "you can't get them in the stores now and Lenicka needs more and more. But you forgot the white plush again..."

"Tomorrow I'm going to Brno, please pack two shirts in the satchel, and no lunch."

R 30 was given permission to leave Prague Main Station only eleven minutes late, but on the plains beyond Kolin it made a fine showing and arrived in Pardubice at exactly 10:34, by the railing in the sun Hanicka Kohoutkova was smiling, she wiped her right palm on her skirt and stepped out to meet him, 192 mins. free.

"Were you good all week?"

"I was, on my honor."

"You didn't upset your father?"

"Yes. On Tuesday instead of doing my German I was staring out the window, and when he tested me I didn't know the second person plural."

"What is the second person plural?"

"*Ihr habet* or *habt, ihr seid, ihr lernet* or *lernt*."

"Good. And why were you staring out the window on Tuesday?"

"I was looking forward to your visit."

On the other side of the lazy Elbe a vaporous blue glow quivered over the yellowing wheat and along the country roadway the red of the poppies cried out, Hanicka stuck one in her mouth, stood with arms akimbo, pulled her belly in, and "Now don't I look like Bizet's Carmen?"

"Not in the least, you lamb. These cornflowers are more your style..."

"That's a bit insulting. I'd like to be like Carmen and dance wildly on tables in some cheap bar, just like her."

"I'd be afraid for you and jealous of those barflies."

"Don't be afraid, anyway I wouldn't be happy, I'm only saying that. I like the *mazurka* best. It must have been wonderful to be a Polish noblewoman!"

"Is that what you tell the children in school?"

"I should say not, that would really do me in! There was a great oppression in those days and the collective farmer had to pull wooden plows with his family."

"Good."

"While the great landowners and later the city manufacturers went from feast to feast. In that case I'd like to have been named Jadwiga."

"And I Tadeusz."

"Hey, that would be just like Mr. Kutil from Rosice! No, wait, I thought up a name for you long ago—Jastrun."

"What do you mean long ago?"

"When I was still a girl, before I got to know you...," and she ran off into the grass, Jacek after her, they chased each other and frolicked until they were out of breath, then they sat down on the warm grass, Hanicka picked flowers and braided two garlands, she put the larger one on Jacek's head and, thus crowned, Jacek glanced at the timetable, Mojmira can't make it today and it's too hot to travel, it isn't so important anyway and a no-show would be a blessing, so he wasted 242 minutes with Hanicka and left at 2:46 on the R 7 for Prague.

No, it isn't so important anyway and a disaster would be a salvation, Jacek was coming back on his usual express from Brno to Usti without actually having been to Brno at all, but at Cottex they'd swallow anything now, their confidence in Jacek was limitless, the director and his deputies had called the factory guard to deal with that crazy shipping clerk come to announce that there was a whole carload of ethyl acetate waiting on our siding, they were convinced that the shipping clerk was soaked to the gills again, but there was the car and two more were confirmed for arrival from Brno, Cottex couldn't use up that lake of ethyl acetate in five years and it couldn't be stored, so it would be traded to Chemopharma for roofing, oxygen, and three hundred porcelain cups for the plant cafeteria, instead of inevitable shortage a gratuitous prosperity, careworn Jacek gazed out of the train at the Elbe, today we're coming home from our trip a day early but next time a day late, Lenka's no longer surprised at anything, so I have to reach for a higher caliber, you compel me to do it, my love—

*Darling:*

*This evening it's raining, I'd like to crawl in beside you and watch the rain with you.*

one from Anna or from Tina

*Expect you definitely 11:00 P.M. Something's come up. Arrange it at home so you can stay till morning*

or best of all from both, in the Lovosice station Jacek decided on the 4:45 to Berlin and he stuck both letters in with the dirty clothes in his satchel so that Lenka could not avoid finding them, the world is calling for us and at home it's always the same old thing, how many years do we want to consume going out to meet that call, how long will that call persist without an answer—

"About the sad pwince!" Lenicka wanted a fairy tale, Jacek stood nervously over her bed, why is it that today Lenka hasn't opened his satchel yet—

"...and he was vewy sad, because he awways had to wide the twain..."

"...train, trrrain..."

"...and in the tunnel they wasn't no wight and out of the woods cwop-cwop-cwop came the auwochs..."

"...aurochs, little one, you say auwochs, aurrrochs..."

"...a gweat gweat big cow and he said, pwince, here is your pwincess and don't cwy, and pwince went boom! And now they was wight in the tunnel and the pwincess gave the pwince a gweat big kiss wike..."

"...great great big like this. And now beddie-bye, darling."

"Daddy don't go way—"

"What's this you've got here...," Lenka said from outside. "Some sort of letters..."

Jacek waited in the dusk of Lenicka's room, her little fist in his hand, and he held his breath, the pwince went boom! And now they was wight in the tunnel—

"Why these are great—whose are they?" Lenka said from the other room.

"Ohh—they're someone's, a pal's."

"I can see they're not yours."

"What's that?" said Jacek from the dusk to the lighted glass panel of the door.

"You'd hardly have stuck them in here so stupidly. *Watch the rain with you,* but when it's raining, Jacek, you just start to yawn, you pull down the blind and go to sleep right where you are—"

"Huh— and what do you make of the other one?"

"There's another one here?— How many women does your pal keep up a correspondence with?"

"Let's see... with seven."

"And it amuses him?"

"Tremendously!"

"Today I'm celebrating," Mojmira called as she stood at the counter of the Brno Main Station cafeteria, from a cellophane bag she poured the remainder of the potato chips into her mouth, finished her beer, and as if it were a handkerchief stuck the crumpled cellophane bag into Jacek's jacket pocket, "after less than seven months they sent me my check! Let's go."

At the Petrov lunch counter they ate two grilled Moravian sausages with their fingers and Jacek clasped his black satchel between his legs, "Today I'm celebrating, they sent me my check!" Mojmira cried across two counters to a young fellow in white-rimmed sunglasses, "Buy me a beer?" the young fellow called, "Make it three," and he got the five crowns change for carfare.

By the time they reached the milk bar on Freedom Square they'd added a freckly archeology student from the Low Tatra Mountains, and Mojmira paid for four strawberry cocktails, "I got it for my translation!" she cried, crossing the square toward a motorcyclist in leather pants and suspenders, the driver stepped on the gas, drove around the square, and held the door open for them at The Four Ruffians, during the goulash soup a bearded radio technician joined them and all six of them went on to The Noblewomen, at a long table fourteen people were sitting and talking quietly, in their midst, like a priest, the poet Oldrich Mikulasek was stroking the edge of his wineglass, "We just heard you're celebrating," a pretty blonde on his right told Mojmira, "I got it for that Spanish story," Mojmira confirmed happily and ordered two bottles of Mikulov Sauvignon, the procession of some eleven people now went to the seafood restaurant on Jakub Square, at their head the motorcyclist in leather pants and in the rear Jacek with Mojmira and the large black satchel, at a necktie store they were joined by a long-haired unisex creature, "The fellows at the Slavie said you got paid for that 'Executioner's Afternoon'—" "Here, take it—" said Mojmira, thrusting a crumpled three-crown note into his (her) proffered hand, and (s)he joined the group, from St. Jakub's on a grey-haired woman limped along on crutches, "I got paid today—" Mojmira called after her. "I heard," the old woman rejoiced, "For that Alvarez translation!" and she hobbled after them, in the Typos Arcade a fellow in a black waterproof hat was pissing into a grate, "Vitek," Mojmira called after him, "today—" "I heard," he muttered and joined the gang, by the portal of the Viceregent's Palace Pavel Vrbka stood with an Admira movie camera around his neck, "Mojmira got paid today—" Jacek called after him, "I can see," said Pavel Vrbka, already in formation, and at the M Club there were almost thirty of us.

"Ten days I worked on it like a mule till late at night," Mojmira cried, kicking a trashcan down the stairs into the Vegetable Market. "I played with it as I would with poetry and I made a hundred and eighty crowns, I've found a job in a dairy, I'll handle butter with a sterilized coal shovel, fifty-five crowns a day, I have to supply my own rolls..."

"We hear you're looking for a job in Brno," wheezed the man in the waterproof hat as he trotted beside Jacek along the rounded cobblestones and down the hill after Mojmira. "I would like something—" Jacek wheezed back, fending off with his knee the jolting satchel, "We could take you onto the editorial staff of the *Technical News*—" "But I—" "We know all that, I've already sent up the proposal—" each of them caught up the trashcan at his side, swung it, and threw it over the edge of the fountain, the latter wasn't on, so Jacek stepped into the fountain and climbed up the possibly Baroque stonework, the Vegetable Market turned upside down, the lights above and the dark below, "I greet you, Brno—" Jacek cried and to the shouting of fifty throats he stretched out his arms like the pope for *Urbi et orbi*.

A flowering linden gazed into the window and around the wall the continuous strip of Impressionists, on a collarbone a hairy leg in a red sock, half-past six in the morning, Jacek extracted his black satchel from beneath the golden-haired admirer of the Great Poet Oldrich and kissed her half-open mouth, Mojmira evidently hadn't made it home yet, into the courtyard onto the trashcan and skip over the fence, along the asphalt, and across the park opposite his house, the old folks were still asleep, in his bookcase Dad kept hidden behind *The Count of Monte Cristo Ten Years Later* a bag of chocolate-covered raisins, Jacek gulped it down and collapsed on his boyhood bed.

A huge tree with reddish leaves gazed into the window, by the window a globe and on the wall the wooden saber, 11:16, and at 11:30 in white shorts on the Luzanky courts, an hour of practice hitting the ball against the wall, now the backhand and then into the shower, at one sharp Jacek, wearing his father's grey English suit, entered the University cafeteria, a well-built girl in rimless glasses made room for him beside her, Jacek silently, carefully, and quickly ate his beef broth with Russian egg, his kipper with three pickled onions, and a pint of warm milk, nothing but protein.

The large park was almost empty at the time, and it was quiet beneath the tops of the century-old trees, one after another was set afloat and simply by walking past you could see a continuous live cyclorama *Trees in the Grass*, and Jacek took a turn through it across the lawn, ta-ta-tatatata, why not snap your fingers, ta-ta-tatatata and, dancing through the treetrunks as far as the playground, he looked at his watch and out of the park at a trot.

At Under the Lookout three old fellows were nodding over their stale beer, evidently they didn't want to go home from work so early, and the bargirl was lazily sucking her wine spritzer from a wineglass, Jacek held his cue and concentrated on the green cloth of a battered and cigarette-burned billiard table, a cushion shot for this one—no, go back to the starting position and again—no, try again, nothing, again and again nothing, at last, chalk up the cue and keep it up, twenty-three caroms is our longest series and now our exhibition game, with fine pecks keep three balls going close to the cushion, a carom is easy enough but the trick is to get the balls back into position again, that's not it, once more— "Mister," someone said behind Jacek's back, "let's play to a hundred and fifty for coffee and rum, I'll spot you thirty-five—" "Excuse me, please," said Jacek without even looking around, "in five minutes I'll finish and give up both tables—," in five minutes he put the cue away, at home he lay on his bed and slept for ninety minutes.

Penetrating into his room from a great distance were radio music, the rumble of motors, and the whiz of pneumatic drills on the pavement, then from many sets the same TV program acoustically reinforced itself, the day was long in coming to an end and, as if uncertain, the city put off its decision to go to sleep, what was the day good for, an invigorating breeze of silence lifted the room from its chance surroundings, over the roofs of the houses and up above the night itself into the space beyond earth's orbit, where it's always light, the desk lamp's halo awakens the old wood to a warm breathing and in an open red binder a white sheet of paper flares up, cigarettes and matches on the left, an ashtray on the right, an eraser and a pencil sharpener in front, Jacek sharpened some graphite and studied how to reckon with the elements all things are made from, physical chemistry is the backbone of the two principal sciences and a serpentine going upward, marked by constantly higher mathematics, heat content $H$, free energy $G$, entropy $S$ is the measure of the chaos of order, with organization it approaches 0, freed from interference it rises to the number 1 of absolute chaos, where are we in this continuum (0-1) and where are we going through sheer inertia—

Jacek walked quickly down the long corridor of the grey palace to the general director's office and marched in through his door, "Did you get my proposal dated the fifth of July?"

"Sit down, please...," the chief said with an affable smile.

"No. What did you think of it?"

"Let's have some coffee, at least..."

"No. What do you plan to do with me?"

"You're a sly one, aren't you!"

"Sly?..."

"You must be the first person in the world to propose the abolition of his own job—hahaha!"

"But I really don't want it anymore."

"So why not hand in your resignation? Hahaha!"

"I've been there for ten years and understand, it isn't easy... People I like..."

"Don't make me cry—hahahaha! Sit down and let's have that coffee!"

"No. I'm asking you to abolish my job—"

"Hahaha—"

"—or I'll start making trouble for you!"

"Hahaha, you needn't do that anymore, you've already snared another two hundred crowns that way and praise from the general director for initiative, and they've put you on the Management Reorganization Committee, we'll be sitting there beside each other and playing tricks together—"

"Ow," said Jacek and he sank down in his chair, instead of the abyss another lift, "so shoot that coffee to me, Anton boy, let me get a grip on myself."

Jacek swayed along the long corridors of the grey palace, another couple of stunts like that and I'll be boss of the whole building, on the stairs a girl in a white apron ahead of him, on a tray she carried six bottles of domestic Gold King whiskey wrapped in cellophane and ribbons, "Come, kitten, let's drink it together in the boiler room." "What's left of it—" she giggled and Jacek set out after her, in front of a pair of tall white doors she stopped helplessly, "Where are you taking that?" "To some West Germans—will you open the door for me?"

Jacek grabbed the handle, but the door was locked, he knocked with his fist, nothing, and then a bit of kicking, both doors flew open and a petty official with a black tie and a stripe on his sleeve, evidently entrusted with watching the door, looked out in fright, "Engineer Werther hasn't gone yet?" Jacek shouted close to his face and walked in, the speech was evidently over and, at the head of the crowd, Franta Docekal was walking toward a table covered with a white cloth, his hand met Jacek's over the Hungarian salami, people always go for the most expensive things first, for the last ones only some disgusting looking meatballs were left, Jacek clinked glasses with an athletic-looking blonde in white silk with diamonds on her neck, ears, breasts, and belt, why drink with the waitress in the boiler room, the party lined up to have its picture taken, "The lady in the center—" the photographer commanded, the blonde wanted a profile and, with a smile, Jacek looked over her shoulder at Franta Docekal, who had just eaten the last meatball, wiped his fingers on the napkin, and placed in his now healthy windpipe a log-like, gold-banded cigar.

"But there's no place to go here," said Tanicka Rambouskova on the bench of the Svitavy station, propping her feet against Jacek's traveling satchel and looking at the tracks, "there's nothing here, it's only for people who don't want anything anymore, only to stuff themselves and sleep—should I hand in my resignation?"

"What would Mom and Dad say about that?"

"We haven't lived together for a long time... It was a great romantic love affair, they addressed one another very formally, every day he kissed her hand and brought her flowers and when he left her a note in the kitchen to say, for instance, that he'd gone out to feed the rabbits, he addressed it to My Beloved..."

"But then why—"

"One day it all collapsed and we had to throw him out."

"But that's awful, really terrible, what must have happened to—"

"He was a thief and a degenerate."

"Really? Explain it to me in detail, I'm immensely—"

"He stole candy from the store, pickles, rum, powdered coconut, and gave it to the boys in the dorm. When should I hand in that resignation?"

"It'll happen this year, I know it—" she whispered up to Jacek at the window of the express, she was magnificently resolved to pick up and leave without a suitcase on that very train, it was already starting and Tanicka began to run beside it, "—I feel it already in my feet, something like a tingling—" and Jacek stroked her on her dark head, Tanicka couldn't reach him, she stroked the train, it was already leaving and Tanicka was left behind, she grew suddenly smaller and with her hand above her head like a soldier's salute she disappeared around the bend, Jacek still returned her salute and now the express carried him off to the west, ta-ta-ta-dum, on green cushions through green meadows and forests, ta-ta-ta-dum, as on the green waves of the Mediterranean from stairs to stairs, the Belvedere, the Jeannette, the Palma, the Stefanie, the Kvarner, and on each tiny beach another naiad waits, Speranza has been realized and the Miramar is no longer merely a dream, ta-ta-ta-dum is a hymn of freedom, only two more cliffs along the way and in the sun beyond them the open strip gleaming toward Africa—

"You forgot the white plush again, didn't you..."

They'll call him a thief and a degenerate, still it's better than inhaling hydrochloric acid, at lunchtime Jacek entered the tow-cloth storeroom, not a soul anywhere, and he pulled down from the shelf a parcel of tow-cloth, more than a sixth of a mile of it, material for white and purple tuxedos for the barons of jazz, and he dropped by the chemical storeroom, "You've got a visitor at the porter's—" he told the old woman, who was hooking a curtain, "Could that be my old man, I wonder—" she cried and she ran off. Jacek took a bottle of mercury under each arm and dripped a bit from one of them—that was how Alois Klecanda had got caught that time and how he'd become Candy, the silver drops ran their crazy course over the concrete, both of us await our triumphant return tour—

In his office Jacek propped the roll of tow-cloth against the shelf with the files, the bottles of mercury on the edge of the lower shelf with the curtain only half concealing them, and he sat down at his antiquated Urania:

Dear Mrs. Jostova:

You don't know me, but I know you very well. We have windows across the way from you and it's terrible to watch what your husband's been up to, the degenerate, when he's in the bedroom by himself and you, poor woman, are working in the kitchen till late at night. I can't even tell it in a letter. Dad said if I didn't write to you, he would inform the Security Police. There are children here, after all!

Your outraged neighbor across the way

On the envelope: MRS. JOSTOVA

and seal it and when Mr. Stefacek comes back from lunch to his burgled tow-cloth storeroom, he'll lend us some photos of nudes.

The letter into our mailbox in the lobby, the pictures into the pocket of my bathrobe, the belt from Lenka's sewing machine, fasten it with wire to the handle of the can opener, and a whip under the pillow.

"It's from that Dvorakova hag," Lenka laughed as she read the letter, "she's mad because Thursday at the cafeteria I grabbed the last milk away from under her nose," and the letter became a paper steamboat for Lenicka and from the bedroom revels and shouting, Grandma was lying on her back, Lenicka sitting astride her and waving the whip, her "fishing wod," the "fish" is Grandma, the poor old woman tried conscientiously to bite the line and so lost her last incisor, "Now you, Daddy—," "With a stomach like that I wouldn't dare have my picture taken," Lenka grinned and tossed aside Mr. Stefacek's photos, "That's Mommy—" Lenicka rejoiced over them and shuffled them like cards, "Here's Mommy and here's another one—," "Let's go eat," Lenka decided, through the closed kitchen ventilator one could see in spite of the curtain the eighty windows of the apartment house across the way, the perpendicular strips of shining kitchen windows, the whole development is eating dinner now and over the apartment house only a crack of sky turning pale, stabbed by antennas, crying from the cage of those antennas—

Outside the open window a magnificently undivided blue hemisphere, the surging crests of the Krusne Mountains and a view as far as Germany, in the bar of the Mosquito Tower music from a tape recorder and weaving among the occupied tables the golden-orange Tina de Modigliani, tourists from four countries watch her go by, she's something to stare at, but you stare in vain, she's mine, in the aisles Tina raised her tray over her head, leaned over, thrust forth her chest and laughed, and no one looked at the beautiful view from the window (the chalet's take was up forty percent from the preceding year).

A bell sounded for the last funicular down, Tina pursed her lips, Jacek nodded imperceptibly, finished his unbilled cinzano bitter, and chewing on a slice of lemon walked slowly out onto the terrace, the sun bled on the mountain chain and in the valley the reddened meadows flamed, beyond them a strip of fields and then a grey imitation mountain where a huge mine was murdering the soil, and beyond the spreading grey corpse of the strewn waste rose the grey-brown crepe of smog beneath which the city of Usti was suffocating, and Jacek turned around, the last tourists were hurrying to catch the funicular, the terrace was empty, buses and cars were going down the serpentine to the valley, and on the slag parking lot only the couple's Renault, the family's Wartburg, and that Opel Admiral.

Jacek slowly lit a Kent and gaped at the increasingly washed-out sky, Tina's window in the tower was open, when he lit another one the family rushed out the door and into the Wartburg and started down the mountain, the couple with the Renault was evidently going to stay the night, Jacek leaned on the railing and smoked slowly, Tina's window was still open and from the valley night was coming on, Jacek approached the glass doors to the bar, the couple were kissing in the corner and the Opel Admiral in the buffet was whispering with Tina.

The blue woods began to turn grey, in the valley the first lights and the first stars in the sky, Jacek glanced at Tina's window and relished a pleasant feeling of tension, his fingers played with another Kent but he didn't light it, it was as if the silence grew stronger and with a bang the window in the tower suddenly slammed shut.

Jacek broke the cigarette and tossed it away on the run, through the side entrance and up the winding stairs, one more landing and he rushed through the peeling door, "Was machst du hier, du Saukerl—" he hissed, Tina grabbed her head and took refuge behind the wardrobe, the Opel Admiral began to protest, Jacek pulled out a camera, Tina screamed, and the fellow dressed quickly, shook his fist at them, and got lost, the start of his engine, the lovers' Renault was left alone in the parking lot, and the lights of the Opel Admiral traced a zigzag down the serpentine.

"Superb," said Tina, she detached a ten-mark note for Jacek and went downstairs to give the couple their check, Jacek took from the green box on the wicker chair a cigarette (Yenidze No. 6 Mild Virginia) and a silver lighter (Hasenlaufer und Sohn), Jacek's new lighter worked marvelously, from deep inside Jacek exhaled the blue smoke out into the night air and waited for Tina.

His whole paycheck transferred to the secret hoard, Jacek walked nervously through the empty apartment and waited for Lenka, nothing at all was happening, LEAVE and TAKE, the various objects unanimously mocked him in the dusk of the drawn blinds, dust was gathering on the cosmonaut's luggage so that he could write on it with his finger BECAUSE OF DAMAGE TO FIRING AP-PARATUS FLIGHT WILL NOT TAKE PLACE—

"Did you bring the money?" the launching pad asks.

"No—" the apparatus begins its countdown.

"How's that?"

"You know, I had a few drinks in Brno with some friends... I had to send them some money."

"Nine hundred crowns' worth?"

"Twelve. Three hundred I'll send next payday."

"As you like," Lenka shrugged her shoulders. "I'll take it out of the savings account and you'll have to put off buying that dark suit another year. Are you coming along to the garden?"

"No!—" and again Jacek roamed through the empty apartment, the rocket was to be held on the launching pad a while yet, the dark suit would have been of use for the first time in his life, again the Lenkas' fortress had repelled the attack, but the besieged can be starved out, like a tornado Jacek burst into the pantry and went through it shelf by shelf, try bacon with cheese and put condensed milk on the sardines, chocolate'll do the trick, but it didn't, and white as a sheet Jacek opened the door for the Lenkas, "You must have been hungry—" Lenka made a wry face, "well, Lenicka, Daddy ate up our supper—" "He just stuffed himself a bit, that's like a man—" Grandma called, "wouldn't you like some garlic soup now?" Lenicka rejoiced that she didn't have to have any din-din, while Lenka and Grandma deliberated whether to cook macaroni, lentils, potato pancakes, canned goulash, toast, braised beef, bilberry dumplings, or dried peas with bacon bits and onion.

"Tomorrow I'm going to Brno," Jacek whispered, "please put two white shirts in the satchel, and no lunch..."

Jacek strode along quickly behind Dr. Janzurova's copper headdress, over the magnificently maintained parquet floor from hall to hall of the Government Information Bureau, Anna's gift to him, enormous ceramic vases hid flowerpots under the windows and across the panes a forest of tropical foliage, the walls were covered up to the ceilings with books bound in black and the ladders to reach them were made of stained wood and ringed in brass, at polished, statesmanlike tables people leafed through illustrated magazines and drank coffee from glass cups, the telephone rang in the hall and no one bothered with it, "Nobody breaks his back here, does he—" said Jacek. "It's quieter at the beginning of the month," Dr. Janzurova smiled charmingly, "now we'll take the elevator down to the ninth floor, where we keep the encyclopedias, dictionaries, and manuals, on the eighth there's only a card-punch machine, the photo lab, and the bindery—" "That's enough for now," said Jacek, "I'm sure I'll like it here..." "Comrade Deputy Bromova gave us the best report imaginable concerning you and we're all looking forward to having you here..." "You too?" "Me... especially, I left that for last, but if you should need anything from the start I'd be most happy to help you..." "I could see at first glance that you were friendly..." "Thank you, I felt the same way and I'm really looking forward...," "My God, they have forced air, real leather everywhere, chrome knobs, even an aquarium," "And here's your desk—" a desk like a steamboat, on the first, glassed-in deck a regular library, on the upper deck two telephones, a metal vase for a smokestack, and as a mast towering above it all a magnificent *Palma areca*.

The chauffeur opened the door of the stretch limousine for Jacek. "What do you think," said Anna, sitting down on the back seat. "Fan-tas-tic—" sighed Jacek and he sank back into the cushions.

Jacek leaped out of his wicker chair and with a look of disbelief took in those nine-by-twelve feet of creaky boards, the roughed-up desk from the days of the Germans, the flower stand with its half-century-old Urania, and the five pine shelves behind a curtain of local manufacture... where was the mercury and the material that would put him in tuxes—

"I stashed it all away when that inspection party was here from Brno," said Vitenka Balvin, "you should be a bit more..." "Till next payday—" said Petrik Hurt, despite his eleven hundred in alimony, he pushed a fifty-crown note into Jacek's hand. "Get lost—"

In the empty office Jacek breathed in deeply and dialed the main office of Cottex, "Security Police, give me the director... Comrade Director? District Office of Public Security, Sergey Sniper speaking. Do you have a certain Jaromir Jost working there?... That must be him. Have you noticed anything suspicious about him lately?— no, I can't tell you on the phone, we only want you to inform us immediately about everything involving this matter, goodbye."

Within five minutes the director came to see Jacek with a newspaper in his hand. "Have you seen the latest issue of *Textile World*? Just look here, at the top..."

> *In the photo, from left to right, Cmrde. General Director Josef Novacek, the central secretary of* UNICAG *Prof. Erika Ursula Marie von Wittig-Hohenmauern, Eng. Jaromir Jost, and the general director of* CHIAG *and president of*

WIPAG *Dr. of Phil. and Dr. of Sci. Siegfried Postolka, all engaged in hearty conversation.*

In the photo were the two general directors and the blonde in the center, all looking in the direction of a smiling Jacek, "I shouldn't tell you this," the director whispered, "but just a little while ago the security police were asking about you, so be careful... we'll all stand up for you, but watch out... You know how in Brno they're always trying to discredit us, we need you badly...," and the old man put his hand on Jacek's shoulder.

On the porcelain tray five checks and three asterisks had arrived, Jacek gulped down his third rye and turned resolutely to the fifth beer, by the door neighbor Mestek pining in his green windbreaker with a hood, still drinking his first beer, and at each of Jacek's successive drinks he shook his head, inside Jacek a cold, damp sense of revulsion suddenly rose up but he drank on heroically, it was necessary to drink up all twenty-five of those crowns stolen from Lenka's rent envelope, in the twilight of the Vseborice tavern the gloomy drinkers looked up from their glasses each time the door opened, a boy came in with a jug for two quarts of beer and two packs of Partisans, as he left he took a deep drink from the jug, and again we look into the fragments of that little round mirror between the floating wisps of stale foam, just stir it and it'll bubble up, the bubbles will float up to the surface, and beneath the thin foam that cruel mirror will disappear for a while, the door creaks and we all look up again quickly, the next guy comes in for beer and enjoys the thick foam, but just wait a while, and silence in the bar waiting for the next arrival even though the preceding ones have been so disappointing, mix it all up by stirring and when the door creaks we'll all look up—

The development blocks were all playing musical chairs and on the walk in front of his apartment house Jacek began to sing, how many more stairs there are now than before, and he scratched at the door like a dog, inside too there was scratching, and when the door opened Lenicka was down on all fours on the carpet, Jacek got down on all fours, too, and barked, "Woof-woof—" Lenicka answered in ecstasy and the two puppies ran into the kitchen, "I'm drunk as a monkey—" Jacek announced triumphantly, "You took twenty-five crowns from my rent money," Lenka accused him, "But how can you leave your husband without a single crown?!—" Grandma spoke sternly to her as she poured Jacek a glass of herb liquor to stop his burping, and when the barking puppies had crawled under the bed, Grandma stuck fifty crowns of her money into Jacek's pocket, "So you don't have to borrow anymore—" Lenka said later and she reached under the bed and stuck a hundred into Jacek's pocket, "Get dwunk again soon, Daddy—" Lenicka whispered in her crib behind the net, "and we'll pway puppy again..."

The official limousine of the director of VUGMT stopped at the Ministry of Heavy Industry, Jacek followed Anna through the vestibule and the passageway to the courtyard, between stacks of old papers out of the building and onto a bus, out of the excavated earth towered ten-story apartment blocks with curtains, twelve-story ones with whitewash crosses on the windows, and fourteen-story ones still only crudely assembled from sections, Anna's high heels disappeared into the masons' rubble of the boxed-in staircase, and here on the sixth floor we're at home, I'd like to have this room with the view of Prague, "This room with the view of Prague is yours," said Anna, "and the first time it rains we'll sit and look at it together..." "And at night Prague will shine in here on the ceiling..." "You know, all my life I've wanted this city so much..." "Take this room, I'd be glad for you to..." "No, I'll come here to see you..."

Outside the frameless window, the hills of the capital spread out at their feet, the boss of the Government Information Bureau with his second wife in their Prague apartment— "Come here, let me show you where we'll put the

dinette," said Anna, happily leading Jacek by the hand,
"... and wouldn't you like a wall-hanging with a large
abstract design? I like to cook in general, but not every
day... although here it will be something entirely different, I don't know how much I'd give just to peel
potatoes and listen to you singing in the bathtub—I still
can't believe it..." "Nonsense, I only have a couple of tri-
fles to take care of—"

"—first you must break off with that Cottex, the pay
there is shameful. At first I thought we could rent a lodge
in the mountains, but I've found something better," Tina
raved, sitting on the bedspread with her knees tucked
under her chin and her dark hair, let down, quivering on
her calves, "a gas station, you know... Instead of at zero
you start at five, at night at ten, but for just one gallon
you get ten crowns, maybe five hundred a day and in
three years half a million..."

"Great," Jacek whispered, "but first I have to break
away and you've got to help me... Throw something over
yourself and let's go down to where there's a telephone..."

Tina led Jacek by the hand down through the sleeping
chalet, from behind a thin door the snoring of the couple
from Krakow resounded along the corridor as if they
were choking to death, and that West German sedan from
Hanover was snoozing decisively after spending eighteen
crowns on his wife and then a hundred marks on Tina,
with the key to the bathroom Tina had no trouble opening
the office door.

"So what will it be?"

"I'll dial the number and as soon as you hear a
woman's voice, say right off, 'Jacinek...,' and then maybe
how wonderful it was yesterday and how next time I
should stay all night..."

"OK, but I'd never call you Jacinek..."

"That's just the point, that's what she calls me at the
moment of climax," and trembling, Jacek dialed his apartment, "You're a real snake," Tina sighed, "well, at night

it'll come in handy at the station—Jacinek...," she whispered passionately, theatrically, into the receiver, "Oh, Jacinek, it was so wonderful yesterday and next time I know you'll stay all night... Jacinek, do you hear me... Jacinek...," and she banged the receiver onto the hook, "She's bawling or something... I can handle a lot, but I don't have the stomach for this..."

"Lenka's crying..."

"But so strangely, as if she were choking or..."

Jacek rushed through the nighttime meadows down to the black forest, on the black sky the brutal stars burned white, the millionfold Milky Way like the road to hell, he rushed over the silvery grass and the heavy traveling satchel struck his legs, thorns like fetters of barbed wire and resilient twigs struck his arms and face, into the evil, tense, lurking forest of the enemy, where from dark damp beds moss-covered boulders roll out their worm-ridden bellies, concealed in daytime, and the dry crackle of dead twigs like shots that have missed, how hard on the soles that road from the forest can be and through grain up to his chest along the field roads, through the sleeping village where all the dogs go crazy on their chains, and along the concrete of the coal-conveyor under those phantasmagoric mountains of uprooted earth and thus murdered soil from which now only strange sparse pale weeds can grow, and around the moon-like craters and dunes from which nothing will ever grow again, through the labyrinth of undermined cave-ins, how ghastly far off home is, the lights of the development have long since gone out and like steamboats the apartment houses are lying in their winter anchorage, the silent pavement between the buildings is still warm with the tramp of children's shoes and again the stairs to our apartment have multiplied, "Lenka, I have to tell—"

"Please don't say anything...," she whispered, sobbing softly, and passionately he kissed her hands, "... and get up, please get up... my Jacinek."

On the bank of the Elbe, on Sunday before noon, three thousand people, there would be more room in back by the wire fence under the poplars, Lenka spreads the checkered blanket out on the grass and Lenicka is already bare, "Cawwy me piggyback, Daddy—," Jacek crawled on all fours and on his back Lenicka exulted, her little legs clasped his ribs and on his shoulderblades that tender little body, they tumbled onto the ground, "Mommy, look, I'm wessling wif Daddy—" and Daddy and his daughter were like lovers in the grass.

Daddy stood in line for a boat, he seated the two Lenkas and pulled on the oars, the heavy rowboat flew with the current, a tanned brunette flashed by in a red canoe and behind her four girls were laughing in a white motorboat, Jacek pulled on the oars and the rowboat made its way heavily through the wake, Lenicka had fallen asleep lying in the prow and Lenka was carefully surveying the banks, the oars creaked in their metal locks and from his soaked brows salty sweat trickled into his mouth, "Look, pears already—" Lenka whispered excitedly and Jacek turned the boat toward some stairs on the bank.

Up the slope to the railway embankment, through the dark, narrow underpass to a forgotten paradise of silence and warm, free grass, Lenka and Lenicka jumped to reach the hard, green pears and Jacek set out to find some hazelnuts for his little girl, he entered the hazel jungle and the springy, sap-filled twigs pressed stiffly against his body, beyond the bushes a small glade with a hut six-by-six feet and in front of it a dark, heavy woman was sunbathing, she sat up slowly and looked Jacek straight in the eye, "I only wanted to pick a few nuts...," he whispered uncertainly, and she got up and gestured—her finger in the hole—toward the door to the hut, Jacek followed her through the high grass and entered with his head bent, the ground inside was spread with sacks except in one corner where there were pots, saucepans, cigarettes, linen with black lace, cold cream, and lipstick in a straw hat along with baby oil and a yellow sandal turned upside down, the woman fished out a bar of cheap chocolate with peanuts and broke Jacek off a piece like a slice of bread, "I meant hazelnuts, from the tree...," he stammered, he tripped over a red parasol and sank on his knees into the sacks in front of her, "Daddy—" they heard from outside, "Daddy, wherre arre you—" "I'm coming—" he shouted and he tore his hand free from the woman's, crossed the lawn, and leaped into the hazel thicket without any idea where he was going till whipped and scourged he found the Lenkas among the pear trees, they took him each by a hand and together they ran down to the boat, Jacek leaped to the oars and pulled at them with all his might, the heavy rowboat turned its snout against the current and Jacek labored conscientiously, the grating of wood against metal and streams of sweat uniting in a hot salty veil over his face like a burst of tears, the old crate crawled against the current and playfully the current pushed its prow now to the right, now to the left, around the bend came a steamboat, aroused waves rocked the rowboat like wind on the sea and the now wet daddy hauled his family back to their dinner.

Over the trampled grass Lenka carried two large bags for her hungry family under the poplars, "And now let's give our faces a good feed—" she laughed, and Lenicka helped her unpack a thermos, bottles, packages, sacks, and a perforated tin box.

In the afternoon heat, yachts sailed out from the jetty on the other side of the wire fence, their keels, polished like jewels, whizzed over the surface and nearly naked, their tanned crews of both sexes hung over the sides and from the rigging, handsome and free as the gulls above their masts, the whole river to the south was full of white sails—

"Hello," Lenka was smiling in some direction, from the boat-rental stand Trost was coming with his family, his wife was unpacking from two bags a perforated tin box, sacks, packages, bottles, and a thermos, Trost played with little Trost on the same checkered blanket we have, "Daddy cawwy me piggyback—" Lenicka cried, she climbed up on Jacek's back and kicked with her heels painfully into his groin, Jacek the Horse snorted on his knees in the warm grass near the wire fence and across the way Trost the Horse was snorting with his screeching jockey on his back urging him on.

One slope below on the left, another slope below on the right, above the point of intersection the crest of a third, dark green needles of two shades: muted and bright, light green foliage of a thousand shades: muted, bright, reflecting, translucent, absorbent, half-, quarter- to 1/2, packed into a complete progression of gradients from 0-360° times the third dimension, all in motion on a conjectured polystructure of spatial branching drawings and a proportionally motionless, static eruption of inelastic explosions in a Niagara of light—

"This is our forest," Lida Adalska smiled, "come—"

Inside, twilight and bright spots surprisingly focused now on the roots and now on the crowns, here in a plain of dead needles sad telephone-pole spruces aren't making it, here the floor of the woods is like a bombarded city square, behind the trunks of the larch trees rise the ruins of forgotten castles and beneath your feet the tips of young spruces growing up out of the ravine, grey stumps, lustful as Turks, roll their huge deformed members into the tender bilberries and from the sprucen' armor trickle stalactites of sugar and rock candy, the spider's diamond lace closes off the dragon's cave, an art gallery of wood sculpture and the path to it spread with pinecones off a grandfather's clock, a forest of fairy tales and happenings—

"... I used to come and meet him here," Lida whispered, "and the children ran here with me. He was so fond of us..."

"... and then there was the time he brought us a fawn on his back," Lida laughed, "Arnostek polished its hooves with boot polish and Janicka made him little silver antlers from the paint we'd used on our stove..."

"... and once when the snow was up to your waist, I put
a kerosene lamp in the window and the children kept
waking up all night long to see whether their daddy had
gotten home..."

"... 'grrr-grrr,' he growled from his hiding place in the
hayloft, and Janicka looked out the window and said, 'Go
way, bear, Daddy's coming and he might be fwightened
of you—'"

"... he lies under that young fir tree, like you he was
thirty-three when he died..."

They walked down the slope together to the ranger's
lodge, up to their calves in flowering grass, and from the
white house a boy and a girl ran out, they were afraid of
the stranger with the black satchel, Lida stooped down in
front of them and there were three faces peeping out from
under her brown hair, Jacek tossed his satchel into the
grass and stooped down with them, he made a rabbit
face, he made Janicka laugh, we've got a way with kids,
he barked at her and she barked timidly back, he didn't
have to ask her twice to climb on his back, and Arnostek
looked on jealously as he observed how his little sister
was playing with her new uncle, "Now me, Uncle—"
"But you're a boy, we should box a bit together—," but
Arnostek didn't know what that was, "My husband
didn't do that with him...," Lida laughed while Jacek explained to her son what's a jab and what's a hook, inside
five minutes Arnostek was a passionate boxer and now it
was Janicka's turn to be jealous, Jacek picked them both
up, "One more time—" Janicka called. "You're as strong
as Daddy, Uncle—" Arnostek whispered.

Daddy's workroom was to be Jacek's temporary
bedroom, outside the window a mass of spruces pierced
the sky like Asiatic towers, and from a wide frame of dark
wood with a black ribbon over the glass the forest ranger,
the late Mr. Adalsky looked down, a thirty-three-year-old
with an oval face, eyes and hair apparently brown, no

special markings, no feature betraying any special quality, an easily exchangeable anybody in the best years of his life and dead at thirty-three, you came to an end right at the time I'm getting my start—

The strong scent of felled pines in the afternoon heat, the wild swirl of the brook, and in the warm grass a half-naked man was eating, like that time eighteen years ago, my God, nothing ever dies, the summer heat beat on the asphalt roof of Forest Building No. 06, outside, the buzz of a circular saw, Jacek played with the jointed weight of the drafting board, tried out the T square, and attempted a couple of drafting techniques, "We'd be very happy and don't worry, I'll break you in myself. I like you—" said a magnificent man with white hair above a deeply furrowed, copper-colored face and the chest of a Laocoon in an unbuttoned Canadian shirt. "Well?" asked Lida on the highway, "I've been taken —" Jacek sighed happily.

Ta-ta-ta-dum, the express tore along through fields and woods, thundered at crossings, and rumbled through village stations overgrown with weeds, after the change of engines it quickly made up for the delay and at Kolin it was already two minutes ahead of schedule, I won't be the one to push our train on to its destination, my love, you take charge of the string of cars, the changing of engines: you be the one to push me off on my way—

"Just one more, this one will really be the last—" Jacek insisted on pouring Lenka another glass of Georgian cognac, "What's gotten into you —" her tongue now tripped confusedly, "you put it into the desserts, into the stewed fruit, the tea, I even tasted it in my mouthwash..." "It only seemed that way, you're acquiring the taste..." "But I don't want to acquire any taste, I'm afraid I'll get drunk..." "But how can you from just this little bit, come on, let's clink glasses—," they clinked glasses and Lenka emptied another pot-bellied glass, she got up with difficulty and staggered off, under her thinning hair the sinking shoulders of a suddenly old woman and on the other side of the wall the revolting sound of splashing, then her sour breath, "Oh, Jacek, I feel so sick—" and she laid her head in his lap, "Mommy," Lenicka called from her crib, "come and give me a kiss... Mommy—" "I can't come now, darling, tomorrow—" "Mommy, pwease come now—" "I can't—" Lenka moaned and collapsed on the floor, her head shook as if at its final gasp, "Mommy, I'm down on my knees, pwease come, pwitty pwease—" the neighbors' brooms were beating on the floors and ceilings as on a tin barrel and like a rat inside it Jacek ran back and forth in the dark, he was afraid to turn on the lights, the Lenkas moaned on the other side of all the walls and, near madness, Jacek howled under his pillow.

"... and greet him nicely and tell Comrade Dr. Mach that Mama and Papa send him their best," Hanicka Kohoutkova repeated her instructions in front of the pale-blue entrance to Kolora, a firm in Pardubice, "in the event of a successful outcome, Mama will fatten up a goose for him, but better not say that, Comrade Doctor's very strict. And don't forget to greet him with 'Honor to Work.' I want so much for you to pass the exam—come around the corner and I'll bless you on the forehead..."

With a glass rod pull the skein out of the boiling dark-red bath, with another rod stretch it out and by twisting it in the opposite direction wring the specimen out to a pink color, untwist it, submerge it, and with both rods put it through the color bath evenly, as when you turn a hoop with a stick, that's the way we learned to do it at school, to get the color even— "It takes a bit of practice, but it'll come, a colorist has to be born," Dr. Mach laughed, "so how about starting on the first of October?"

In a small, cheerful lab with windows looking right out onto fields ("We tore down that terra-cotta smokestack across the way, so it wouldn't throw a red reflection into the lab—"), bright skeins were hung everywhere and the dyed pieces looked like garlands and streamers, there are only four shades of black, no one knows how many whites there are, and no one has ever counted the browns, the keyboard of colored tones is over half a mile long, life as a colorist is a life of visual music, come here mornings, compose a Spanish moss or a bishop's cyclamen in silk and we'll put sixty crowns a day toward your account, on the wooden racks saturnine brown, bittersweet, Victorian blue, passion auburn, salmon pink, and cardinal red had dried, and on the pole below Jacek's first harmonious chord after fifteen years, the color of flesh from that dark-red bath— "Starting on the first of October!"

By the entrance Hanicka was fidgeting and biting her nails in agitation, "Jacek—" she cried and she ran toward him, "well—did they take you?" "They took me!" "Was it hard?" "I absolutely pulverized him." "Oh, Jacek, I suffered as much as when I took my college entrance exams. Mama will start right away fattening that goose for Comrade Dr. Mach, and for you too we have a reward—"

A warm breeze blew over the solitary tract of beardless wheat from horizon to horizon under the hot clear sky and wave after wave rushed across that endless sea of grain, the path through the fields fluidly turned into a quiet street of well-swept clay and neat green fences with red knobs on top of the poles, behind each fence a little garden with a circle of flowers in the middle and a wooden bench and from each green gate, surrounded by roses, stairs up to a pretty little house, ours is that pink one with wild roses along the stairs, on a concrete plat-form under the apple tree on a bench Mr. Kohoutek my father in a clean white shirt, his skin like a young wom-an's, not even a single grey hair and a dry, firm palm, and out of the house comes my mother, Mrs. Kohoutkova, in a clean white apron, a thousand lively wrinkles from so much smiling and a palm soft and warm, in the parlor on a clean white tablecloth four deep dishes on four shallow ones and four settings of heavy, antique silver.

A nice little house, a nice new job, a nice little garden, Jacek looks and Hanicka is beautiful, she was full of joy and the eyes of all four were damp, touched, Jacek fought for the huge glass jug so that he could go for beer but he wrested it from them only to find a ten-crown note on the bottom ("We're entertaining *you*—"), a quiet, pretty tavern with a sparkling brass spigot, in front under a linden tree sat tanned, sturdy men in white shirts on red garden chairs on yellow sand under the green linden tree, all the tones unbroken and rejoicing together, from all the windows came the clean smell of roasting and frying, today we're having fried cutlet and roast capon, walnut cake and strawberries with cream.

When dinner was over it was already six in the evening, Papa went out to drink beer and Mama disappeared into the kitchen, Hanicka wiped her mouth thoroughly with a stiff napkin, but even so her conscientious kisses tasted of strawberries and cream. Today she must sleep downstairs between Papa and Mama, but she can go out for a while on the bench in front of the house, on all the benches in front of the houses there are couples in the twilight, "I want to have three children," she whispered, "two at least. The first one will be called Jastrun or Jadwiga. It's practical too, they'll have the same monogram as you do, that is, as we will. I've already started to embroider two red J's."

"So go ahead and kiss each other, you're as good as engaged now—" Mama smiled, one more warm silver goodnight spoonful of strawberries and cream and up the wooden stairs behind Mama, she showed him where the toilet was and also stuck a porcelain pot striped with flowers under his bed, the black traveling satchel rested like a purring cat on the little round cushioned armchair, a white basin and a white pitcher as in a summer cottage, the warm stars squeezed their way through the little window in the slanting wall, and out of the perfect silence rose the breathing of the dark earthenware oven of the endless Elbe plain.

The morning was shining vigorously as Jacek ran down the stairs of the pink house, down the sleeping clay avenue to the train, he stayed out in the corridor by the

window and again ta-ta-ta-dum, the express pulled out
with an insignificant delay from the grey platform
deserts of the new Pardubice station and it rumbled west-
ward through meadows and fields, ta-ta-ta-dum, past
green tablecloths and endless fields wave after wave to
the stairs leading to the platform gardens with benches
around the houses with their loving bright facades, it's
the hymn of freedom, this ta-ta-ta-dum, or is it only the
theme song of parting—
"Did you bring the white plush?"

Out of the ridged mud in front of Cottex a scaffold was
raised and with latex paint an ancient mason was potem-
kinizing the facade of the electric plant, but the wall had
only contempt for this vain endeavor, the paint rotted,
peeled, and fell off, and beneath it the inexorably naked
bricks of that old barn which should have collapsed long
ago, like the gaping teeth of a corpse that is overgrown
with grass and yet still unburied—
At the ring of the phone Jacek started, perhaps this was
it— "Petrik?..." said Verka Hurtova, "Darling Verka...,"
Jacek mumbled like Petrik Hurt. "I'm looking at the wall
clock and the time doesn't move, I wish I were at the
square watching you jump off the streetcar, Petrik?..."
"Darling Verka..." "I thought that crazy Jacek was with
you, Petrik, I can't wait for the afternoon anymore, you'll
buy me ice cream first, won't you, darling, and we'll lick
it together, one lick for you and one for me, why must we
leave each other in the morning and spend so much of the
day apart..."
Petrik Hurt rushed into the office and Jacek handed
him the receiver in full stream, for another half hour they
chirped and then Petrik was wiping the sweat from his
brow, "Excuse me," said Jacek, "but what are you doing
this afternoon?" "We're going to the swings!" "And
then?" "Why home—" "I accidentally overheard and got
the impression that you're doing something special
today..." "With us, you see, every day is special. Verka

is... but you wouldn't understand. Verka, you see..." "It sounded like a poem." "Verka writes poems." "About what, for heaven's sake?" "Why, about the two of us—"

Jacek dialed the director's office, "It's Jacek Jost; greetings, Jozef," he spoke quickly into the speaker as Verka had done earlier, "I can't wait any longer to break with this Cottex, I look at the wall-clock and the time doesn't move, I wish I were at the square in front of our institute in Prague, I can't wait for the time I'll start to work there, meanwhile you should supply me with a new typewriter for the lab, in ten years of service here all I've got is this old Urania from the time of Franz Josef—" Bang! and the director hung up.

He simply hung up and when they met he pretended that nothing had happened, he only upped his affability, the old man has refused to collaborate so we'll force it out of him, Jacek rushed to Cottex with Tina's camera, at 12:00 sharp he conspicuously stepped straight from the courtyard onto the fire ladder and up onto the roof of the electric plant and, in full view from the director's windows, he whipped off two rolls of factory espionage, twenty-four shots so perfect they could go directly to the desk of the director of the CIA—"What stop are you using, Mr. Jost?" the hulking guard with the heavy revolver in his belt took an interest, "You haven't seen anything—" Jacek in a theatrically threatening half-voice tried to provoke some action against himself and out of despair he even hinted at a possible flight, "Today I'd step down as far as f22," the warrior yawned instead of shooting and climbed into his glassed-in cage, it was maddening—

"Booooo—" went Jacek to Lenka in the doorway when she came to open the door for him and right after that he kissed her, as usual, "But I said hi to you—" Lenka said in surprise, "But I gave you a kiss—" "But why did you bellow so?" "I bellowed?—" "You did, right when I opened the door—" "I didn't bellow, are you mad?—" "But I heard you with my own ears, you went boooo—" "I'm really scared, Lenka, what's wrong with you?"

Lenka was doing laundry in the bathroom, Jacek stole into the kitchen, turned on the mixer, and stole out to the bedroom, Lenka went to the kitchen and the mixer was silent again, she went back to her laundry, Jacek stole into the kitchen, turned on the mixer, and disappeared, Lenka went to turn off the mixer and went back to the laundry, Jacek turned on the mixer and hid behind the bathroom door, Lenka went to the kitchen, in the bathroom like lightning Jacek turned on the wringer and the washer and rushed into the kitchen after Lenka, "Are you turning this on?" she asked in confusion over the screeching machine, "Why would I do a thing like that?" "Well, for no reason at all—," the mixer was silent but in the bathroom the roar of the two motors and Lenka stiffened, "What's that—" "You've left on the washer, dear." "But I'm done with the laundry—," together we run to the bathroom and are horrified at the two motors running, "What's wrong with you, dear?"

And at night lay out on the sideboard all the knives with the handles together and the points facing outwards, a fan of blades pointed toward anyone who comes near them, in the morning when Lenka gets up not a word from her, only Lenicka's voice from behind the wall, "Mommy, why don't you talk to me today, even when I make you angry—"

Tanicka's room was noodle-shaped, about 140 sq. ft., only an iron bed, a wardrobe, a stove which would never warm anyone, outside the window facing the Svitavy station modest little parcels wrapped in oiled paper and on the wall a prewar tin poster advertising the Papez Company with the legspread of the Eiffel Tower against a yellow Parisian sky, "This is where I'm dying—" in a theatrical posture Tanicka stretched out her skinny arms clad in a none too clean blouse, "Of impatience," said Jacek, "Completely!" she cried, collapsing on the bed to show just how completely, but she couldn't endure lying quietly longer than two seconds and was already churning in the air with her legs like a cyclist and she burst into laughter, magnificently unaware what dying was.

"Would you like some bread spread with lard?" she said from the bed. "I've started to write a novel."

"I'll take a slice. Of course it's about the two of us."

"The knife's on the wardrobe. You come in in Chapter Two."

"How many chapters do I last? Don't you have any salt?"

"No. I'd like to have lots of lovers..."

"I'm not enough for you? So advertise."

"What woman wouldn't want to have lots of lovers? The novel will have a hundred chapters."

"Seriously, at our place there's a couple by the name of Hurt and the wife writes poems... about the two of them. Really, I wouldn't believe that in the world..."

"There really isn't any novel, I made that up, maybe I will write one, but I've already got more than thirty poems about us. For instance:

> *I don't care*
> *for crumbs*
> *fallen from the table*
> *I want to be a feast*
> *for you the unsated*
> *I am virgin soil*

"What do you say to that? Would it do for a blues song by Vasicek Neckar?"

"You write poems about the two of us...," Jacek whispered in enchantment.

"Did you bring the money?" Lenka said and she went to the bathroom to do the laundry, Jacek stole into the kitchen and turned on the mixer.

And before the pale Lenka could go downstairs to hang out the wash, Jacek had gone for cigarettes then slipped back into the empty apartment, turned on the washer, the wringer, the mixer, the radio, and the TV, a fan made of knives on the sideboard and away quick, with his cigarettes he went down to the drying room for Lenka and helped her hang out Lenicka's shirts and tights, who will do your wash, little one, when they take Mommy away—

One step behind Lenka up to our place, in the hallway the roar from our apartment, "Someone must be in there—" she whispered, "But who could—" "Don't go in there, wait—" she leaped to the door opposite hers, bearing the nameplate JAROMIR MESTEK, and leaned with all her weight against the bell.

In his green windbreaker with a hood and with his carved cane neighbor Mestek came out at once, evidently prepared for an excursion, but quite willingly he let himself be led into our apartment, "It's happened again," Lenka whispered to him, "just like last time…"

Mr. Mestek seems to know his way around our apartment well enough, he looked it over expertly and turned off all the roaring electric appliances, then went back to the hallway to check the fuse and returned right away, "It's nothing," he smiled, "just the current acting up." "But look here—" Lenka whispered with horror, pointing to the knife fan on the sideboard, "just like last time…"

"But it's nothing," Mestek smiled comfortingly, "it's just Lenicka playing, or Grandma being absentminded…"

"But they're both at the movies and when they left it wasn't happening—" Lenka whispered in a terrified voice. "Exactly like last time—"

"You've been terribly overwrought lately," Jacek intervened, "and evidently so preoccupied you…"

"But then it wouldn't be—" and Lenka tried to swallow, "quite normal…"

"But what are you thinking of," Mestek intervened, "why should you imagine such negative things…"

"There must have been someone in the house…" Lenka whispered.

"Well, since it disturbs you so," said Mestek, "it's nothing, of course, but for the sake of your peace of mind—" and he took a clean dishcloth out of a drawer, he really knows his way around here, and with expertise he wrapped all the knives in it without touching a single one, "—I'll take this to the police, the fingerprints will explain everything—"

"Give that here—" Jacek exclaimed and in a cold sweat he grabbed the bundle out of Mestek's hand, "I'll take it there myself."

"And so the movie's over," Mestek smiled good-heartedly, "or did the ghost do something else? Who put that balloon up there on the sideboard?"

"But you put it there...," Lenka was smiling now and turning rosy, "so Lenicka could see it from every direction..."

"Maybe I did that thing with the knives too," said Mestek, "you know, I do occasionally have blanks..."

"But what are you thinking of," Lenka intervened, "why should you imagine such negative things..." and she was laughing now, in a little while Lenicka and her grandmother came back from the movies and straight up to Mestek, "Uncle, gwab me—" Lenicka insisted and Mestek held her a while and then seated her up on the cupboard, Lenicka was afraid and ecstastic, "Uncle don't go way—," he wouldn't go yet, Mommy has to pour him a bit of cognac to thank him for his help and Grandma brings him a plate of brittle cookies, Lenka and Mestek clink glasses and right away she's poured another one, for herself as well, conversation and laughter from the room, the two of them sitting on the sofa and the husband outside the door, swell, what woman wouldn't want to have a host of lovers, swell, but not like this, unproductively and without guilt— In the middle of the table a pink rum cake for Lenka's birthday with a twenty-eight made of Dutch cocoa icing, around it are neighbor Mestek (the timid suitor), Vitenka Balvin (the experienced seducer), Mija Balvinova (as a bad example), and we two Josts (fissionable material), Jacek (the procurer), who has unpacked from his black traveling satchel onto the white tablecloth one bottle of Georgian cognac after another, until there were ten of them in all (66 crowns a bottle—, his last special bonus was 900, so 240 left over for the secret hoard, the special bonuses from Cottex had become a sure thing now), "But they're only pints—" Jacek called as he poured out the second, Lenka was chatting with Mestek about baby powder and Mija was doing her best to no avail, "It's kind of dead here...," Jacek whispered to Vitenka, the expert on relaxed parties.

"Table and chairs out of the way—" Vitenka cried and he clapped his hands, "take apart the sofa, the mattress goes on the floor and from now on everyone onto the floor—" Lenka was for it and with the third bottle the party moved down to the floor, Jacek put his head on Mija's breasts, but across the way Lenka and Mestek had just gotten onto the cementing of linoleum, "Vitenka—" Jacek addressed the master of the revels.

"The light really gets in your eyes," Vitenka cried and he clapped his hands, "haven't you got a candle—," Jacek brought one at once and conscientiously loosened all the bulbs in their sockets, he sat down by Mija and kissed her hair, Mija put her arm around his shoulders, she was cooperating marvelously, and Jacek strained his ears, "... on a hill the mornings are always the finest," Mestek prattled on, "Yes, the air is clearer then," Lenka babbled. "Vitenka—" Jacek almost burst into tears.

"Everyone drink up his drink and the men change ladies clockwise—" Vitenka cried and he clapped his hands, "hop-a-hoppity-hop," movement and laughter, Vitenka sat down by Lenka and took things expertly in hand, in a while they were lying beside one another and from the halflight Lenka's quiet laugh could be heard, Mija lay on her back and drew Jacek toward her, she was really outdoing herself and Vitenka too was exerting himself, at first they hadn't even wanted to come and now they were almost conquerors, the vessel was taking wind into her sails, Jacek emptied the third bottle from the burning slopes of Georgia and opened a fourth.

"I'll go make coffee," said Lenka and she got up, "I'll go with Lenka and we'll come back soon, in no more than half an hour—" Vitenka cried and he jumped up, "If you don't find Jacek and me when you come back we'll be behind this door and please don't disturb us!" Mija called to him, and already she was pulling Jacek in that direction, one couple in the kitchen and the other in the bedroom, poor Mestek was the odd man out.

"Let go—" Mija hissed on the other side of the door and firmly she pushed Jacek away, "But Mija..." "Just sit here and enough of this low comedy routine, we haven't got an audience anymore—," they sat on the bed in the halflight of the bedroom, a whole yard apart, minute after minute, Mija bent over until her forehead touched her knees and she wept quietly, "Mija, what's happened—," a quiet sob, "Mijenka, please—" Mija's broken into tears, but don't make noise, please, there's no acoustic insulation here like you have in your white room at home.

Both couples came back to the living room in silence, Mestek, sadly sipping his drink, was shaking his head in disapproval, "Vitenka...," Jacek whispered in despair, "do you know anything else to do?"

"Why are you so anxious to turn your place into a whorehouse?"

"I like the way you keep yours."

"If I had a wife like Lenka..."

"Come on, then—And pour yourself some more—" and Jacek got up, clapped his hands, and ran around the room pouring diligently, he drank with each of them in turn and with all of them together, he was as pathetically assiduous as the owner of a tavern on the eve of bankruptcy, Lenka quickly cheered up again, she stroked the limp Vitenka as if he were Lenicka refusing to eat, and Vitenka revived and snapped at her stroking hand, Mija kicked her legs in the air and her shoes flew off into the darkness, Jacek rubbed his hands, he lit their cigarettes, freshened their drinks, asked what they wanted, drank with all of them, and smacked his guests on the back, he bent down to them and laughed officiously, keep the action up the way a hoop is kept going with a stick, up the stairs to the platform near the little pink house for strawberries and cream, "But certainly, Mr. Mestek, make yourself at home here—" and Mestek unfastened his shoelaces, kneel down and officiously remove those stinking shoes, for the Government Information Bureau and an apartment with another wife with a window overlooking the metropolis, "I've had one too many—" Vitenka sighed, intoxicated, lead him off to the bathroom, take attentive care of him, refresh his breath with our own toothbrush and wash him with our own washcloth—the Balvins' great improvement was somehow collapsing—if only his respect could be that of a rival, I want to be a feast for you the unsated underneath a yellow Parisian sky, meanwhile Mestek's gone down, lead him off to the bathroom, a cold shower, rub his back and belly provocatively with the fine sponge reserved for Lenicka's face, I have a girl-friend by Modigliani, but all of a sudden they're tired out and want to go home, what's so wonderful there, don't run out on me yet, green waves from stairs to stairs and on each terrace another naiad waits, they're all in the doorway all of a sudden, they tie up my boat and lock my plane in a hangar, they're running down the stairs, they've stolen my sea and my air and in the sudden silence after the closing of the door Lenka is coming toward me with a smile.

"That was a wonderful evening, I want to thank you very much for thinking of it," she whispered and with her hair disheveled she looked inordinately pretty, "I had a nice talk with Mr. Mestek and Vitenka really courted me in the kitchen—," she giggled and her eyes gleamed, that's her hand stroking me again and petting me, her sensuality is aroused but, as if to spite me, in the wrong direction, but how newly beautiful Lenka looks today, newly aroused, "Jacinek, my darling—" she whispers the magic greeting and her arms are firmly around his body, "Lenunka—," like milk and like that cognac, how sweetly it had failed this time, it'd never been like that before, "It's never been like that before," Lenka whispered and she went to open the curtains, the aviation-blue sky was already bright and Jacek ran to catch his R 12 with cars direct to Brno, "... and don't forget the white plush..."

Like an airplane hangar and over each metal entrance laminated glass like an outstretched wing, excitedly Jacek climbed the stairs of his classmate Bena Smrcek's institute in Brno, a hodgepodge of concrete, glass, and steel, around him up and down rushed young men in white gowns, the uniform here, physical chemistry is on the fifth floor, "I've just come to look since I'm one of the applicants for the fellowship..." "Our new fellow will have this desk—," in streams of light a white-and-pale-blue laboratory desk with silver taps for water, gas, vacuum, and coolant, silver burners and under a cover a row of electrical outlets, inside, on black shelves, the gleam of laboratory glass, that almost forgotten glass with which one could always make a hole opening onto the world, at the next desk a hirsute young man looking fixedly into a golden brew as if it were a spinning roulette wheel, and by the large window in the corner a cheerful scholarly debate, presenting for your approval our new fellow, I'm not dead yet, Jacek walked out of the lab and back down as slowly as possible so that he could imprint as much as possible of that blue-and-white room where intellect still lives and where there's still adventure, of that room prepared and waiting in this airport of a building.

Outside the window in the mud-ridged Cottex courtyard the ancient mason was asleep under his crooked scaffold with his mouth wide open, and on the speckled desk from the days of the Germans work that had piled up for two days: a directive from the general director's office, sent again in error.

Jacek sat down at his Urania and, mentally counting up how much was available from the secret hoard, mechanically replied that we will proceed without delay, paragraph, As we have informed you many times before, we cannot proceed in the foreseeable future, five spaces and in the center the greeting, Peace on Earth, just then the telephone rang, this was it—some Carmen Pospisilova was calling angrily to ask where her daughter was, she hadn't been home for two days and her name was Carmen too.

Jacek banged down the phone, pulled out of his drawer the twenty-four spy shots of Cottex enlarged to map size, for two days he'd fiddled with them in the factory darkroom, he put them between fiery red covers with the letter to the general director's office, added a ten-mark note from Tina, and tossed it all onto the director's desk, a time bomb ready to go off—he went back to his office, lit a stolen Winston cigarette, and waited happily for his stage-call.

Outside the door at last a stomping, there was more than one of them—the dyer Patocka come with a suggestion for improvement: fire the color-room foreman and we'll save twenty thousand a year, his explanations weren't convincing, the dyer stood on his rights and so Jacek had to write it up in two copies, record it in the log, write a receipt, and thank the man for his initiative.

The phone rang, I'm coming and I'll take all the responsibility—Lenka was calling to say that Grandma had gone off to Brvany for unknown reasons and Lenicka had run through a closed door, you must buy mat glass, twenty-seven by forty-four-and-a-half inches, beige enamel paint, crepe paper, and especially the white plush, the telephone rang and informed him that the boys had pulled out lab assistant Palanova's chair as a prank and that she'd suffered a light concussion, the telephone rang and officially informed him that tomorrow Dr. Bruno Deleschall would arrive from the Basel firm of Ciba, he had nowhere to stay and tactfully take away his camera right at the entrance, so that's how you want to frame me, OK, I accept your game and out of all the stalemates up till now I'll squeeze out a checkmate—

Heavy steps outside the door, there are at least two of them coming—three arrived, first the director with the fiery red covers and, now liberated, Jacek stood up, I'm ready—the director placed the covers on his desk, "The letter to Brno is marvelous—" he said and then whispered, "Those shots of our grounds are handsome, but for security's sake I locked them in the vault—," behind him an aged secretary and the firm's legal expert made sour faces as they carried off the fifty-year-old Urania and left in its place on the plant stand a brand new blue-grey Zeta, the director winked archly, the doors banged shut, and Jacek was left alone with his new typewriter, for another fifty years there would be peace between Cottex and his department, blue-grey is the color of aviation, CAPTAIN, I DON'T UNDERSTAND YOUR CODE—

Outside the window a mass of spruces pierced the blue blue sky like Asiatic towers and behind the glass with the black ribbon the portrait of the dead thirty-three-year-old Adalsky, how delightful sheets bleached in the sun feel against the body, how young it is to be only thirty-three—

Jacek dashed through the blossoming meadow from the forest ranger's to the slope, through the woods, and by bus to the station, on the platform deserts loud-speakers summoned passengers to board trains for the west and the east, Jacek with his black satchel going up and down the stairs, the greatest torment is not to be able to decide, but if deciding fetters one so then isn't that torment one's last remaining liberty, depart by the first train that stops here to pick us up, Jacek laughed into the faces of the hurrying throngs and snapped his fingers, so quick, quick, children, off to school, the bell's rung and the teacher's already raging on the podium, she'll put a black mark in her record book, Jacek set his satchel down at his feet and raised his finger like a preacher, they had to go round him and Jacek guffawed in their faces, life is such a wonderful game of chance and so terribly one and the same for all time, everything that passes you by, you who never venture anything, and where do you get your firm belief that you couldn't live MAGNIFICENTLY SOME-WHERE ELSE than where you live according to a con-catenation of chances, you maggots and roundworms, MY FAITH IS IN FLIGHT, ta-ta-ta-dum, on the green cushions into the green waves of the sea which never ends, ta-ta-ta-dum, I TEAR UP MY SEAT CHECK and sit wherever I like, ta-ta-ta-dum, what, we're in Usti? Train, ride on—the train stopped.

And the crowd had already surged from the cars, all by the shortest routes to their Lenickas and Lenkas, ride on, train, I beg you, my Poseidon, from your compartment I pray to you, ride on, I must go to the end of the line, Sper-anza is there waiting for me on the first terrace behind the Residence, from where we once swam, we'll sit on chairs facing one another and call on you, ch-ch-ch-ch—I wasn't asleep then, ch-ch-ch-ch—I can't fall asleep anymore, ch-ch-ch-ch—I don't just want to sleep until I die, I've al-ready torn up my seat check, ride on, train, ride on, ch-ch-ch-ch—

## IV — fifteen

*T*he stream of passengers leaving the Decin station poured quickly onto buses and streetcars, we've only got a short walk from the station, Jacek hurried down the street past our third-category, on the staircase that stinks of sauerkraut he pulled out of his pocket a metal ring with a mass of keys, the Decin key is the gold one and this tiny beach is the Naiad's, in the foyer he kicked off his shoes and slipped into waiting leather slippers, Nada was reading Páral's novel *The Trade Fair of Wishes Come True*, and already she was tossing it aside, "Jacek, you've come—"

"I'm here now, my love—"

"Wouldn't you like something to eat? I have a big can of herring in oil—"

"Later, now all I want is to look at you and listen to you talk. Sit here on this chair and I'll bring the other one from the foyer... ch-ch-ch-ch—I love you so ch-ch—repeat after me: ch-ch-ch-ch—" The overturned chairs laughed with their legs in the air while the lovers lay on mattresses as if on waves.

A cigarette by the window, the barges on the Elbe sailed out from the docks and formed into a convoy, the afternoon sun with its golden trapezoids moved through the room and the room was full of light, "Jacek," Nada whispered behind him, "I've already signed up for the new co-op they're building, in your name... In three years we'll have our own apartment, two rooms, a bathroom with hot water, central heating, a telephone..."

Jacek jumped out of the bus and hurried across the excavated plain up the hill past the ten-story buildings with curtains and now with antennas as well, the twelve-story buildings have curtains already, and in our fourteen-story the windows are in with whitewash crosses on the glass, on the spattered staircase he pulled out the metal ring with its mass of keys, the Prague key is this silver one with the notch and this lofty beach is the Palma's, Anna was kneeling on an old coat, varnishing the wood floors with a brush, and already she was tossing it aside, "Jacek, darling—"

"I'm here now, my love—"

"Wouldn't you like to take a bath? They're trying out the hot water system today—"

"Later, now I can help you. What should I do?"

"First change your shoes, darling. The blue ones in the foyer are for you..."

"Anci, you know, it would be great if we had a phone here—"

"I've already applied for one... in your name."

On air mattresses Jacek and Anna lay side by side on the floor and their shoulders touched, "As if we were floating on the sea...," said Jacek, "Farther and farther away from the shore...," said Anna and they lay on compressed air as if on waves.

A cigarette by the window, out of the night the metropolis shone from its invisible hills, the lights blended with the noises of the enormous development and in thus permeated waves they shrilly broke on our ceiling like the tide, "Jacek," Anna whispered behind him, "I'd like to have a cottage somewhere in the country, you know, where it's dark at night and quiet and where even the open air goes to sleep..."

On the path through the fields Jacek hurried across an endless expanse stretching from horizon to horizon, huge red farm machines drove into the yellow sea and sacks of harvested grain lined their incursions, on the steps between the wild roses Jacek pulled out the ring of harvested keys, the Pardubice key is this homemade one, already Hanicka is running full tilt onto the platform with the circle of flowers, "Jacek, this is so wonderful—"

"I'm here now, my love—"

"Wouldn't you like to go see the rabbits?"

"Later, first I'll go say hello to your parents."

In the corridor Jacek tossed off his shoes and put on a checkered slipper with a tassle, "Don't take off your shoes—" Mrs. Kohoutkova said, "we've been holding supper for you, you can go right away for beer—," the clean scent of roast meat and the glass jug with the ten-crown note on the bottom.

On all the benches in front of the houses couples in the twilight, "The goose for Comrade Dr. Mach will be remarkable," said Hanicka, "Mama thinks fifteen pounds is big enough. I've been arguing that it ought to weigh at least eighteen pounds... Why don't you say anything?"

"I'm listening to the magnificent quiet here..."

"I'll be quiet too. It *is* magnificent..."

A cigarette and blow the smoke into the prism of light coming from the window, the couples got up from their benches and entered their houses, downstairs the lights went out, in a short time they went on upstairs, and then one light after another went out into the majestic quiet. "Jacek," Hanicka whispered, "we must wait a while yet, but I'm so looking forward to having children... First a boy, he'll look like you and go out into the world, and then a girl, she'll stay home with me..."

Through the blossoming grass Jacek sped down the slope to the forest ranger's and involuntarily reached for his key ring, but here they don't lock the doors, with a cry of joy Arnostek slid down a ladder and from the wood-shed Janicka came running, in the yard Lida was feeding the hens from a wicker basket and already she was toss-ing it aside, "Jacek, you've come—"

"I'm here now, my love—"

"Wouldn't you like to go for a walk?"

"Later, first I'll quiz Arnostek on his new vocabulary."

In the foyer Jacek took off his shoes and put his feet into the enormous leather slippers of the late Adalsky, "Uncle gwab me—" Janicka begged, so hold her in his arms a while and then set her up on the cupboard the way neighbor Mestek does, Janicka was afraid and ecstatic, "Uncle don't go way—," he wouldn't go, but now Arnos-tek must recite the thirty new words he's learned, the boy must get ready to go out into the world.

In early evening behind Lida along the path to the woods, then turn off the path and straight up through the glades to the grassy dunes, "My husband used to call this our Nude Beach...," Lida said, "It must be nice to sun-bathe here...," Jacek said, "It is, people come here from Prague and some of them don't bother wearing suits..."

A cigarette on a stump in front of the forest ranger's, in the lighted window two children's silhouettes and their little faces pressed to the glass, "You're a good man, Jacek," Lida whispered, "but here life isn't easy, there's a lot of work to do, the house, the farming, the children... It would be fine to begin again from nothing, to be young again from the very beginning..."

Jacek stepped out of the express and hurried across the tracks of the Svitavy station, it's right across the street, on the warm dark staircase grope and find in the bunch of keys the one for this place, big as a church key, under the tin picture of the Eiffel Tower the little Jeannette beach, Tanicka was mending a stocking and already she was tossing it aside, "Jacek, you devil—"

"I'm here now, my love—"

"Wouldn't you like to hear what I've written?"

"Later, first I'd like to change my shoes..."

Jacek took off his shoes and looked around in vain for something to put on, all Tanicka had were three pairs of shoes under the bed and otherwise nothing, "I go bare-foot at home, but I've heard that in Prague they've got real Chinese sandals for sale..."

"Wouldn't it be better to first buy a table and chairs?"

"They're dull, unnecessary things, look here—" Tanicka threw all the bedding off her bed and under the yellow tin Parisian sky they rocked on the cross-wires as on a canoe, Tanicka read eighteen new poems and then suddenly fell asleep. Scarcely had Jacek begun to read than a skinny arm slipped before his eyes a chewed-up piece of paper containing the nineteenth:

> *With my longest nail*
> *on my master's back*
> *I'll engrave*
> *childish obscenities.*
> *Surely*
> *it will get through to him then*
> *that*
> *this is no time*
> *to read the paper!*

A cigarette by the window looking out onto the sad Svitavy station, through the air-bubbly glass modest little parcels in oiled paper, "Jacek," Tanicka whispered, "I'll die here longing for the big city, where the store windows shine and the streetcars clang..."

Jacek stepped out of the express and hurried with the crowd through the din of the Brno station to the buffet, over a stale beer Mojmira was reading *The Trade Fair of Wishes Come True* and suddenly she lit up, "Jacek, welcome, all happiness—"

"I'm here now, my love—"

"Wouldn't you like to go to the publisher's, I have to take you there sometime to explain to them that you're not ready to come right now..."

"Later, first let's stuff ourselves. I'm so huuungry—"

The magnificence of the city of Brno begins right outside the station, streetcar after streetcar in three rows, directly across the square the airline office with its heavy chrome swinging doors, and on both sides a gleaming, unending strip of shop windows and glass doors.

Through glass doors, swinging doors, and turnstiles, down from glass refrigerated shelves, out of bowls and out from behind curtains, onto spattered counters, onto wood, and onto ever new damask tablecloths and paper trays, plates made of plastic and of gilded porcelain, with crackling sausages, crunchy french fries, and meat from the spit, and into steins, paper cups, crystal goblets everything that can conceivably flow, at first icy and then ever warmer, "You're the last man left who knows how to eat—" Mojmira said, "You're the first woman I've enjoyed food so much with—" said Jacek and gargantuan kisses in front of the dried-up cloakroom attendant at the Hotel Continental.

A cigarette inside the glass doors, along the garden wall down under the tops of the old trees the street leads to our house, the street is pasted up with a thousand posters on which long ago we used to dream of seeing our name in huge letters, "I'm ashamed now I made such a hog of myself," Mojmira whispered, "but I've been hungry all my life, before the war, during the war, since the war, and now I'm still hungry, it's wonderful not to have any money, but sometimes a sense of horror comes over me..."

Jacek jumped from the funicular seat and hurried up the hill to Mosquito Tower, on the spiral stairs he took out the key ring, from the round windows now the crests of the Krusne Mountains, now the tips of the Czech Central Range, and now the view into Germany, this thin skeleton key belongs to the Belvedere beach, Tina lying on the bed smoking a cigarette and already she was tossing it aside, "Jacek—"

"I'm here now, my love—"

"Wouldn't you like to go down to the bar? We just got our quota of Dubonnet—"

"Later, now I'd like to be with you. Do you have anything for me?"

Tina gave Jacek some paper money fastened with a hairpin, each bill from a different country and the prettiest of all, like a postage stamp, a colorful franc note, "But now you have to go down to the bar, Jacek. Right away."

Without a word Jacek changed into heavy half-boots with tire-tread soles, in these he could go up and down the stairs like a ghost, they could serve for attack or defense, "You won't need them today," said Tina firmly, "wait till I come down. Scoot!"

On the stairs going down Jacek passed a huge fellow with a thick cigar in his bared, vulgar teeth, in the bar Jacek drank Dubonnet and in hot breakers again and again he beheld Tina's tormenting gold-and-orange skin, he breathed in deeply like a drowning man that hitherto unknown smarting sensation and again hot wave after wave.

A cigarette by the window, Tina's hair let down and quivering like an animal's, he poured another two glassfuls and looked out in silence, "Jacek," Tina whispered behind him, "I'd like some milk now, sweet white warm milk..."

The funicular down to Bohosudov, the bus at 5:34 and in Usti at 6:05 as if from the 4:45 to Berlin, streetcar No. 5 to Vseborice, Jacek hurried along the roadway past the

children's playground, on the well-scrubbed staircase he
pulled out a bundle of keys, opened the Residence with
the one with the letters FAB and the dog's head, Lenka
was wiping the foyer with a rag and already she was tossing it aside, "Jacek, you came back today, already—"

"I'm here now, my love—"

"Wouldn't you like some strawberries, they're fresh
from our garden..."

"Later, first I'd like something to drink. You didn't forget the milk... No hot cereal, just warm up the milk for me
and put in five cubes of sugar..."

"You forgot the white plush again, didn't you—"

"Yes, I did, darling, but I'll bring it, really I will—" said
Jacek, putting on his old slippers worn smooth to a shine.

"Daddy—" our little darling calls, her chin on the brass
pole, down with the net at once and his rough chin on her
sweet little tummy, Lenicka cried out with pleasure,
nothing's so sweet to kiss as our little one, "Daddy gwab
me—" cries our pretty little girl, and so swing her back
and forth and set her up on top of the cupboard, Lenicka
is afraid and ecstatic, but now she must go beddie-bye,
"Daddy don't go way—" and stay by her bedside until
she goes to sleep with her thumb in her mouth.

A cigarette by the window, outside children being
called home to bed and now the stars like urchins on a
fence slide on their rumps down the antennas into cribs
with nets, just across the way Trost with a cigarette by the
window... that fellow's gawking right this way, from that
window he's goggling right into my face—

By bus at 3:55 from the main square through the
canyon of facades none of which can be omitted, down
the row of old chestnuts, around the sharp curve past the
gas works, and through mountains of dead soil torn up
from the earth to the monument with the lion eaten up by
verdigris, now the linden tree with the sign and along the
clay road up to the retreat, the yellow house isn't ours, it
belongs to Mrs. Heymerova, who'll come back again very
soon, on the oval table and on the wall stags bellowing in

rut, they don't bellow but they're embroidered with open jaws, and out the window of the retreat the undulation of gleaming emerald grass rearing up to the gleaming sky like the coast to the sea, we've already set sail, but we forgot to pull up the anchor, the boat has only a lookout deck and the train keeps hauling us around and around and back onto the ramp at home, try it once on foot or perhaps on a horse, MY KINGDOM FOR A HORSE that will carry us away from the plain of too many victories and hurl us into the bloodspill of salvation because it is the bloodspill of a single defeat, MY KINGDOM FOR A KICK-OFF so that instead of going a little way with a satchel of dirty clothes we can take off once and for all with the cosmonaut's luggage, I already know the timetable by heart, CAPTAIN, I REQUEST THE SIGNAL TO TAKE OFF— This is the last time I'll ask.

## Part V — Autosynthesis — sixteen

With its usual delay, express No. 7 from Bucharest, Budapest, and Bratislava was just pulling into Platform One at Brno Main Station. In the midst of the usual confused rush of travelers Jacek took in the always unexpected sequence of numbers on the reserved cars until, sufficiently amused, he finally caught sight of his own car, No. 53, hooked up between Nos. 28 and 32.

In compartment F by the window on seat No. 67 a fat old man looked up, we have No. 68 across from him, Jacek put his traveling satchel up into the net, hung his beige iridescent raincoat beneath it, and when he sat down another passenger entered the compartment with a seat check in hand, he had the odd number 69, alongside the fat man, he put his suitcase into the net and he hung beneath it his blue-grey raincoat of the same material and cut as Jacek's.

"Excuse me, gentlemen," said the fat man by the window, "do either of you play chess by any chance?"

"I do, " Jacek said.

"I wouldn't mind a game," the third passenger said simultaneously, he and Jacek looked at each other, laughed, and the train pulled quietly out.

"So you two come to an agreement which of you I'm to demolish," roared the fat man joyously, "meanwhile I'll set up the pieces—" and he was already sticking them into his portable chess board.

"You play, since you're sitting there," the third passenger said to Jacek, "I'll kibitz. To myself."

"You can do it out loud," Jacek smiled as he opened P-Q4.

The fat man opened up on the same column, P-Q4, mechanically Jacek moved P-KB4, the fat man again the mirror image, P-KB4, another couple of moves and similar countermoves and we've achieved that double interlocking barrier known as a stonewall.

The train rushed on through meadows and forests, a girl flashed by, she was wearing a red polka-dot dress and waiting behind a lowered barrier, and on the little table by the window two players sweating over their total blockade, nothing could come of it, both were waiting for their opponent to make a mistake and that's a terrible bore, "I've got to step out a minute...," Jacek grumbled a good quarter hour before reaching the Svitavy station and he stood all that time by a window in the corridor.

Tanicka Rambouskova had been waiting at one end of the Svitavy station and she ran up to Jacek's window, we stop here for just a minute, "Don't think I came here just to see you—" she lied, out of breath from her gallop.

"I wouldn't have imagined it even in my sleep—do you sell lemonade here?"

"You're a disgusting cynic and I don't want to see you ever again, ever—understand!"

"I'll jump off the train!"

"That would be wonderful... I'd lay your bloody head in my lap... Jacek, please, get out—"

"It isn't that simple..."

The train pulled quietly out and Jacek waved to Tanicka until she disappeared around the bend, actually why didn't we get out, he sighed and went back to his compartment, on the table that nightmarish unfinished game and both passengers preoccupied, making faces over it, "You said you'd like to play," Jacek told the third passenger, "so if you're still inclined—"

"If it's OK with you—" said the third passenger and he eagerly moved over into Jacek's seat No. 68 opposite the indefatigable chess player while Jacek moved into the thus emptied No. 69, and with relief he now observed how his replacement was tormenting himself, he tormented himself another hour, as far as Chocen, where the two of them, quite exhausted, settled for a draw rather than an endless repetition of the same moves.

The third passenger fished a timetable out of his suit-case and compared it with his watch, "Twenty minutes late, right—" said Jacek. "Yep," the passenger agreed, "I wonder if we'll catch the 4:45 to Berlin—" "You can rely on it—" Jacek assured him, "are you going to Usti by any chance?" "Yes, and you?" "Me too. For a long time?" "Possibly for good. You know the place?" "For ten years now almost too well. What would you like to know?" "Do you know anything about the chemical plant?" "Everything, I work next door at Cottex. You're a chemist?" "Yes. If you'll permit—" and the passenger pulled a card out of his wallet and handed it to Jacek,

ENGINEER NORBERT HRADNIK

Jacek read the card, got up and almost embraced him. "We're in the same profession then, I'm very happy..." "It really is a lucky coincidence..." "Most happy to do anything for you..." "You're really very kind...." "With the greatest pleasure..." expressing their affability they rushed to the dining car and shared a large dinner, Hrad-nik was running away from his wife and two children, from an awful job in Brno to Usti, we from Usti to Brno, two more beers, "I'm Jacek—" "I'm Nora—" and two small carafes of wine, "I'll find you jobs, Nora, as many as you want—" "I'm more worried about a place to stay, Jacek, they'll stick me in some dorm—" "Tonight you can stay at our place—" "At home, Jacek, I had to cook hot meals twice a day—" "Nora, I've got fantastic chicks in Svitavy and Brno—" "Two cognacs!" cried Nora, "Geor-gian!" cried Jacek and just before Prague they stumbled back to their compartment, in the dark of the tunnel they fell laughing into their exchanged seats and here was Prague Main Station already, both got up and put on their raincoats, "But Jacek, you've got on mine—" Nora guf-fawed in Jacek's beige iridescent, "And you've got on mine, Nora—" Jacek giggled in Nora's aviation blue-grey, they fit and suit us, CAPTAIN, NOW I UNDERSTAND YOUR CODE—

"Why you're like twins," the fat man grinned from his window, "Let's exchange them," Jacek cried, "I'm awfully fond of this aviation color—" "Sold!" cried Nora, "we've both got a new coat for free—"

"Darling—" Anna Bromova called from the exit of Prague Main Station and she ran up to Nora, only a step away from him did she realize her error, "Jacek...," she whispered in terrible embarrassment, Jacek laughed and took her around her thin shoulders, "Jacek, stay in Prague today...," she said on their swift trip through the little park, "... you know no one's expecting you in Usti..." "Today I've got something very important to arrange," Jacek muttered like a conspirator, "for both of us...," and at least Anna was able to see him off at Prague Central Station, Jacek and Nora easily caught the 4:45 to Berlin and Jacek had time to come out to the window in the corridor, Anna stood for a long time by the car, she kissed her palm, blew the kiss up to him, and the train pulled quietly out over bridges high above the streets of Prague, it passed through the green shadows of Stromovka Park and then beneath a hillside of millionaires' mansions and the Byzantine skyscraper of the Hotel International.

"With your right foot!—" Jacek cried at the Usti station and Nora had to step out right foot first for good luck, streetcar No. 5 to Vseborice, the last stop, the two men hurried past the children's playground, the steps up to our place have multiplied considerably again, "You go first—" Jacek pushed Nora, reshod in his old slippers and carrying Jacek's black satchel, into the dark foyer, Lenka came out to meet them with a smile, "Who are you bringing home, Jacek?" she said to Nora, she took the traveling satchel from him and went back into the kitchen, Jacek stepped ahead of Nora and entered behind Lenka, "Mr. N. Hradnik."

Nora kissed Lenka's hand and she took it unexpectedly well, heaven knows when the last time was that anyone had greeted her that way, Nora moved through the kitchen with agility and prepared a marvelous omelet, but then he's had the training provided by five years of married life, Lenka clapped her hands in admiration, Nora took Lenicka by the legs and taught her to do backward somersaults, you can see the routine of a father of two children left behind in Brno, after supper he talked about the Margrave Jost and Lenka showed a surprising familiarity with Moravian history, she must have read up on it sometime, the substitute had taken and they put him to bed in the living room with two pillows under his head, depleting Jacek's customarily high head of the bed.

From Cottex home as slowly as possible through the town, at the Hranicar movie house they're playing *No One Will Laugh* for the third week in a row so let's go to the movies for a change, herring and onions at the Svet Cafeteria and a small carafe of white Burgundy at the Zdar, everywhere he goes a bachelor lives it up, even when he's alone, paradise must be solitude with the possibility of choice, Jacek stopped in at the barbershop and spent a pleasant time in Kamilka's soothing hands, "Why didn't you come that day at ten...," she whispered when he kissed her on the elbow, "That day I couldn't, but today's no problem..." "Today my Dad's here from Mimon, but come tomorrow—," Jacek inhaled his cologne and gazed contentedly at the travel agency display next to the notice agency, two pretty girls invite us to visit the Czech Paradise and over the green sea a white boat sails along, on the column a new poster with Candy in a red tux, LAST APPEARANCE BEFORE OUR GRAND TOUR—

Toward evening Jacek came home, in no way missed, in Jacek's T-shirt with Lenka's apron tied around his waist Nora was preparing Hungarian fish soup and Mexican goulash, Lenka merrily grated the cheese, and together they went to bathe Lenicka, "I thought that kind of husband had long since died out...," Lenka laughed, "That's nothing," Nora laughed, "I used to do the ironing and one winter I even did embroidery with my wife..."

After supper each of them took a cup of wild-rose tea with jam into the living room and talked about Stravinsky and Kandinsky, what sort of men they were, Jacek went out onto the balcony with a chair and a glass of cognac and facing the strip of dark blue sky he smoked cigarette after cigarette, the couple on the sofa and the husband outside, it would be only an occasional release from the barracks to visit the town's dance hall and besides that Lenka doesn't want to sin, but to bring a new husband into the apartment and so preserve the numerical status quo, soldier for soldier, CAPTAIN, THANKS FOR THE SIGNAL, when the bottom of a gasoline storage tank cracks it's best to call the firefighters, all that has to be done is to let water in, and then out of the hole in the bottom only water will flow, it's heavier, and the gasoline will remain undisturbed in the cracked storage tank until you pump it into a new tank—since Lenka and Nora had forgotten about Jacek, they were almost frightened when he suddenly appeared from the balcony, "Don't bother getting up—" said Jacek, "tomorrow I'm going to Brno, please put two white shirts in my satchel, and no lunch..."

"Don't forget the white plush..."

Out the window over the houses a shining blue hangar, Jacek tiptoed through the apartment, away from the sleeping Lenka past the sleeping Nora to the foyer, take the traveling satchel and the blue-grey raincoat, CAPTAIN, THANKS FOR THE UNIFORM—

A great four-day cruise on the green cushions of the black steamship from beach to beach along the entire coast, Jacek stepped out of the sea and up the steps with his black satchel like a trident in his hand, like Neptune himself, greeted and welcomed by naiad after naiad, fed, indulged, fondled, loved, and respected, the Belvedere, the Jeannette, the Palma, the Stefanie, the Kvarner, the Naiad, the Speranza, and in exchange for just the one beach at the Residence he got the Miramar as a point of departure for Africa—

"What's happened here?" Jacek was frightened, Lenka locked in the kitchen and Nora throwing into his suitcase the things he'd laid out on a chair, "Nothing, to be precise."

"You want to leave?  Why?" Jacek whispered, crushed.

"Didn't you know that tomorrow Grandma's coming back from the hot springs?"

"But that can be taken care of... Would you rather live in the chem plant dorm, in a room for four with bunkbeds?"

"I've been living in one for three days now and there are nine of us in a room."

"Did Lenka do anything..."

"Lenka didn't do anything. When you described her to me on the train you said that she's intelligent, decent, a good cook..."

"And isn't all of that true?"

"It is, anyone can tell that in half an hour himself. But you forgot to tell me the main thing about her."

"What main thing?"

With a sigh Nora picked up the suitcase and shook it, it was almost empty, he carried it into the foyer, tore his blue-grey raincoat off the coat tree and threw it over his shoulders, CAPTAIN, WHY DOES HE GET TO MAKE THE FLIGHT INSTEAD OF ME, "Couldn't you possibly change your mind...," Jacek groaned, "if I were to ask you—"

"I might learn to be afraid of you," N. Hradnik said, "Farewell, Mrs. Jostova, and thanks for everything—" he called to the glass panel of the locked door and he left in silence.

"Nora was swell at first," Lenka said, holding Lenicka in her arms, "but when you went away he tried to take advantage of the situation, I had to go for Jarda Mestek at once..."

"Jarda?"

"... and in the meantime Mr. Hradnik had vanished. Today he only came back for the things he'd left behind

in his haste. Jacek, when are you going to bring me that
white plush—"

"Next time, definitely."

Post another man at once in the deserter's place, "And
so I'm extremely grateful to you, Mr. Mestek," Jacek said
in his neighbor's bachelor apartment, "you've done so
much for us already..."

"But it's nothing, I was glad to..." Mr. Mestek smiled.
Jarda.

"And why shouldn't we call each other by our nick-
names, after all, when we're almost like members of the
same family. Mine is Jacek—"

"Mine is Jarda—

"I know. Lenka uses it more and more often lately:
Jarda says this, Jarda thinks that, Jarda would never—she
likes you, you know..."

"I'm not so sure myself..."

"But she does. Just now she was saying how surprised
she was that you're alone all the time. Such an intelligent,
decent man—those were her words—and then such a
good-looking one, very good-looking, in fact... Why once
in the middle of the night she whispered your name in
her sleep..."

"Oh, that's hard to believe!"

"She did, but I'm not jealous, on the contrary—"

"You'd have no reason to be."

"But you see I'm very glad to know that Lenka has
someone to depend on when I'm not around, someone
who... who..."

"You don't know her very well, Jacek. Not very well at
all."

Jacek got up, took in at a glance the saucepans with old,
hardened grease, the bundle of filigree carved canes, the
piles of crossword puzzles, the socks drying on the string
hung from the windowlatch to the latch on the door, all
that bachelor squalor, he sighed and stole away.

DARLING, COME, PLEASE PLEASE PLEASE, wrote Anna, COME LIKE LAST TIME, Tina wired, and from Tanicka a call from Svitavy

> *Sweet drop of honey*
> *Trickle into the comb!*

Jacek paced his office at Cottex like a beast in a cage, CAPTAIN, I REQUEST INSTRUCTIONS, your parachutist has deserted and the next man from the local reserves is unsuited for the task, how can I attack without troops—

On his desk Tanicka's poem, the telegram, and the envelope from Prague, did we dream it or did a ray of sunlight really fall on the blue-grey metal, the Zeta flashed a gleam and Jacek stopped short in the middle of the room, CAPTAIN, SIGNAL RECEIVED, carry out a paratroop recruitment drive, the escalation will culminate in a mass parachute drop, and already Jacek was pressing the corresponding keys of the newly assigned Zeta:

28-YEAR-OLD wom. off. work., divor. with 3-year-old charm. daught. and own furn. apart. 1st-cat. seeks partner, key word: "LIVE!"

and then on the envelope the address of the Personals section of *Prace*, Jacek tenderly caressed the aviation-blue machine, *zeta* is the last letter of the alphabet, and he stopped to reflect: flight wouldn't be as easy as an ocean voyage, the failures up to now dictate a revision of the old maps, one must get to know the squadron assigned and, most important, become familiar with the terrain to be conquered, to learn where the stores of oil are, where the communications, the junctions, and the dams, where the artillery units and where the staff, perhaps our conjectures concerning the territory are incorrect—

## V — seventeen

Alarge yellow envelope, METERED MAIL, was already
there, not much more than a pound, Jacek tore open
the paper and from the large yellow envelope a stream of
dozens of variously colored smaller ones splattered onto
his desk, on all them in different hands and in different
places the same thing:

    Live! 64063-v

Jacek piled up the letters and then he counted only 62,
that's because of Lenicka, he took his letter opener out of
the drawer and began to open the paratroopers' applica-
tions:

    Dear Lady!
    I read your ad in Prace and I'm in just as bad a
    fix as you, my girl is six, only we don't have a
    1st-cat. apartment and that is certainly a
    basis and condition for

Dismissed, next—

    Madame:
    Your advertisement today strongly attracted
    my interest. Although I'm 44 and I limp a little
    on my right leg

    Dear Comrade!
    I'm also an office worker, to be precise the
    assistant chief of the top contract division of
    an important consumer co-op handling the
    manufacture of durable feedstuffs and first of
    all
    My three children, Svatopluk, Zdislava and
    Zaboj
    I am taking the liberty of answering you.
    Please send me the precise dimensions of your
    apartment, i.e., including bathroom, toilet
    I'm 34 a yung felow you see and lively to. I'm
    surching for a lively girlfriend I've got a boy
    but they dont make me pay for him

I'd like very much to meet you and I'd like
your picture. For the time being I don't enclose
my own for understandable reasons. I'm big in
build, the photo and a detailed description of
the apartment with information on whether a
garage can be built nearby
    I too was deceived and I believed in her so
much. I'd like to believe again, or at least
hope, for what can life do to us now
    still feel young and I'd like to try a third
time if the apartment isn't on the top floor
We don't have anybody to do the cooking and the
two children need warm food    not yet forty
I'd be glad to move    2 children also deceived
and so    By a first-category apartment we surely both understand central heating, a bathroom
with hot water and a gas or electric    They need
a mamma    in your apartment    we fix our food
all sorts of ways    in your apartment    with
your apartment    your apartment

With a sigh Jacek classified the letters into acceptable,
marginal, and discards, he transferred the sheets from
one pile to another like cards and sighed more and more,
at one point the acceptable pile had vanished entirely and
everything was in the discards, the divorced, the retired,
and the fathers of several children were only interested in
a cook and someone to take care of their children, and all
of them wanted to marry the apartment, what a pitiful
squadron of mercenaries and retired paratroopers, Jacek
drank strong coffee and with a cigarette he sat down at
the blue-grey Zeta, he prepared 16 draft calls, first of all
some recruitment slogans, From a hundred letters
just your letter    revealing real intelligence
and an unusual    you surely won't be disappointed, then a tactical comment, for reasons which
you will certainly appreciate I am compelled
for the time being to act for the woman advertising, and a Napoleonic ("Soldiers! I will lead you on

to fertile plains...") conclusion: for contentment, happiness and a new life, and he dropped 16 letters into the mailbox.

Only 11 replies, of which 2 broke off the correspondence (is that office worker of yours literate? Unfortunately I have a lot to do with the authorities and I wouldn't be a bit surprised if, and I've turned your letter over to the police to check up on the suspicious circumstances), what poverty compared with the music of the women's offers, but the existence of a go-between had awakened fears even among eight of the nine acceptables, two had procedural doubts why doesn't she write herself, she wouldn't have to give her name does she really know you're acting for her in this rather important business, but one remaining one felt, on the contrary, joy I am a passionate adherent of psychoanalysis and find it a fascinating idea to penetrate through an intermediary who is an intimate friend, from all nine acceptables, however, came nine tidal waves of insistent questions

I'd like to believe in spite of this, but I'd be happy to find out more please write in more detail about her character, interests and preferences does she prefer company or being alone? what are her ideas about marriage and does she really want is she lively or quiet? the main thing is her interests does she like to read and if so which present-day Czech authors her character is she sincere? does she like classical music and specifically what without using big words describe her personality and inclinations truthfully and specifically her attitude towards nature about history and cultural monuments specifically and in great detail describe her character and her significant features more

about her psychic personality and in more
detail    what she expects from her partner and
what she longs to give     her ideals and her
dreams    what more specifically she actually
understands by the slogan "Live!" what she's
really like—

the territory put up for annexation, what its mountains
are like, its lowlands and rivers, how is it populated and
what mineral wealth does it have, what fauna and flora,
what grain it grows and what vegetables, how terribly little we know about the evacuated territory—

In the bathroom an alternately hot and cold shower,
Jacek then unscrewed the head from the shower and
turned the swift stream straight on his body, hot and cold
showers whip you up to peak efficiency, and with his hair
wet he sat down again at his flying machine, Dear Sir,
thanks for your    I assure you completely    she
is fond of company, but not even while alone
does she    she is lively and at the same time
restrained    she likes to read and reads almost
exclusively present-day Czech writers— "What
present-day Czech writers do you know?" Jacek
telephoned Mija, "... what's that? *The Dictionary of Czech
Writers*... aha... in the town library, many thanks and so
long," you can't do it all in one day, so then the next,
Jacek pulled the sheet out of the typewriter and again,
Dear Sir, thanks for your    I can assure you
completely    she's a close student of history
and knows all about the Moravian rulers Jost
and, hell, which other ones were there, how do I cross out
the and and were they really rulers, wish I'd asked her
sometime, but there  wasn't time, Jacek pulled the sheet
out of the typewriter and so let's just answer the things
we know about Lenka, classical music probably not,
well, we used to listen to it, but not so much anymore,
attitude towards nature, she likes gardening, of
course, and she used to go to the woods with me, good
God, why did she give that up, of course it was the child,

but then Grandma was always happy to, is she lively
or quiet? she's quiet and she's lively too, in detail
describe her personality her interests her
character truthfully and specifically her
character and her significant features about
her psychic personality more and in more
detail what she expects I don't know what she
longs to give her ideals and dreams I don't
know what she actually understands I don't know
what she's really like I DON'T KNOW HER AT ALL,
Jacek bit hard into his cheeks and twisted the sweaty hair
on his temples as painfully as he could, the damp of the
shower had now been replaced by sweat, can I still profile
MY OWN WIFE, eat this paper if you can't do at least ten
lines, Jacek pushed another sheet into the machine as if
the last cartridge into a barrel pointed at himself, Dear
Sir, thanks for your I can assure you completely and now for your question as to what she's
really like She's

The keys of the typewriter were like forty jeering eye-
balls, for a long time Jacek pushed the space bar with his
finger and finally he took out the sheet and began to
thoughtfully chew it up.

"We can go to bed," Nada said in the room overlooking
the Decin harbor, "but even then you must answer one
very important question..."

"Truthfully and specifically...," Jacek whispered and
he shivered.

"The co-op I applied to wants to know our wedding
date. If it isn't this year or next, they'll cross us off the
list."

"But Nadezda, isn't getting married too convention-
al..."

"It's insane, but we'll sleep better in a first-category
apartment than we do in this dump. I'll buy an apron for
the first time in my life and a cookbook and a feather-
duster and a vacuum cleaner—I'm looking forward to the
first time I vacuum *our first carpet* as if it were my wed-

ding night, those I've already had—you'll be amazed what all will pick its way out of me, why you're looking at me as if you were seeing me for the first time—oh Jacek, you've still got to learn so much about me..."

"I can't catch the afternoon train, but *we* can still catch it—"

"But first that date—"

At last the Ford Taunus came out of Tina's room and unceremoniously Jacek squeezed into the still open door, "You were standing outside the door—" comb in hand, Tina was astounded, she was painfully beautiful and torturingly disheveled, "But you kept him here a whole eternity!" "Not at all, he flew out of here like a bat out of hell..." "Darling, couldn't you really give it up, I'll pay you out of my salary—" "With every cent you're paid we'd have to save for years to buy that gas station, lover boy!"

"... you're like a little boy, like a schoolboy...," Tina whispered, caressing Jacek's head on her lap, "but it'll soon be over, never fear, I want that gas station mainly so we'll be rid of this bar for good and rid of all this, believe me, more for that than for the money, someday I want to be the guest and not one of the staff, to have an honest profit instead of two-bit tips and crumpled hundred notes, and most of all I want to have my peace of mind and like a banded middle-class wife go afternoons for my coffee with whipped cream and cake with a husband who has the same band I've got, two bands they take off only in the coffin—"

"They opened a new café on Strekov Hill last month," said Lenka, wringing a rag out into a bucket, "and if it stays rainy, we could go there sometime..."

"For coffee with whipped cream and cake!"

"That's it! So let's go?"

"But you could have gone there long ago, when I was away, with the little one, or Grandma could have babysat with her..."

"But I want to go with you—"

Jacek watched Lenka bending over, how little you have in common with that illegal hard-currency whore Tina, she should have a traveling husband, one who brings home lovers and suitors to her apartment—but what do we really know about you, behind the wall the vacuum roared in the bedroom and Lenka was singing to its roar, in the bedroom *our first carpet*—Jacek was afraid to go into the bedroom after Lenka, I AM NO LONGER SURE WHOM I WOULD MEET THERE—

## V — eighteen

Out of the thickening dusk stairs ran up to our bench in front of the pink house and on all the tiny platforms in front of the houses with their shining facades quiet couples, "Happiness is such a strong feeling," whispered Hanicka Kohoutkova, "I've read many leading writers, Czech and foreign, but so far none of them has ever given an accurate description of... Jacek, which month will we hold the wedding?"

"Do you need the date this evening?"

"No. But soon. I have to have a white dress made and there'll be lots of shopping to do. Dad would like to combine it with a slaughtering—"

"That would probably be best..."

On the meadow in front of the forest ranger's Jacek pitched a tent with Arnostek, they stole through the high grass to the garden, burst out with the battle cry of the Iroquois, and took Janicka captive, Lida tried to ransom her with a bilberry tart, Arnostek accepted the ransom but Jacek grabbed the little girl and ran off with her to the woods, she held on to him with her little arms and legs, "Cawwy me, Uncle, and we'll build a gingerbwead house in the woods and we won't wet Mummy and Arnostek come—"

Jacek and Lida sat on the stump and the two children's heads showed in the window above them, "Go to bed, children—" Lida called, "or Uncle won't come anymore," and the little heads disappeared at once, in a minute, though, Janicka's looked out once more, "Can Uncle come give me a kiss?" "You know he'll come." "And can Uncle tell a stowy?" "You know he will."

"She's so terribly attached to you," Lida whispered, touched, "Arnostek too, but he's a boy and doesn't show it, but Janicka— Jacek, she'll be going to school soon and I'd be so happy… if she had your name, Arnostek can keep the Adalsky name, but Janicka could have yours, at least one of them would…"

"Today we've got to go to the publisher's," the beaming Mojmira cried in the Brno Main Station buffet, "and you don't know why, but I'll spill it to you: we're going to work together there, I'll do translations and you'll choose and edit them. Jacek, you know what it's like to earn money every month on the dot, precisely on the day? It must be a fantastic feeling…"

In the hurrying crowd, Jacek and Mojmira walked out of the station, "… it's fun to work for a publisher, you get to know a million terrific people," Mojmira was ecstatic, "and together we'll earn almost four thousand—month by month the whole year long and the next year and all the time—from our first paycheck we'll buy a suckling pig, for New Year's half a pig, and every summer we'll go to the seashore—Jacek, let's go get married right now—"

Right across the street the enormous airline building and out of its heavy chrome swinging doors came three officers in flight uniforms—comrades, I've already sent out nine calls to mobilize and day after tomorrow I'll deploy my paratroops, a blue-grey airline minibus pulled up in front and the captains rode off, I am ready to go with you—

Of the nine, only five paratroopers heeded the mobilization order and presented themselves in the Zdar café at 4:00 p.m. on the succeeding specified days, "And otherwise it's quite simple," Jacek repeated to Tuesday's, Wednesday's, Thursday's, Friday's (Saturday and Sunday were days of rest), and Monday's paratroopers, "so let's go around to the development right now, without obligation you can have a look at the mother and daughter from a distance and in case you're interested I'll take you up to the apartment as a friend from the train..."

"I had a hunch she didn't know anything about it..." Tuesday's whispered, a faded balding blond with fingers stained walnut-brown from nicotine, he drank up his Pilsner and slunk away without paying or saying goodbye.

"So let's go!" Wednesday's said emphatically, a sweaty and smelly divorced guy with a big build and a low forehead running straight back into a greying wire thicket, the whole endless trip on the streetcar he was doggedly silent and in mounting fear Jacek looked askance at his gloomy profile, wasn't it a bit crazy to bring this brute home to Lenka... and Lenicka—

"Excuse me, I've changed my mind, this isn't really the way to do it—" would have sufficed to call off the frightful deed, anyway it doesn't have to be this one, we have three more in reserve, Jacek thought feverishly, but he said nothing and already they were standing at the observation post behind the substation, between the buildings with their delicate pastel shades where the broad roadway leads past the children's playground to our home—

"So which windows is it?—" the fellow growled.

"There, over the left entrance on the third floor...," Jacek whispered in a choked voice.

"And when's she get home?"

"She comes home every day around five..."

"What?!"

"Around five... she comes home then..."

But today it was half-past five, the two figures, large and small, along the walk in front of the wall as if for an execution squad, "There—" Jacek pointed with a concentration of his last efforts, Lenka was dragging two heavy bags and Lenicka, with her doll, was holding on to one of the handles of one of the bags.

"The one with the bags and the brat?"

All Jacek could do was nod, Lenka bent her head to wipe her forehead on her sleeve and Lenicka ran ahead home... "And now we're supposed to go and pretend we've just come in from the train...," the fellow grumbled, Jacek just stood there, "—for that I ain't got the nerve," the fellow whispered, he turned and cleared out across the grass, Jacek took a deep breath and ran across the grass in the opposite direction, "Lenka...," he cried from afar, "darling... wait for Daddy—"

A kiss for Lenka even before they were home, "You know what, let's go to that new café for coffee with whipped cream—no, let's make today a home day and not go anywhere..." "At least carry these bags upstairs," said Lenka.

And today we'll have a good romp with Lenicka, till evening or even later, she can go to bed an hour late for a change, "Darling, tell Daddy what you'd like and you'll have it—"

"I want a wowwypop!"

"But we'd have to take the streetcar again..."

"I want a wowwypop!"

"You'll have five of them, but now let's go home..."

Jacek set the little girl down on a step, he bent over and tried to take off her little shoe, it was terribly tight, he jerked a little and Lenicka started screaming, "It's too small for her...," Jacek told Lenka, "No it isn't, it's just that you've gotten out of the habit," Lenka sighed.

"So what do you want to play with Daddy tonight?"

"Optical course and house."

"First let's do the obstacle course...," and already Jacek had laid two mattresses down flat on the floor and a third one vertically between them, the little girl climbed over it, fell down, and again climbed up, just then the bell rang and in the foyer neighbor Mestek's voice could be heard, he's come to change the washer in the faucet, "Uncle gwab me—" cried Lenicka and she ran off after him, "Little one, stay here with Daddy—," but the little one was already off after Mestek and was working on the plumbing with him, "And now wet's go see Punchinjudy—" "Where is it she wants to go?" asked Jacek, "Every Wednesday they have a children's theater here," said Lenka, "and Jarda Mestek has been good enough to take her when you're away." "We won't go today, Lenicka," Mestek said, "your daddy's here, see!" "I'll give a show for you myself—" Jacek cried and already he was pulling out the puppets of the water goblin, the princess, and the king, "I want to go with Uncle—" the little one screamed and she struck the poor puppets with her fist, the king's head and his crown flew off and out of his neck popped a copper spring, pitifully Jacek stood over the beheaded monarch, "You'll spend the evening with your Daddy," Mestek said sharply and went away, Jacek caught the girl and carried her to the living room, "Don't want optical course!" she screamed and she struck her Daddy on the face with her tiny fists, how strong she is for her age, she tore away from him and pushed with all her weight against the obstacle course until she'd demolished it, "—I want to go with Uncle!" "I'll take the kitchen spoon to you—" Lenka threatened her and the squealing Lenicka rolled around on the floor as if in a fit, struck her head against the carpet, and turned the color of raw meat, "... that's what happens when you're away all the time," said Lenka.

"Some jobs demand it, and what if I were a sailor or a pilot—"

"Then you've got a problem...," Lenka remarked and Jacek tried for the last time to lift his daughter up, she scratched him under the ear till the blood came and then administered what was almost a kick to the groin, "So go along with Uncle—" Jacek said decisively and Lenicka jumped right up and was running off, Jacek rubbed his groin over the ruins of the obstacle course, thanks, my clever little one, for this warrior-like support.

"... and otherwise it's quite simple," Jacek repeated on Thursday at four o'clock in the Zdar café, "so let's go around to the development..."

"But it's a real horror story what you're telling me," Thursday's paratrooper said in agitation, curd white with goggly watery eyes (an interest in history and cultural monuments), "in essence you're offering your wife to me, though you're not even divorced yet and you're still living with her even!"

"That's only a question of time, you understand, I've been transferred to Brno and I'd like to leave everything in order here before I go."

"Does your wife know anything about the ad?"

"Of course not, otherwise she would have placed it herself."

"What makes you think she'd be interested in another husband?"

"What makes you think she won't need one?"

"So this is what I came here from Teplice for! I hope you'll at least pay for my round trip and for the waste of my time at the going rate for business travel. And my double coffee and the double cognac I'm about to order— I should have a whole bottle, tonight I won't be able to sleep—"

CAPTAIN, THE PARATROOP RECRUITMENT DRIVE IS COLLAPSING, enough reason to abandon it, but when wasted chances torment you so painfully, and after them neurosis and depression, "... so then let's go around to the development," Jacek repeated mechanically on Friday at 4:00 in the Zdar café, "so that without obligation you can have a look at the mother and daughter from a distance..."

"I'm a passionate adherent of psychoanalysis," said Friday's paratrooper, Tomas Roll, a dwarf with tousled black hair which seemed to be fleeing in horror from his strangely crumpled face, "and I find it a fascinating idea to penetrate through an intermediary who is an intimate friend, even a husband—"

As if hypnotized Jacek observed his eager counterpart, but when the fatherly and kind Mestek and the elegant and perfect N. Hradnik have failed us, what hope can there be with this bungled imp, "It's terribly far away, it's the last stop on the streetcar, so let's let it go for another day...," Jacek said, "No trouble, I've got my car here—," the tiny man had a tiny bright red Fiat 600, he dragged Jacek into it and shortly before five they were standing at the observation post behind the substation.

"Sun, light, air...," croaked the dwarf as he greedily looked the development over, "do you know, I've spent my whole life in a basement with a window looking out on a row of trashcans—and which are the windows of your dwelling, please?"

"There on the third floor," Jacek pointed, now quite apathetically.

"It's a fine habitation...," Tomas Roll nodded.

"And here they are at last, the woman with two bags and the little girl running after her..."

"A beautiful, fascinating woman and a really charming little girl," the midget grew excited, "do you know, well-built women are my type and I never—and I'm awfully fond of children and I couldn't—"

Some of Lenicka's friends were playing in the sandbox, so Lenka let her play outside, Lenicka climbed up onto the concrete rim and leaped down, "Look how the nimble little girl climbed up there all by herself—" Tomas Roll sentimentalized, "and now she's going to jump, you'll break your leg, you little rabbit, hop—did you see her? And now she's climbing out again—hop! Boy, she's a real ballet dancer—you've got to let me see her closer up, you've really got to!"

And the tiny paratrooper ran out of the hideout by himself, he limped, and Jacek had to run ahead of him to keep him from climbing into the sandbox, "Little girl—" he called to Lenicka and she came, today charming to the letter of the ad, she had evidently taken a fancy to the midget as to a new toy, they made faces at one another,

Lenicka made a curtsey and even sang a song "from kin-dagarden" *The Wittle Fish Swims in the Water*, Tomas Roll was carried away and, "Come, little one, Uncle Roll will show you his car—"

Lenicka crawled through the red Fiat and sobbed with ecstasy and she was even more ecstatic when the midget taught her to make honk-honk on the horn, "If you would be so kind, Mr. Jost, and show me how to pick the girl up safely and properly..." "Not that way, turn her face towards you, put one arm under her arm this way, the other under her bottom, you've got it and now she's sit-ting in your arms...," already Lenicka was sitting in the midget's arms, for his size he had surprisingly long, strong arms, like a gorilla's, he pouted with his lips to make a horrifying grimace and Lenicka ran her finger over his mouth to see how Uncle Woll made that with his wips, they both liked it so much that Jacek had to tear them apart from each other and by sheer force stuff the imp into his car, but its honk-honk was still to be heard when the Fiat was no more than a speeding red dot far off down the highway.

"... the mother and daughter from a distance," Jacek repeated on Monday at 4:00 at the Zdar café, rested and with new strength from the weekend, "and in case you're interested I'll take you to the apartment as an acquain-tance from the train."

"Why not," said Monday's paratrooper, the last of the five mobilized, an obsequious, snake-like fellow with cruel yellowish-grey eyes, evidently an experienced, ruthless bastard, and when he'd obtained detailed infor-mation concerning the apartment, its furnishings, Lenka's salary, and Grandma's pension, he stubbed out his cigarette and grinned, "So what's keeping us?"

With mounting distaste, Jacek observed his so easily won-over counterpart, you've got the swing of it, you must be a real sharpie, too much so—

"It's already five—" said the paratrooper and he tapped on the glass of his watch as if impatient for the jump, but you're in too much of a hurry to climb into my bed, to see you there with Lenka, with my love, and as Lenicka's daddy—CAPTAIN, THE TASK IS BEYOND MY CAPABILITIES—

"So what's doing, mister?"

"Nothing," Jacek sighed. "Do you like cognac? Waiter!— A double cognac for this gentleman and for me soda and ice, and I'll pay for everything."

With Lenka to the new café on Strekov Hill for coffee with whipped cream and cake, the Josts exchanged news of the troubles that had befallen their two firms and their mutual acquaintances, of whom there were hardly more than five in all, and then they read the torn old magazines under the ugly, yellowed polyvinylchloride covers hung on the walls of this unsuccessful enterprise where you had to wait half an hour for coffee, they brought it cold and the icing on the cake was turning, "Daddy don't go way—" Lenicka babbled automatically behind her net like a wound-up toy, she yawned and fell asleep.

In the office over the blue-grey Zeta a new plastic cover and in addition to unanswered letters from Mojmira, Hanicka, and Lida, Anna had written:

Jacek,

You probably don't know—I didn't—what a certain man named Benoit did a hundred years ago with snails… He paired off fifty snails, left each pair together for some time so that they would get used to each other, then he painted identical letters on their houses and one of the pair he sent off to America, while the other one remained in Paris. After a certain time that devil Benoit exposed snail A in Paris to an electric shock—and snail B in America reacted the same way at the same moment… BE GLAD YOU'RE NOT A SNAIL!

Fists pressed to his temples and a tormented face, for three days now they walked through the technical division on tiptoes and better not to go there at all,

"Jacek's got neurosis," and on the horizon the colorless prairie sky of depression, at 1:59 Jacek got up mechanically and at 2:00 the shriek of the siren propelled him out, right outside the gate a bright red Fiat gleamed and in a blue-grey waterproof jacket Tomas Roll leaped out of its little door, CAPTAIN—

"Climb in at once!" cried the dwarf, jumping around Jacek, and he shoved him into the door, resigned Jacek sank back in the cushioned seat behind the dashboard of the car sent for him, *Fiat* in Latin means *let it happen* and with magnificent acceleration the little car took off toward the highway to the mountains.

Lke a red beetle it went in and out of the mountainous dunes of yellowing late summer grass, while again and again the large man and the small one in agreement went in and then in disagreement went out of the waves of yellowing grass, "... we must know how to stimulate Lenka's interest, her rebirth, her conceptions, her desire," the importunate reader of ads insisted, "we must find someone who's succeeded at it and find out how he did it, we need a model, an example, a precedent..."

"Vitenka Balvin failed," Jacek whispered, "so did Mestek and Nora Hradnik..."

"Didn't Lenka love anybody before she married you?"

"It all went out the window the day we met..."

"She must have loved you very much, but no matter, we'll figure out how to bring this to a head—We've got one person left who didn't fail..."

"Who could that be?"

"You yourself! And now to business—how do you do it?"

"How do I do what?"

"Not fail. Let's look at the details: afternoons you come home from work, well—"

"Very rarely nowadays... Well, in the afternoon I come home from work, I say a couple of meaningless sentences to Lenka, I play a while with Lenicka, but Grandma does that more, then we eat, we watch TV, I go to bed and go

to sleep before Lenka comes to bed, only on Saturday—
and then not every week, well, and on Sunday we take
Lenicka into bed with us and after dinner we go with
Grandma to the zoo. Sometimes we go to the garden, the
other day we went to that new café on Strekov Hill..."

"Don't tease me, you must give me all your techniques
and recipes, your strategies and tactics, your dodges and
tricks—"

"But I really..."

"Do you mean to say that you're loved just because
you're you? It almost looks that way, but no matter, we'll
simply imitate you. So let's go—what are you like,
anyway?"

"Me?... Quite normal... though in some respects perhaps... on the whole... but then not quite... on the other
hand, of course... to tell the truth... still... there are certain but it's hard... I think I'd... I don't think I'd... more
or less..."

"You'll be forced to train me in your likeness," in the
car Tomas Roll grinned and pressed on the accelerator,
"but first, sir, what is that likeness made of, anyway, besides some canvas, a frame, and a hook for hanging up?"


## V — nineteen

Jacek hurried across the excavated plain past the ten
and twelve-story buildings shining above him with
their fresh facades, in our fourteen-story on the eighth
floor left, the first white curtain has appeared, "We'll be
the last to hang ours up," Anna laughed in the white-
and-blue kitchen, in the corner an electric refrigerator
purred quietly, the apartment all ready to be moved into,
only by the door to the bathroom a big hole in the wall,
"I had them move the outlet higher so you wouldn't have
to use an extension cord when you shave... Just so I don't
forget, yesterday they called me from the prime

minister's office, when are you going to take over that chemical department at the information institute—"

"Anci, you know, I'm not really sure I'm up to that..."

"Don't be crazy, before you an ordinary druggist had the position and he was in it eleven years... you just have a little inferiority complex, right? Don't be afraid, Jacek, you're really too good for a sinecure like that, usually they sweep the worn-out big shots into those jobs, but you've got something upstairs and you can make something of it, you'll show them what you're worth..." TAKE IT DOWN, DWARF, THERE'S MORE WHERE THAT CAME FROM.

"... and Comrade Dr. Mach was very satisfied with the goose, though he didn't show it," Hanicka Kohoutkova told him in the evening on the bench in front of the pink little house. "Dad thinks you're going to live here under his wing till your pension and he wants to have a serious talk with you soon— Jacek, you haven't asked him for my hand yet!"

"Have you thought it over well, Hanicka?"

"Very thoroughly. At the end of the school year we always prepare reports on all the pupils, on their conduct, personality, potential for development, talents, character traits, a whole profile. Every year over thirty reports, several hundred pages. I'm good at doing profiles."

"And what's mine?"

"You're an ideal husband. Mama says so too." NOTE IT DOWN, MIDGET, "because you're mature now and you've sown your wild oats."

A cigarette on the stump in front of the forest ranger's, "Wait, I have to light up—" Jacek said, he extracted his hand from Lida's clasp and the cigarette gleamed in the twilight, "You said I'm a good man, but you also said that life here isn't easy, the house, the farming, the children... Lida, I'm beginning to think seriously whether I really..."

"You're a good man and life here isn't easy, but when you love children and the forest... and if you'll love me a little bit, too..."

"Uncle, come give me a kiss too!" Janicka called from the window, "March to bed!—" cried Lida, "I'll grab you—where it hurts!" cried Jacek and he ran up the stairs to the children's room, of all the children all over the world Arnostek and Janicka went to sleep the fastest, but on both their faces their eyelids quivered as they artlessly tried to fool their Uncle who comes to court their Mama, Jacek stroked the apparently sleeping Arnostek and gave Janicka a kiss on the forehead, the little girl tenderly took hold of his ear so he couldn't escape her yet, "When you go way, Uncle, I've got you here on the pitcher..." "On what picture, Janicka?" "On that one there—" and the child's finger pointed towards the well-known picture of an angel guiding a little boy and girl over a broken footbridge, "—that's Arnostek and me and you—" WRITE IT DOWN, IMP!

From the Svitavy station Tanicka Rambouskova rushed to the door of the car with an enormous suitcase in one hand, in the other two umbrellas and a parasol, "Move over, Jacek, I'm coming along!" "But I'm going to Brno!" "Well, I'll find some place to stay." "But the trade fair's coming and everything's full up." "So I'll sleep in the waiting room at the station." "The police'll pick you up!" "Then I'll sleep at the police station!" she kept shoving onto the train and Jacek was forced to push her off the steps, the suitcase struck her on the knee, Tanicka let go of the suitcase and stabbed Jacek in the stomach with the umbrellas and the parasol, fortunately the train was already starting up, but the return trip from Brno would be safer on a plane, "On the way back from Brno I'll definitely stop off for you, my love—" "You bastard, you disgusting old billy goat—" "Darling—" "You fiend—" YOU NEEDN'T BOTHER WITH THIS, SHRIMP.

"... and you don't write, you don't answer, do you think that for you they'll keep a job like that on ice till Christmas?" Mojmira was getting upset, "I don't feel up to it—" Jacek said, weaving his way through Brno Main Station with his traveling satchel in his hand, "but can't you read and type, you ox?!" "And as for the two of us, Mojenda, you need at least thirty people to have any fun and I'm only one..." "If you're going to give me the gate, say so right out—" "You know so many people, people more interesting than I am, so why do you think I should be—"

Mojmira clawed at Jacek's satchel and violently pulled it toward her so that he had to whirl around and face her, "And if I'm fond of you?" "Who in Brno aren't you fond of?" "But they're—hell, OK, I love you!" "Why?" "Think I know? Maybe because you're somebody different, you're not just made of cardboard, maybe because you're simply a man—" WRITE THAT DOWN, YOU WHIPPERSNAPPER, in front of the airline building across the street stood a blue-grey airport bus and a man in uniform was dusting off the seats.

In a blue-and-white room a blue-grey electric fan was humming and five men in white gowns were gazing across a wide table somewhere over Jacek's head, "It's easy to calculate according to the Gibbs-Helmholtz proportion," the sweat-drenched Jacek completed the last question of his fellowship interview, swallowed air, and glanced stealthily at Benedikt Smrcek, who was presiding, "Perhaps that will suffice," Bena said and the men around him murmured something, "We'll inform you of the results in writing within a week," said the institute secretary, "Wait in the anteroom—" Bena added and Jacek got up, bowed smartly, went out the door into the anteroom of aluminum and plate glass, and with a feeling of relief sank into a foam shell on metal legs.

From a pile of magazines on an asymmetrical table a recognizable face smiled out at Jacek from the cover of *Atomic Technology*, on a strange-looking little balcony in a forest of cables our château tennis player and the master of two billiard tables with the high-protein diet, Jozef *completing the preparatory phase for the final stage of thermonuclear synthesis*, we dined together that day and what have you accomplished in the meantime and what have I accomplished, but already now they're deliberating whether to take me on as a soldier in your Grand Army—

Five men in white smocks passed through the anteroom, Bena came last and slowed down till the others had disappeared, "The Party, the Union, and the Scientific Council still have to give their blessing," he smiled. "That means—" Jacek took a deep breath, "I voted for you," replied Benedikt the Great, "of the seven you were the best. Now all you've got to do is bore your way in—" "Like a laser beam—" WRITE IT DOWN, IMP!

From under the daybed Nada pulled out a box as big as suitcase and from under tissue paper a blue-grey vacuum cleaner gleamed, "... and it's got a mass of attachments with brushes and without them, this nozzle is for sucking dirt out of cracks, see, and what a beautiful color..."

"A wonderful color—" "Don't touch it! It's for the new apartment, for the time being we'll only look at it, a wet rag's enough for these rotten old planks, it isn't worth buying carpet for this place...," and tenderly Nada wiped off the attachments and the body of the machine, covered them with paper, and pushed them back again, kneeling as before a monstrance.

"Why you?" Nada grinned. "A woman's got to marry someone, so why not you?" IMPORTUNATE ADVERTISER. "Besides, I'll be twenty-four next year and my pelvis is beginning to stiffen—it hurts then, you know." ARE YOU TAKING THIS DOWN? "And now come to bed—you've only got a few months till the long intermission... with a child we can get an apartment sooner!"

The bell sounded for the last funicular down, the tourists paid and left, the big white Mercedes 250S strolled right up to the tap, casually looked around the empty bar, and roughly pulled Tina toward him, by the window Jacek ran his palms over his face, a noise, the white giant tried to pull the golden-orange Tina over the counter and Jacek jumped in through the open window, "Jacek—" Tina cried, "see this gentleman out!" and Jacek rushed through the bar to the counter, "Heraus, du

Saukerl!" he roared with gusto and then he corrected himself, even more cheerfully, "I mean—HINAUS!"

Tina tossed the keys into the office, in full stride she untied her apron and tossed it over a chair, she took Jacek by the hand and *on the double,* let's catch the funicular, on the seat together they were borne aloft over clearings and forests and on each pylon a jerk up and then a drop down and on the next pylon the count was down one again, in Bohosudov they serve coffee with whipped cream and cake right by the bus stop, Tina carefully wiped her fingers and drew out a small blue etui, on the black velvet two golden bands, "Just take it," she smiled, "it isn't legally binding and for the trade it's better to have one than not... carry it in your wallet with your change..."

"... and you're as insanely jealous as Othello, Jacek."

"But not a bit where Lenka's at stake."

"You trust her," Tina sighed, "and that's a greater sign of love than being angry that she's fooling around with someone else or afraid that she's enjoying it more than with you..." YOU DON'T HAVE TO TAKE EVERYTHING DOWN, MY DEAR SIR—

In front of our building on the rim of the sandbox Tomas Roll, dressed in a black sweater and black jeans, like a little devil in the circle of children having a wonderful time, in his hand a glass ball filled with water, in the water a mountain, and when you shake it up snow starts to fall on the mountain, Roll winked at Jacek and gave the ball to the ecstatic Lenicka.

"Who's he?" asked Lenka, pointing at the dwarf from the kitchen window, "he told me he knows you well..."

"He said that?"

"Those very words. When he tried to pull Lenicka into his car I ran out to complain, but he was very well behaved and he apologized, he said you'd given him permission to play with her. Did you?"

"I came close to hiring him for that."

"I hope you didn't, but he is touchingly fond of children and he's lots of fun—"

"Depends on how you take it. If you'd like I'll ask him in."

"Why not," Lenka laughed. "You know, Jacek, the wonderful thing about you is you're never jealous..."

MR. ROLL, RESPECTED SIR, "I trust you," Jacek whispered, "and that's a greater sign of lo—" DON'T WRITE THIS DOWN and bring me back my child on the double, "Lenicka!" Jacek roared at the window, "Come home!" the little girl was playing with the imp's glass ball and didn't want to come home for anything in the world, "You must always listen to your daddy—" croaked the dwarf, deftly and easily he picked up the little girl in his gorilla-like arms, he was extremely easy to train, and he carried her to Jacek in the doorway, "Please come in—" Lenka smiled at him and Jacek had to introduce them, Tomas Roll kissed Lenka's hand and she took it very nicely, Grandma served him butter cookies on a tray and Lenicka pulled him away to show him her toys, the three females almost came to blows over him as the dwarf outdid himself, he turned somersaults and walked through the kitchen on his hands, the apartment turned into a vaudeville theater and Jacek himself yielded for a time to the charm of the little acrobat, the clown, and then suddenly he clapped his hands, "That's enough—"

With a cartwheel Tomas Roll again stood on his legs, bowed and scraped, and at once obligingly disappeared, Jacek stood by the window and pressed the warm little body against his own, the black imp jumped into his red car and drove off with a loud honk-honk through the pastel-colored buildings of the development, "Daddy, when will Uncle Woll come again—"

"Never, little one, never fear..." "But Daddy—," in the window across the way Trost appeared with his child in his arms, as if on purpose stuck into a denim shirt washed to a blue-grey, CAPTAIN, ARE YOU MAKING FUN OF ME, OR IS THIS A WARNING SIGNAL IN MY MIRROR—

Jacek walked through his office and impatiently looked at his watch, when will they come, alcohol is necessary as milk today, finally Vitenka Balvin entered the room with Petrik Hurt staggering behind him, Jacek shoved at him, for his signature, a red issue slip for our 300 grams of absolute alcohol, Petrik's hand was shaking so that he couldn't hit the blank spaces, "What's the matter with him?" "He ran away from Verka and spent the night in the tow-cloth storeroom... he's been lapping it up since morning..." "But that isn't possible, from his Verka—"

With a slant like that of a pneumatic drill Petrik wrote on the blank line Quantity: *3,000* and, rocking, he signed the slip, "I'm drinking down my troubles—" he said in a deep voice, "Once again I've got no place to stay..." "For the time being I've still got a place," Vitenka sighed, "but I may be worse off than you..." "You can't be worse off than me...," Jacek whispered.

"Today there won't be any sixty-forty!"

"Today no diluting!"

"We'll drink our alcohol straight!"

The murderous drink burned the throat frightfully and without any delaying filtration or other detours it went straight to the neurons, "We won't be calling each other up anymore, 'Verenka darling,' 'Petrik darling,'" Petrik Hurt howled, "we won't go on the swings or for ice cream, you won't write poems about the two of us and you won't wait for me at the square by the column..."

"I can't go on this way anymore," whispered Vitenka Balvin, "one half of the apartment an amusement park and bordello, the other a cell for solitary confinement, that's how our improvement has ended up—you don't realize, Jacek, what you've got at home, getting up and going to bed you should kneel and pound your head against the floor in gratitude..."

"Vitenka, do you really think you'd get a kick out of playing dad and, instead of going to the woods with Milenka Cerna, taking Mom and the kid to the zoo every Sunday..."

"In three weeks Milenka Cerna's a bore, in four she's poison, and in five it's total despair—you've no idea, Jacek, what you've got in Lenka and Lenicka..."

"So I'll sign it all over to you with the apartment and the furnishings and all the papers!"

"Jacek, you're crazy—"

"I'm serious, I'd like to clear out for Brno and begin life over again myself, you see— I've been taken on there as a graduate fellow. Vitenka, on my knees I beg you, take Lenicka and Lenka off my hands, you aren't a midget, the apartment is first-category, it's got a balcony and a telephone, a refrigerator, a charming little girl, a TV set, and a grandma—and that's a treasure these days—carpets everywhere and in the kitchen linoleum at a hundred sixty a yard—it even goes under the sideboard where you can't see it—a thermometer and a cast of a red hippopotamus on the wall, ten Christmas neckties, all sorts of glass and china, I'll even leave you my slippers, my gardening jacket, the ficus plant, the funnels, mashers, glass spoons, saucers, spatulas, strainers, and pots... take it all off my hands or it'll drive me nuts—"

"Then why don't you get a divorce?"

"Why don't you?"

"It wouldn't do—I'm fond of Mija."

"Darling, the sun's shining here, it's shining on you too, it's shining on me as it's shining on you, let's hold hands and go for ice cream and on the swings we'll both fly right up to the sky, Verka, Petrik, Verka—the old goat, the fattened Danish cow—" Petrik Hurt roared as the siren sounded for lunch, and he banged his fist on the acrid drying puddles of alcohol, "Fellows, it was like puking to live with that cluck!"

"Talk if it helps, but you don't have to insult her..." "Why Petrik, you two have the finest marriage in all Usti..." "He'll sleep it off."

"I've slept it off already, I'm just pulling myself out of all this pink shit, fellows, you've got no idea what a hell it was, like two disabled soldiers when we met and we hooked on to one another with our artificial arms, we'd call one another up out of terror, we were worried the other might already be packing his suitcase, we'd both been divorced twice and all told we've attended six of our own weddings, what goes bang all of a sudden no one can patch up, but you can lie and go on acting till you're blue in the face, today you called up less than yesterday, today you came later than yesterday, you came over to me as if you didn't want to, your note wasn't warm as the last one, and that terror makes you phone daily for an hour, jump off the streetcar before the stop, and write poems about the two of us, more and more of them, phone for two hours, jump off the streetcar at full speed, write operas about the two of us, phone for three hours, Petrik, I called and I was looking at my watch, Verka, I was just counting the minutes in terror— Jacek, you haven't the slightest idea what you've got at home..."

Jacek fled through the ridged mud of the Cottex courtyard, onto the bus and away along the highway, the monument with the lion, the linden with its sign, the clay path, and up the steps of stormy waves to the little beach of the pension Splendid Isolation, THERE IS NO LIKENESS, BROTHER TOM, THERE'S ONLY BLOOD SAUSAGE—

## V — twenty

Quick, down with the net of the crib and the rough chin on her sweet little tummy, nothing's so sweet to kiss as our little one, "Uncle gwab me—" our pretty little girl calls, take her in your arms and rock her.

"Uncle don't go way—"

"I'm just going to give Mama a kiss."

"Uncle come back—"

"You know he'll come right back."

"Uncle tell a stowy—"

"You know he will!"

Lida was already heating the milk for the hot cereal, "Look what I brought you—" "How wonderful, you're too kind, thanks—" and joy at an additional supply of Dutch cocoa, a water pistol for Arnostek, and a blow-up squirrel for Janicka, trampling her nightgown with her heels the little girl got all tangled up with the squirrel in the kitchen while Arnostek sprayed the walls liberally, "To put that thing in his hand—" said Lida, "—means an immediate call to workmen to repaint the house!" Jacek laughed.

"And why did you choose to come today?" Lida asked.

"Uncle tell a stowy—" Janicka called from her crib.

"Chema made up its mind again it wouldn't raise the OMZ's balance allotment—"

"Just a second, please," said Lida, "I have to run and shut up the hens, the fox is making his rounds..."

"Uncle tell a stowy—"

"I'll just go put her to bed—" said Jacek. "So which one shall we tell, kids?"

"The sad pwince!" Janicka cried, "The sad prince!" Arnostek cried.

"Once upon a time there was a prince and he was very sad...," Jacek began.

"Because he had to wide the twain so much," Janicka whispered and Arnostek: "Through eleven dark tunnels."

"... and in each of those tunnels a princess was walled up...," Jacek continued.

"In each of them they was one." "Eleven princesses in all."

"... and the prince rode from princess to princess..."

"And aways cwied." "Then where did he live?"

"... and he kept waiting until from the woods he would hear cwop-cwop-cwop..."

"And the auwochs'd come!" "Uncle, aren't there some aurochses in the Tatras?"

"Only in the zoo. Aurochs, little one, you're saying auwochs, aurrrochs..."

"And he was all golden—-" "But Uncle, I've seen a photo of a Tatra aurochs in the woods—" "and he said, pwince—" "But an aurochs wouldn't go into a tunnel!" and the children started to argue, "—here's your pwincess!" cried Janicka, "But which of the eleven was it?" Arnostek shouted at her, "And the pwince went boom like this!" Janicka squealed and hit Arnostek on the head, "And that tunnel went bang on top of him!" yelled Arnostek and jumped toward Janicka and so because of the fairy tale fighting and tears.

Outside the window a mass of spruces pierced the morning sky with its Asiatic towers and from the wide dark-wood frame with the black ribbon the late Adalsky looked at them through the glass, on the other side of the wall a child crying, objects falling, and shouts.

"Uncle come today?"

"But he came last evening."

"Uncle didn't come!"

"But you've got that pistol he gave you, I mean, that squirrel. So hop into your pants!"

"Uncle put on pants!"

"Shh—Uncle's still beddie-bye and we mustn't wake him..."

"... and we mustn't wake him...," Janicka whispered on the other side of the wall, did we imagine it or did the face on the picture really move, the thirty-three-year-old forest ranger was grinning behind the glass and with horror Jacek hid his head under the pillow for his second sleep.

Outside the window the mass of spruces and across the strip of morning sky, over the Asiatic towers, a jet plane flew in supersonic silence, it disappeared behind the towers and shortly thereafter the empty blue-grey sky grew stormy, Jacek shivered and again his head under the pillow.

"...and today I'd like to go somewhere we haven't been yet," Mojmira said as they left Brno Main Station, "Great!" Jacek agreed, "How about something sweet?" Mojmira proposed, "Coffee with whipped cream and cake!" Jacek said and burst into laughter, "Great!" Mojmira agreed, but Jacek suddenly stopped laughing, "What's the matter?" Jacek froze as he looked at the airline building across the street, did we imagine it or did those heavy chrome swinging doors really open by themselves—

We haven't gone yet to Tomans' pâtisserie, Jacek ordered two coffees with whipped cream and Mojmira Parisian cake and cream rolls, "What's the matter now... Jacek?" "Nothing, I only imagined...," but he didn't imagine it, among the boisterous cluster of heads in the corner diagonally across, Nora Hradnik was reading the paper, now he shoved it aside, drank his mineral water, and again vanished behind his paper sail, he couldn't have seen us—

"... and so it comes to six thousand," Mojmira prattled on and the crumbs from her cream rolls fell on her breasts, "the apartment I've taken care of, all we need is to buy a couple more things, I'd like a new carpet and..."

"... and a vacuum for it..."

"Great, that would come in handy for dusting the pictures and the books...," Mojmira gibbered with chocolate-stained lips, and with greasy fingers she scratched her hair, Comrade N. Hradnik, how about this 29-year-old translator and editor, intell. no child. with own apart., take this one at least, let my holdings diminish a bit, "... do you know what we'll buy out of our first paycheck?" Mojmira whispered, "But it's plain as plain," Jacek said wearily, "wedding rings." "How'd you guess?"

Nora Hradnik suddenly laid aside his paper and got up, a pretty woman came toward his table, she might have been 28, with two children, they borrowed a fourth chair and all of them sat down at the round table, "But Jacek, you aren't listening to me at all and these things matter to a woman...," N. Hradnik had come back home and at his table the waiter was serving two coffees with whipped cream and four small slices of cake, Lenicka was so fond of store pastry and so far she'd never been to a pâtisserie with her daddy and her mommy, "Jacek, what's wrong with you today..." "I forgot that I have to go back to Usti immediately, if I leave now I can just catch the R 7—"

Express R 7 from Bucharest, Budapest, and Bratislava was arriving two minutes early today on Platform One. "A reserved seat to Usti nad Labem—" Jacek shouted into the ticket window, he received his ticket at once and in relief rushed along the row of eccentrically numbered cars till he found his own car, No. 100, compartment G, except for two seats the whole compartment was taken, the trade fair had just opened, Jacek placed his traveling satchel up into the net, hung his beige iridescent raincoat beneath it, and as he was sitting down an air force officer entered the compartment, IS HE SUPPOSED TO GUARD ME, CAPTAIN, OR GIVE ME A MESSAGE—

The air force lieutenant, seat check in hand, gave Jacek a sharp look, he had the even number opposite, he placed his own satchel made of light leather—on duty, of course—into the net and hung his blue-gray raincoat beneath it, on his uniform the golden emblems of the air force shone, the train pulled quietly out, the officer took his seat, and he looked straight ahead.

"We're on time...," Jacek said casually and directed a smile of blandishment at his counterpart, the lieutenant neither returned the smile nor turned away, insolently he looked straight ahead and Jacek blushed, well, so a pilot's going by train, when you travel so often there's nothing mysterious about one trip with an officer, and angrily Jacek dug himself in behind his coat, today there's no view anyway and we know this whole stretch by heart.

In Svitavy Tanicka Jostova, in Pardubice Hanicka Jostova, Lida Jostova waiting in the woods and in Prague
Anna Jostova is trembling for us, in Decin lies the victim
Nadezda Jostova, and besides them there's Tina Jostova
in her tower, let's not forget Mojmira Jostova either, and
then Jost the graduate fellow who's trying to conquer the
world, you didn't stick in the two Lenka Jostovas yet, and
the Jost retreat in Ritin would make an even ten, but
weren't these ten Josts still too few, why not take out
another ad—

Ta-ta-ta-dum the train went through meadows and
woods to the east and to the west, ch-ch-ch-ch it moved
slowly along the coast from beach to beach, ta-ta-ta-dum
is the dream of a man who's wide awake and ch-ch-ch-ch
is an awakening for the timid, ta-ta-ta-dum is the sign of
a weary traveling man in love and ch-ch-ch-ch is a boat
sailing to a fabled continent where one lives only for
play, hunting, and loving, ch-ch—close your eyes and
repeat after me: ch-ch-ch-ch—

At the terminal, Prague Main, Jacek waited hidden behind his coat until the compartment was safely empty
and then he mingled with the hurrying throng, looking
around from time to time to see whether he was being followed, outside in front of the station he stood for a while,
uncertain, we could try to ask for Lenka's white plush,
but a train doesn't wait and Jacek hastened by the shortest path through the park to Prague Central Station and
climbed onto the 4:45 to Berlin, as always there was time
to spare and in the corridor he leaned out of the window,
behind the rail at the entrance gate a blue-grey air force
uniform seemed to flash by in the crowd, Jacek jumped
back into the corridor and banged the window shut.

Through the early Indian summer evening the train
rushed along past the sand and the white stones of the
now ebbing river, during droughts the river is at its
lowest point, beyond the empty harvested fields the copper-colored woods of Varhost and below Strekov Castle

the first leafless trees, the first lights in the first houses of our town, and on the express we've made it home—

Standing right in front of the door of the car were two air force officers looking at the faces of those descending, Jacek slunk back into the corridor and pressed his face against the dirty wall, YOU WON'T LET ME GO HOME, CAPTAIN, EVEN FOR A TWO-DAY LEAVE, and the train pulled quietly out along the bank of the falling river.

So the meeting with Speranza was ordained from on high, now the high command was taking responsibility for opening fire, Jacek was the first to jump off the train onto the Decin platform and he drew a deep breath, but suddenly he felt the impossibility of leaving the station, minute after minute flew by, outside in front of the building Speranza was still waiting and inside the station Jacek ran back and forth, CAPTAIN, S-O-S, "This is a customs area," a man in uniform shouted at Jacek, "you have to exit that way—" and Jacek left.

On the sidewalk in front of the station Nada was waiting, just now her back is turned toward us, and the familiar air force lieutenant with the special light leather satchel, the one who got on at Brno, is looking right at us, of course it's me, the officer verified this with a short concentrated look, walked on in Nada's direction, and came up close behind her by the rail, both of them turned around and already they were walking back together towards us, he's really bringing her here, who'll fire first, it would be enough to press the trigger—

"There's no point in lying anymore, Nada, because I'll never marry you, I love my wife and daughter and besides them I've got six more women and two kids all along the line to Brno, why should I save up for years with you for a co-op apartment in this hole when I've got a better one in Prague, ready to move into, two more furnished ones in Brno, a family house is being readied for me in Pardubice, and I even have at my disposal a real forest ranger's lodge in the woods I love so much, why should I train as a case maker's apprentice in your Wood-

Pak when I can be the head of a government office, amuse myself as a colorist or an editor, or rake in money like hay at a gas station, and besides I've been accepted in Brno as a graduate fellow, I have a girlfriend who writes poems about the two of us, and I've got two girlfriends with college degrees, I've got a simple, pretty girl who's younger than you and still a virgin and I've got an experienced Venus with skin like gold and like oranges...," all I have to do is say it, a jeep with a canvas top drove up to the sidewalk, the officer jumped in, and quickly the car drove off, CAPTAIN, WHY MUST I MYSELF— "You're looking at me," Nada Houskova laughed, "as if you had something very special to say—" "Let's go to bed—" Jacek finally managed to articulate.

The next day, as if from the 4:45 to Berlin, Jacek hurried past the children's playground along the wide concrete roadway, the staircase to our apartment is once again quite a bit higher, perhaps with time it will grow up into the clouds and there will be peace and quiet, Lenka has the lights on, but what's with her that she doesn't come to greet me—Lenka was sitting in the kitchen with Grandma and the two of them were whispering with Tomas Roll.

The women didn't even stir to welcome Jacek, but the dwarf joyfully leaped up and greeted Jacek like a king, "I had to stop off in Prague...," Jacek whispered into the women's silence, "... and forgive me, Lenka, I didn't bring the white plush, but next time definitely—"

"I don't need it anymore," Lenka said softly and behind her Grandma looked angrily at Jacek, only the dwarf croaked merrily in the rude silence and Lenicka was already asleep, don't wake her, "Get something in the pantry—" said Lenka, "we're going to the living room to sit a while." "You aren't even going to warm up my milk...," Jacek whispered. "Take it out of the refrigerator," said Lenka, "but it won't go very well on top of fried mushrooms!"

"On top of what fried mushrooms...," Jacek was astonished, but behind the women's backs the dwarf put a finger to his lips and gestured zealously, what tricks are you up to here, Mr. Roll, what have you talked these two good souls into believing—but the dwarf was already being led by the women into the living room—or rather it was he who conducted them, an unexpectedly efficient paratrooper, in the living room whispers and smothered laughter while in the kitchen Jacek drank his milk, frozen solid as ice.

On his desk at Cottex several days' worth of mail had accumulated, a pile of letters as if replying to an ad, FOREST CONSTRUCTION 06 requests confirmation your arrival by Oct. 1, by 10/1 KOLORA 04 PAR-DUBICE, signed Dr. Bivoj Mach, Dear Comrade, we're looking forward to your coming, wrote the TECHNICAL NEWS, *a 20th-century fortnightly*, it's a great pleasure to congratulate you on your new appointment, Bena's RESEARCH INSTITUTE FOR COTTON TECHNOLOGY congratulated him, cable address Brno RIFCOT, the 5th Citizens' Apartment Cooperative in Decin requests the date of your wedding without delay, and THE COMMUNICATIONS OFFICE OF THE CAPITAL CITY OF PRAGUE insists that you fill out, in your own handwriting, the enclosed application for telephone service, from Brno his mom and dad were inquiring whether *they should get rid of their lodger right away or by Oct. 1*, and I'm sending you this cargo of memories and of my longing for the sun, may it reflect at a sine angle and fall on your shoulders as a hot and heavy mantle, Anna wrote from Prague, and Hanicka from Pardubice, that *Mama is of the opinion that it's good to have both children soon after the wedding*,

> *I am already*
> *melted gold*
> *which under your*
> *hands finds*
> *its own form*

Tanicka wrote of her frame of mind in Svitavy and in Svitavy, as in Usti,

*The river in which*
*I drown is not enough*
*A deluge*

a flotilla of lips come to attack like Hitchcock's Birds and a terrifying siege one can only shoot his way out of, at a distance it would be easier, Jacek tore the cover off his typewriter, the blue-grey metal gleamed cold and the rattle of its keys was like a machine gun:

Dear Madam:
I can no longer deceive you. I have concealed from you the fact that I have been married for a long time, that I have a good wife and a clever, pretty little daughter. I won't leave them. Forget me and try to forgive.

in six copies, the seventh to Tina by telephone, place an order for an urgent call to the Mosquito Tower and, while waiting for it to go through, type out six envelopes, Miss Nadezda Houskova, Dr. Anna Bromova, Miss Hanicka Kohoutkova, Mrs. Lida Adalska, Miss Tanicka Rambouskova, Dr. Mojmira Stratilova and seal up the letters and we're all finished with your pirds, Mr. Hitchcock, and your tomfoolery, mudget, we've fired off all the rockets and tomorrow—I'm sending them special delivery—they'll thunder from Brno to Decin, in Usti there's only a pygmy to deal with, YOU BET I'VE CERTIFIED MY LOVE FOR MY WIFE AND MY DAUGHTER— "Happiness isn't necessary," the cardinal told Fellini in a film—AND MY UNHAPPINESS.

Jacek started at the ring of the phone as if it were a shot, CAPTAIN, —"Your call to Mosquito Tower is ready," the receiver sounded and then, "Jacek—," Tina's familiar subdued voice, "it's good you called, I've got the gas station, it's near Harrachov, a marvelous area for tourists, we'll live at the Hotel Belvedere... you must come and see me this evening!"

"I'll come," Jacek sighed, on the table the six blue letters, Jacek pasted a sixty-heller stamp on each of them and locked them up in his desk, he sat down, his fists on his temples and his face tormented, "Jacek's got neurosis," and the final symptom of depression— THE PAINTING COMMISSIONED BY T. ROLL IS READY TO BE PICKED UP.

# INTO OVERTIME

*Everyone will eventually
find the sort of paradise
he is able to imagine.*
　　—*Armand Lanoux*

## Part VI — Flight — twenty-one

Jacek laughed till the tears ran down his cheeks, he poured out into pot-bellied glasses another cognac for himself and one for Tomas Roll: "...and what was that you told them about fried mushrooms, Tom?"

"I told them about that widow of yours in Teplice," the imp grinned.

"Who? I keep a file, but I can't remember any widow in Teplice..."

"She'll never see forty again, you often go visit her instead of going to Brno, all night long you two fry mushrooms and play duets on the ocarina...," the dwarf giggled.

"But why a widow of forty..."

"It has more effect on them than a broad from a hotel or a young eighteen-year-old chick," the imp explained, with his horse's teeth he clasped the thin edge of the glass and sucked the cognac out through a gap where once an incisor had been, Jacek laughed till he choked, a widow with an ocarina is in the last analysis only a dry insert by comparison with an illustrated Oriental fairy tale with seven naiads, Jacek poured again and raised his glass in a toast, "Here's to freedom, Tom—" "to the two Lenkas, my lord Jost—"

The two Lenkas came home with Grandma at twilight, every day they come home later and later, "Uncle Woll make a circus—" Lenicka cried, the midget jumped down from his chair onto his hands and somersaulted through the kitchen and the living room, with a single wave of his monstrously strong arms he swept the mattresses and cushions from the sofa onto the carpet, nimbly he arranged them in a semicircle and with his teeth he placed the kitchen chair before the audience, "And what will it be, little one?" he croaked, "A show," Lenicka breathed and she clapped her hands in joy, the dwarf picked her up and tenderly seated her, Lenka and Grandma were already seated and the imp was serving them full pot-bellied glasses, only Jacek didn't feel like sitting on the floor with his chin on his knees watching those silly puppets— "They aren't silly!" croaked the pygmy, for just an instant Jacek felt the clasp of his gorilla arms and then he too was sitting on the pillow-strewn floor with a glass in his hand.

Holding the puppets' copper wires, Roll's hands flashed over the back of the chair and on the bright seat that acted as the stage, between a china mug and a box of matches, figure after figure appeared and greeted the public, the king, the queen, the princess, and the nice old lady, "She gets eaten up by the wolf—" Lenicka cried, "—and then Wed Widing Hood comes—," but Tomas Roll was enacting a new tale, the queen and the nice old lady jumped around the box of matches and stuck one match after another into the white mug, each match required tremendous exertion and the princess was jumping around behind them like a puppy, she wanted to play with them but there was no time for play, match after match followed the hard road and dropped with great effort into the mug, by the chair leg the king was lying and going -zzzz-, now he gets up and enters the action—no, he doesn't get up but only turns onto his other side and goes on snoring, meanwhile match after match over and into the mug, the little princess climbed up to the very top of the chair, then she fell down on her back like a beetle and the dwarf faithfully screeched on her account, it's nothing, one more match and, with all their efforts, the last one—just then the king jumped up and snatch! there were no more matches in the mug (the dwarf had put them back in the box) and at once the weird ballet of the queen and the old lady commenced again around the box, the princess was once again clambering up to the top of the chair, she'll fall down again in no time and by the chair leg the king was snoring again, and again match after match over and into the white mug, the princess had fallen down boom! again and the dwarf had squealed again, this time Lenicka squealed too, and now Lenicka got up and went for the king, "... he's still beddie-bye and we mustn't wake him!" the dwarf croaked, "... and we mustn't wake him...," Lenicka repeated in a whisper and then she squealed, "—that's Daddy!" .

Lenka drank her glass straight down and even Grandma took a mighty slurp, from behind the chair back two powerful arms reached out and filled their glasses to the brim, Jacek didn't get any, the dwarf threw the wires of the three female figures over his arm and with a mere jerk of his elbow kept the three figures incessantly dancing, with one hand he grabbed the king's wires and with his other he fished for something behind him, the king sat up and traveled on his bottom across the chair seat, ch-ch-ch-ch went the dwarf, ch-ch-ch-ch and suddenly hop hop, a water nymph leaped onto the stage, a new figure, she and the king grabbed at each other and hoppity-hop a dance together, they sat down together and shoveled it in, "They're eating fried mushrooms from the Black Forest," the dwarf commented and again he raised them for a new dance, hop hop, hop hop, and hoppity-hop, Lenka drank her glass straight down and Grandma took a mighty slurp, quick as lightning the powerful arms had filled their glasses to the brim and quick as lightning they were back behind the stage, Jacek didn't get any, hop hop, hop hop, and hoppity-hop, exhausted from this hellish dance the king sank onto his back and again to the sound of ch-ch-ch-ch he traveled across the shining seat, ch-ch-ch-ch to the white mug and again made a—

"Gwab!" screeched Lenicka, "Grab," Grandma whispered, captivated by the story, "Grab!" said Lenka and she drank her glass straight down, and Grandma too had downed the hatch.

The king was snoring again by the chair leg, the queen and the nice old lady were carrying match after match to the mug, and the princess was lying on her back like a beetle, "Ith the king coming home today?" the dwarf lisped.

"But he came back yesterday evening," Lenka said and now she did the pouring for herself, for Grandma too, Jacek didn't get any.

"Daddy didn't come!" Lenicka squealed.

"But you've got your third pistol from him and I've got my fourth cocoa," Lenka called, "so hop into your pants!"

"Daddy put on pants!" cried Lenicka.

"Shh—Daddy's still beddie-bye and we mustn't wake him!" cried Lenka, "I want to wake him!" cried Lenicka, ch-ch-ch-ch— the dwarf responded and already the king was riding again over the smooth surface and here again was the water nymph and they grabbed each other, hop hop and hoppity-hop, the king exhausted on his rear and ch-ch-ch-ch back to the white mug, "We won't give you any!" shrieked Lenicka, she jumped up and grabbed the cup with both hands, the king kept trying to reach it, "Go way—" squealed Lenicka and boom! her fist struck the king till his head flew off, the head which had only been temporarily fastened on after that last trouncing, and out of his neck popped a copper spring, "Let him gorge himself," the half-drunk Lenka clamored and she crammed the remains of the king into the mug, "Take that—" Lenicka cried and she and the queen beat him into the mug, the imp was ready and handed her the figure of the water nymph and Lenicka stuffed it into the mug as well, "And both of you take that—" and she thumped them around in the mug as if it were a mortar, the six women's hands took over and the fairy tale turned into a bloody bacchanalia, Jacek put his empty glass down on the carpet and clapped his hands, "That's enough!"

Obligingly the dwarf pulled up all the wires and the puppets were borne aloft, the story was almost over, so sit down again, the queen and the princess and the nice old lady were kind enough to sit.

All of a sudden clop-clop-clop and now the prince is here, he kisses the queen's hand and a kiss to Lenicka and Grandma, the puppets grabbed each other's hands and together hoppity-hop around the mug, hoppity-hop, hoppity-hop, hoppity-hop dancing around the porcelain grave, Lenicka must go beddie-bye now, hoppity-hop and that's the happy ending of our fairy tale.

Tomas Roll tossed the puppets into a box and took Lenicka off to her crib for beddie-bye, with Grandma he picked over the rice and with Lenka he made Swiss steak, he soaked some peas for tomorrow, at the next meal he told a dozen amusing stories, after dinner he sent Grandma to bed and went off to wash the dishes and wipe up the floor.

"He's beginning to get on my nerves," Jacek whispered when he was left alone on the living room couch with Lenka.

"You're the one who brought him home...," she whispered, we have to whisper in our house now on Mr. Roll's account, and now the imp's back in here again.

"It was an awful lot of fun," said Lenka.

"Terrific," Jacek said.

"You can never get too much fun," croaked the dwarf, "and you must get it, even if they hang your old man— Just sit there, I'll turn down the covers for you," and he disappeared through the glass doors of the bedroom.

"What have you got to tell me, Jacek?"

"Tomorrow I'm going to Brno and please put two white shirts—"

"Can I help with anything, dear?" they heard from the other side of the door.

"Go to bed, you've had enough with your trip," Lenka called mechanically and then she caught herself, "Excuse me, Jacek...," she whispered.

"OK. OK now," the imp continued his tomfoolery, "Beddie-bye and good night, dear."

Lenka stared fixedly at Jacek, Jacek avoided her glance and poured himself another drink.

"Tomorrow I'm going to Brno," they heard through the door, "pack two white shirts in my satchel, and don't give me any lunch..."

"OK," said Lenka, "and don't forget to bring me the white plush!"

"This time I really won't forget," the dwarf croaked through the door.

"It's just a trifle," Lenka said, "and I don't ask anything else from you..."

"I'll bring it, really I will," Tomas Roll promised.

"You've promised it to me for so long...," Lenka whispered.

"You know how it is, when a man has to travel...," the imp sighed insincerely.

"Then don't bring it," said Lenka. "Do you hear? I don't want to give you any trouble!"

"Ch-ch-ch-ch," Tomas Roll sounded behind the door. "I'm here now, my love—but I forgot that plush again!"

"I told you I didn't want it."

"OK. OK now," the imp mocked from behind the door. "Zzzz, I don't feel sleepy yet, yesterday she couldn't... come give me a kiss! Lenunka..."

"You even told him that?" Lenka hissed from the sofa.

"Lenunka, darling...," croaked the dwarf through the door of our bedroom, luckily he couldn't have anything left to lampoon, "It's never been like that before...," croaked the imp, "... and now I'm off to Brno. Pack two white shirts in my satchel, and no lunch..."

The best cure for depression is good cognac, the depression doesn't go away but it no longer bothers you so much, Jacek and Tomas Roll were drinking cognac in the living room while in the kitchen Grandma was beating the pans as a sign of defiance, the dusk was already coming through the balcony door when the pygmy left to get another pint, but suddenly he dashed back into the living room, "Come and look at something—," with a powerful tug he raised Jacek from the sofa and pushed him into the kitchen, Grandma was pounding the lids and directly beneath the window, on the playground, the two Lenkas with Trost.

Trost was actually trying to pick up those two dear creatures, he lifted Lenicka onto his shoulders and Lenicka laughed and grabbed him by his ears, he whispered something to Lenka and Lenka laughed and shamelessly leaned his way. "What are they up to with that slob...," Jacek whispered in horror.

"As chance would have it, he's a respectable man!" said Grandma and bang! with the lids.

"Let him talk to his own Mrs. and play with his own brat!"

"But he's got his little Pavel out there, too," said Grandma and with her dried-up finger she pointed out some kid who was Lenicka's age, "and now he's the boy's papa and mama both, for Mrs. Trostova's taken to sleeping around."

"No wonder she's sleeping around, with a jerk like him..."

"He's a respectable man!" Grandma shouted and bang! with the lids, "You could never touch him, Jacek! As those things happen, she was transferred out of her office and put on the road and she started sleeping around, they say she took up with some Ethiopian...," and Grandma crossed herself.

"Just so he doesn't hang around Lenka...," Jacek stormed dejectedly and hiccuped, "let him place an ad..."

"It isn't easy, Jacek," said Grandma, "you're always away and there isn't even anyone to help with the laundry, now Mr. Mestek's on vacation. And Mr. Trost fixed the switch for us and made us a skeleton key for the drying room and he knocked down those boxes on the balcony so Lenicka wouldn't trip over them—he's a crackerjack with his hands, O Lord!"

"I'll knock them off him...," Jacek muttered as he was seized by a powerful attack of hiccups, the dwarf hit him on the back until it passed, at last Lenka and Lenicka came home, but only for a second, Mr. Trost has promised to take them to see the monument with the lion, which they'd never seen though he said it was very close, "Uncle Twost's got a gweat gweat big motocycle," Lenicka pointed, "wif a great big sidecar on it—" "I'll take you to see the lion in my car," squeaked the dwarf, "Don't want any car, want motocycle—" Lenicka cried and she bit the imp on the arm.

"The gentlemen are having a good time—" Lenka grinned and she tapped her finger on the empty bottle of Georgian cognac, Jacek received a perceptible whack on the back from the dwarf, he opened his mouth but only a mighty hiccup came out, "Huwwy, Mommy," called Lenicka, "We mustn't let Uncle Twost get way—" and the door banged after the Lenkas, Grandma clattered the pot covers like cymbals on Corpus Christi, the dwarf planted cruel blows on Jacek's back, and down the concrete highway past the children's playground Trost drove off with the Lenkas, if you ever bring him into my home I'll turn on the gas but only till it makes an explosive mixture with the air, then I'll light a match, IF NOT ALONE, CAPTAIN, THEN I'LL MAKE THE FLIGHT WITH MY ENTIRE FAMILY—

# VI — twenty-two

Stylish pearl-grey furniture on blue shag carpets and a bluish-silver brocade on the king-size bed, dark Anna in a silvery dressing gown by the illuminated mirrored cavern of the bar, and perfect stereo music from two speakers, the roar, muted by the window, of the far-off capital, and on the ceiling the shadow play of car lights, *stay here—*

DO NOT OPEN UNTIL THE TRAIN STOPS!

Reddening wild roses around the steps up to the house, a pure kiss, a clean white apron, four heavy antique place settings, the clean smell of roast meat and the glass jug with the ten-crown note on the bottom, strong tan men in clean white shirts on red garden chairs under a green linden in the silence of an eternally blue canopy and clean sheets for the clean strawberry loving of purity itself, *or here—*

NICHT ÖFFNEN BEVOR DER ZUG HÄLT!

Arnostek and Janicka in Indian headbands took Lida captive at the edge of the woods and led her through the tall grass to her martyr's stake, Arnostek expertly tied up his mother with the laundry cord while Janicka approached her with a box of clothes pins, she attached the first one to the hem of her skirt, she attached the second to her shin, "That hurts—" Lida cried, "you're leaving again, don't go—," *how 'bout here—*

NE PAS OUVRIR AVANT L'ARRET DU TRAIN!

Tanicka's eager face turned upwards toward the window of the car, the train stops here for just two minutes, her slender shoulders and slim body at the very start of its life, hungry for instruction, eager to give itself and to go through the entire alphabet, "Everything is so terrifically wonderful—," *here—*

NON APRIRE PRIMA CHE IL TRENO SIA FERMO!

"I'm so huungry—" cried Mojmira from the exit of Brno Main Station, right across the street in the airline building the heavy chrome swinging doors stirred, for a moment a red No. 1 streetcar passed and hid the view, we used to ride that line to and from our school, that line goes past the theater and the Kiosk to the old Luzanky Park behind my home, I have a room there all to myself, a desk and a lamp that illuminates just the surface of the desk, and on the wall a wooden saber and a globe from Dad, with a briefcase in his hand an air force officer jumped off the platform of the streetcar and ran straight this way, Mojmira drew Jacek to the left toward the Petrov buffet and Jacek kept looking back, the red streetcar was pulling away, he had time to jump on, and on the other side the heavy chrome swinging doors into the airline building stirred and remained ajar, "Watch where you're going!—" Mojmira shouted when Jacek, still looking back, banged into a passerby, "That's just what I'm doing," said Jacek and Mojmira had to drag him by force into the Petrov restaurant and up to the second floor.

"Since when do you drink red wine?" Mojmira wondered aloud when Jacek ordered some. "In the army I was once a commissary officer and each branch of the service had different rations. The pilots had it best, they got chocolate, red wine, and game," Jacek explained to her.

Just then in the entry two noncoms in blue-grey uniforms stopped, they had submachine guns and red armbands, and Jacek stiffened, "A patrol," Mojmira said, the airmen gave a sharp look over the room, "An escort," Jacek whispered. "They must be looking for someone who's gone AWOL," Mojmira laughed. "I know him," said Jacek, "perfectly now," and at once he got up, "I'll be right back," he said and smiled at Mojmira, "I'll be back again," and he went out of the restaurant behind the two men and down the stairs to the street, the escort stopped in front of the Petrov and Jacek ran on alone, he made his way through the crowd and rushed through the heavy chrome swinging doors, down the corridor, through the doors with wings painted on them, and up to the counter, "A ticket, please."

"Where to?" asked a girl in a blue-grey uniform.

"To Brno!—" and Jacek bit his lips, we're *in* Brno—but the girl was not the least bit surprised, and quite matter-of-factly she asked: "From where and on what day?"

"From Usti, but no, there's no airport there. From Prague. For October 1, in the morning."

The girl turned a circular ticket holder and from one of the compartments she took out a ticket and stamped it. "Ninety-two crowns," she said and Jacek paid, well, if you want to fly you have to buy a ticket, how magically simple it all is—

On the street Jacek remembered Mojmira and shrugged his shoulders, we've got less than twenty-four hours and many matters need to be taken care of, R 7 leaves in eighteen minutes so let's hurry and look for the white plush, Jacek bounded into the store across from the station, they didn't have any white plush, next door our toy shop's display window and Jacek bounded in, "No water pistols, no squirrels, something different—" and he bought a brand new novelty, Arf-Arf, a rubber dog that's supposed to bark, there was no time to try it because in eleven minutes R 7 pulled out, the last train in our direction.

In Prague Jacek ran through the park from one station to the other and as usual he boarded the 4:45 to Berlin with time to spare, the white plush we can buy in Brno and send it back by mail, and the train pulled quietly out along the shallows and sands of the ebbing river.

And on streetcar No. 5 to Vseborice, to the last stop, and past the children's playground, on the broad roadway neighbor Tosnar was waddling with his six daughters, there are as many conceptions of paradise as there are people, the staircase up to the apartment has turned into a tall barrier, Jacek took out of his pocket the ring with its flock of keys, it's this one with the letters FAB and the dog's head, on the way out toss it into the mailbox downstairs, on the door ENGINEER JAROMIR JOST, in Brno we'll have new business cards printed, day after tomorrow is the first of October and the flight—

A diminutive ghost emerged from the dusk of the quiet apartment, "They left me here so the water the giblets are cooking in wouldn't boil away...," Tomas Roll whimpered.

"Where are they all?"

"With Trost... She didn't even buy your milk..."

Every decision destroys all doubts with retroactive effect, at least there'll be quiet for packing, Jacek drew his suitcase out of the chest like a sword from its sheath, everything in it was long since packed and the space perfectly utilized to the last inch as with a cosmonaut's luggage, Jacek took off his shoes and for the last time picked up the suede shoes he'd been married in, still the same as they'd been five years ago, a sense of horror, how awfully permanent the LEAVE things are, he trembled and cautiously put the shoes away.

Outside the door a child's voice, the little one's here, and he fished out of the black traveling satchel—it's served us now for the last time, and Jacek trembled—the box with the new toy, Arf-Arf, he tore it open and rushed to try it out at once, the white rubber dog had a label stuck to it—

> WARNING: *The balloon installed in our product is made of low-grade rubber, which stiffens in freezing temperatures. In severe cold Arf-Arf will not bark. In winter or other cold a strong pressure on the front paws can tear Arf-Arf apart. Do not use our product in severe cold.*
> Co-op Trendex

A rattling in the doorlock and Trost was the first to enter the kitchen: "Ah—Mr. Jost!" "Ah—Mr. Trost!"

"Did you catch the 4:45 to Berlin in Prague?"

"Sure. Of course."

"You make the trip often, don't you?"

"That's just what I don't like."

"The weather's nice, isn't it?"

"It is now. Look, little one, what Daddy brought you—this is Arf-Arf, you see? You push it here—this way—and see how it barks!"

"I'll bark it—" said Lenicka, she snatched Arf-Arf up in her awkward paws, she pressed—crack! and that was the end of its barking. Now Arf-Arf was dismembered and contemptuously Lenicka tossed aside the new toy from Brno.

"I asked for white plush in Brno, but they didn't have any, but—"

"You didn't have to," said Lenka. "Mr. Trost's having dinner here this evening."

"I'm not hungry," said Jacek and with his kitchen chair and a pack of cigarettes he went out onto the balcony.

A minute later a scratching on the glass balcony door, Tomas Roll stole out and whispered: "She bought him a side of pork and now she's putting it into the oven..."

"I wouldn't mind having some," sighed Jacek, "but I couldn't stand sharing a table with that— Tom, bring me something to eat."

Nimbly the imp ran off and in a while he returned with a bottle of Georgian cognac, "Lenka sent this, Mr. Jost, she says it's your favorite food, and Trost was laughing."

"Get a glass for yourself, too," said Jacek, the dwarf ran off and at once came back with a second pot-bellied glass, "They're making liver and bacon for supper," he whispered as he poured, "and roasted potatoes. I wanted to scrape them, but Trost took the scraper away from me and even shook his fist at me."

"So pour some more. And then bring me the sleeping bag from the cellar and a blanket from the bedroom, I'm going to sleep out here tonight."

Nine-by-twelve feet of squeaking planks, but the squeaking's ours, and a roughed-up desk made of soft wood, but the Germans weren't the ones who roughed it up like that, and on the plant stand the new blue-grey Zeta, to tell the truth it has a very hard action and this elite type is so unpleasant to read, besides that you could still read the seventh carbon from the Urania, Jacek sighed as he wrote up his final travel report, pulled it out of the roller, and inserted a blank resignation form

**Name of resignee:**  Jaromir Jost
**Born:** Brno 1933
**Reason for resignation:**

and Jacek pushed down the space bar again and again
with his finger, Good God, what can I write on the spur
of the moment—that competition is a perfectly adequate
and valid reason, of course—Petrik Hurt bounded into
his office and straight to the phone, "Verka...," he lisped
into the receiver, "of course it's Petrik, Verka, the sun just
began to shine in the color room and I rushed here to tell
you—" and already Petrik was lying again, minute after
minute.

Vitenka Balvin bounded into the office and straight up
to Jacek, Jacek tore the resignation form out of the
machine and threw it into the wastebasket, "You're the
light-fingered expert here," Vitenka Balvin roared, "tell
me where I can find some green paint." "Polak's got
some in the workshop. Are you tired of that purple color
in your room?" "It's the most disgusting color imaginable," Vitenka exulted, "I'm doing the entire apartment over in green, the entire apartment, both rooms and
the whole bathroom and the whole kitchen and the whole
john, it'll all be green as May—" "I'm amazed, Vitenka,
won't Mija miss her beautiful pure cerise?" "I found her
out—" Vitenka whispered ecstatically, "I suspected it all
along..." "Found her out?" "She took one tile off my
isolation wall and put her ear to it, it wasn't really all the
same to her what I was up to, nor was I really all that indifferent to her antics, and I caught her at it. She turned
completely white, grabbed the scissors—" "That's the
second time, I believe—" "I've still got the scar from the
first time, look—but this time she didn't stab me. You say
Polak's got some," and Vitenka ran off, "... and then let's
go boating," Petrik Hurt was still on the phone, he
glanced at his watch, "but first I'll buy you some ice
cream..."

"Are you hooked up with that artificial limb again?" Jacek grinned when Petrik had finished the long conversation.

"Don't ever say that to me again!" said Petrik Hurt impetuously, "or to anybody else, understand?!"

"But excuse me, I was just quoting you..."

"You must have been imagining things, Jacek."

"Or you've been, no?"

"Perhaps, why not? Everything's relative, who knows where imagination ends and true... the true... Don't you ever imagine anything?"

"Right now, in fact: I've bought an airplane ticket to Brno for tomorrow."

"But the firm can't reimburse you for that," Petrik Hurt said in a voice suddenly that of an office superior.

"Just ninety-two crowns to get rid of a clown like you, it's a real bargain," Jacek felt like saying, but Petr Hurt's got to sign our travel order for tomorrow, no, now he no longer has to, but he does have to sign our resignation—

"They're saying in the director's office," Petrik Hurt began slowly, "that you're overdoing it a bit with those trips to Brno. I won't ask you about anything yet, but watch out, Jacek..."

Petr Hurt left and listlessly Jacek opened the drawer with the resignation form, it wasn't getting any easier to fill it out like this in a rush, under it lay six blue envelopes, six cancellation letters to six unsuspecting naiads, the seventh Tina by telephone, just then the phone rang and there was Tina's familiar subdued voice, this really is telepathy or mysticism, "I can't come today, I'm on the eve of a big trip," Jacek said into the receiver, "I'll write you." We've already written letters to the others and all we have to do is throw them into the mailbox, the resignation can also be mailed—Jacek filled it out, signed it, and put it in an envelope addressed to Cottex, seven letters in all and he put them into his breast-pocket folder, in its soft black leather a white ticket:

Date: 10/1/66
**Route:** OK 035
**Sector: Prague-Brno**
**Airport bus departs:** 7:15 a.m.
**Flight departure:** 8:15 a.m.
Check all data at time of purchase.
No subsequent adjustments.
**CZECHOSLOVAK AIRLINES**

Seven blue envelopes are seven possible lives, seven freedoms taken together are no more than one aggravated solitary confinement with a crazy dream for every day of the week, but in the morning you've got to wake up and get to your feet—

"Express call to Prague, Czechoslovak Airlines," Jacek placed the call and before it came he shuffled the seven blue envelopes like cards, why not this one, that one, or these two, what a frightful risk it would be to waste another fifteen years of one's life, the last ones, then we'll be fifty already, why just these two, that one, this one, or this one here, and quite different ones would reply if an ad were placed on a different day and, perhaps, in a different paper, must DIFFERENT always be BETTER—

"Czechoslovak Airlines? Jost. I have a reservation for Brno tomorrow. Can I still get a refund?"

"If the passenger notifies us less than three hours and at least fifteen minutes before departure, he can claim a refund with a twenty-five-percent penalty. Does that answer your question?"

"Completely."

When a siren sounded, Jacek walked out slowly through the ridged mud toward the porter's gate and toward the corner with the orange mailbox, he took the seven blue envelopes out of his folder and raised the first one up to the slot,

Miss Nadezda Houskova

on his last visit Nada had dragged her new vacuum cleaner out of the box under the daybed and for the first time she'd turned it on, its nozzle had rattled over the old planks of the floor and Nada had started to sing to its rattle, *our first carpet*, BUT I'VE GOT ONE ALREADY, AT HOME—

Jacek took a deep breath and dropped envelope after envelope into the slot, Miss Nadezda Houskova, Dr. Anna Bromova, Miss Hanicka Kohoutkova, Mrs. Lida Adalska, Miss Tanicka Rambouskova, Dr. Mojmira Stratilova, Cottex, Usti nad Labem— wait on the last one, that one we have to keep for a while and if we still make the flight, just for the fun of it, we won't come back from Brno until we find that white plush, hell, we've been in cotton for ten years, and when we can scare up three carloads of ethyl acetate from West Germany— and the seventh one, Tina by phone. Now only the white plush, a trifle, it's nothing actually—

It glows softly on our kitchen table, soft as the fleece of the most highly bred Australian merino lamb, how supple and delicate the cloth is, in fascination Lenka takes it in her hands and strokes it, Lenicka insists on stroking it right away, and Grandma strokes it too—in his blue-grey denim shirt Trost grins triumphantly over the entire scene.

"It was nothing at all," he blares, "by chance I was passing by and I said, Hey, they've got it here—where but in that new store right down the street—"

"Don't touch that with your dirty hands!" Lenka told Jacek, it would be a coat for Lenicka and because of it Lenicka "woves Uncle Twost!" and how unwilling she is to come and play with Daddy in the living room, she no longer wants to go through the obstacle course, "So wet's pway house, OK?" Jacek lisped ingratiatingly, "wet's put up our pwayhouse—"

And right away, so that Lenicka wouldn't run off after Trost, pull the mattresses from the couch onto the floor, Tomas Roll is an irreplaceable helper in all this, and Lenicka doesn't run off because Trost and Lenka have now come into the living room for her, the mattresses turn into the walls of our cottage, the coverlet into the roof, and the cushions into a balcony, "I'll build you a finer one, out of wood, a real one—" Trost wooed and pursued Lenicka.

"We've got our pwayhouse all weady, cwawl into it, wittle one—," but Lenicka suddenly preferred "a weal one out of wood," "Just cwawl into ours, wook, Daddy's cwawling in and he's waiting for you there—" "Your feet stick out, Daddy—" the little one laughed. "And it's a bit flimsy, look here—" Trost brayed and he smacked the house with his knee, a mattress collapsed on Jacek's back, the second one fell under the weight of the coverlet, and fumbling Jacek was entangled in the blanket like a gladiator in a retiarius's net, above him guffaws and horselaughter, and with difficulty he crawled out into the light, "Let's do the obstacle course now, little one—" and with the dwarf's devoted assistance the two mattresses were laid flat on the floor and the third one perpendicular between them, quick, on the double, but Lenicka had already turned her back on the two frenzied builders and behind her Lenka and Trost brought up the rear of the procession, Jacek was left beside his obstacle course face to face with his pygmy. The dwarf croaked and walked over it on his hands, a somersault and he lay on his back like an overturned beetle.

Jacek took a pack of cigarettes onto the balcony, he lit them one after another and blew the smoke out toward the sky, at least there's the advantage that Trost won't be gawking at us from his window across the way now that he's safely within our own walls and behind our back, at least there's an unimpeded view of the eighty windows, let's have a look, but who's that on the fourth floor of section two in the fourth window from the left—some fellow our age is sitting there on his balcony, smoking and gaping straight this way, "Cognac!" Jacek roared into the apartment and the imp brought some quickly, this time with two glasses, "It's the last bottle," he whispered, "they're carving the side of pork for him now and Grandma's opening some beer for him, they wouldn't give me any."

Jacek drank the last bottle from the warm slopes of Georgia and lit one cigarette after another, the dwarf kept running out onto the balcony with new reports, "He's taken your chair, Jacek, you shouldn't stand for it!" "So pull it out here!" and the pygmy ran back to the kitchen but soon he returned without the chair, "He didn't want to give it to me, he's already sitting on it," he announced, "and he's eating that side of pork with his fingers and Lenka's laughing at him, but not maliciously, and Grandma said: that's right, a man takes meat in his hands, and Lenicka's laughing and Trost is feeding her like you do an animal, with his fingers..."

"Go tell her that I don't think children should eat fatty pork. She'll get sick on it! And have them send out that ham in the pantry!"

The dwarf ran off and came right back, "They say the ham's for Lenicka's lunch and Trost says that you can easily buy your own when you have so much left over from your travel expenses, he says the child needs it more than you do and Grandma says that's God's sacred truth and Lenka nods and Lenicka says we won't give Daddy any ham."

"Bring her here!"

The dwarf ran off and came right back, "She's eating now and they won't let her go and they said we shouldn't nag them anymore."

"This is my home—" Jacek stormed gloomily and he took a drink straight from the bottle, "go back, Tom, and tell them..."

The faithful imp went on carrying messages and he kept bringing back worse and worse reports from occupied territory, Trost in the kitchen was like the Vandals in Rome and Jacek on the balcony resembled the last Byzantine emperor, "Bring me my daughter!—" he roared at last when he'd finished the bottle.

The dwarf finally succeeded in bringing Lenicka all the way through the living room and up to the glass door, throughout the journey she'd resisted with a fearful screeching and now Trost appeared, behind him Grandma and Lenka, without getting up Jacek opened the door from the balcony to the living room.

"Let the kid go, OK?!" Trost roared at Tomas Roll, but the dwarf went on trying to bring the child to its father, he seized it in his gorilla-like arms, but Trost stormed out in open battle and began to shake the dwarf violently and Lenicka fled, "We're fed up with you, up to the neck!" Trost thundered at the imp, "Uncle Woll go way!" Lenicka shouted, "It's high time now," Grandma said and Lenka nodded, "Do you hear?!" Trost roared, "Clear out—" and he grabbed the pygmy by the shoulder, the imp jerked loose but Trost snagged him around the waist, the dwarf had powerful arms but his body was skinny and his legs were like a child's, laughing Trost picked him up and carried him out.

Jacek followed them slowly down the stairs, already Trost was coming up the stairs and Jacek was forced to make way for him, on the concrete roadway Tomas Roll was dusting off his black sweater and his black jeans, "Forgive me, Tom," Jacek said sympathetically, "I'm terribly sorry but..."

"Go to hell, Mr. Jost!" Tomas Roll said firmly, he jumped into his red Fiat and this time without any honk-honk he drove quickly through the development, Jacek dragged himself towards the main highway, the Fiat was now no more than a red period at the end of a fairy tale, our *let it happen* is gone, what will come now, right in front of Jacek a bus stopped and the door opened automatically, listlessly Jacek glanced at the tin stairs and mechanically climbed them up to the metal platform, "Last stop," he told the driver and paid three crowns.

Along the row of old chestnut trees, around the gas works and the pyramid of dead soil torn from the earth, the monument with the moldering lion, what time can do

to metal, the linden tree with its sign and on the slope of
the hill our yellow retreat, but it isn't ours, it's only
rented, and Jacek rode on to the end of the line, tore his
way through the underbrush and over rocks upward until
a swift stream stopped him, the strong whirl of white
foam over well-washed boulders, the water rushed over
pebbles and was quiet only in the sandy shallows, once
there were no valleys, only mountain chains, and their
peaks sprouted up from the depths of the earth, but time
and water had divided mountain from mountain and cut
into them ever more deeply and wide, what fate was the
water preparing for the rock, how systematically it carried out its fearful, patient torture, rock turns against its
fellow rock, thigh-joint crushes collar-bone, rib pierces
shoulder-blade, and the vertebrae mill themselves into
bone meal, sand is the epilogue of the rigid mountain,
sandstorms appease entropy with time, and duration is
the highway to a desert.

Over the mountain stream it began to get dark, the
foamy water caressed the rocks and rubbed off molecule
after molecule, the monotonous splash of the irreversible
victory of water, but one thinking man with a pick and
shovel has power enough compared with the division of
mountains and the diversion of waters.

Jacek came back on the last bus and silently he walked
through the apartment that bore his nameplate and out
onto his balcony, to fly or not to fly, not to fly is the end,
but how to take off, down from the mountains a heavy
cloud front had covered the whole sky and suddenly it
began to thunder, the first drops fell on Jacek's feet and
he didn't bother to draw them in, after all, a man doesn't
dissolve in water, Lenka came through the door out onto
the balcony, it flashed and thundered again, now right
above their heads, and Lenka fled the balcony, my wife is
afraid of storms and inside Lenicka squeals with terror.

"It ain't nothing—" Trost bawled over the storm and he
led the frightened Lenka back onto the balcony, "rain-
water gives you a pretty mug—," Trost neighed like a

horse and he leaned out over the rail, he let the heavy drops of water fall on his face, beneath the protecting arch formed by his body the now calm and laughing Lenka took the laundry down from the line and with cries of joy Lenicka caught the water in her palms.

"Come in," Lenka called onto the balcony late that evening, "he's gone."

Jacek put the mattresses from the obstacle course back onto the couch and sat heavily down on it, late at night Lenka came for him in her blue-grey apron and Jacek went down before her on his knees.

"I understand, Jacek," Lenka whispered, "you're not happy at home anymore and you're afraid to admit it—we can't go on like this any longer. I won't drive you away, but it might be better for everybody if you were to go yourself."

CATAPULTED and in his soul there sounded forth a military anthem, CAPTAIN, TOMORROW I FLY—

"Tomorrow I'm flying to Brno, and please..."

"Two white shirts in your satchel, and no lunch. And this—" and Lenka pulled out of the pocket of her blue-grey apron a small clay monster with many pairs of eyes, the good-hearted imp had given us an ocarina.

"I'm flying with my suitcase, it's already packed."


## VI — twenty-three

The unbuttoned iridescent raincoat shows off the suede leather of the jacket and the narrow stripe of the black leather tie highlights the dazzling whiteness of the nylon shirt, Graduate Fellow (today was October 1) Engineer Jaromir Jost clicked his tongue in the mirror, walked with his suitcase slowly up the steps to Platform Two at Usti Main Station, and at 5:14 he left on the R 10 express to Prague.

Sitting by the window, facing forward, Jacek read the headlines of the newspaper and glanced at the back page of the *Black Chronicle,*

> *Although 24-year-old Ludovit Feher did not know how to swim, he attempted to cross the fish pond near Turnanske Podhradi on a raft. He fell into the water and drowned.*

From Prague Central Station to the airline building, in the airport bus no one asked him for his ticket and by comparison with the sooty train station the airport was like a concert hall, outside on the other side of the red-and-white railing as far as the eye could see in all directions a concrete wasteland of runways for takeoff and landing, a yellow truck drives among the waiting planes and a red lead car with FOLLOW ME in big letters rushes toward the horizon.

Roaring, a giant Pan Am Boeing taxied in, slowly turned, and was silent, a motorized stairway pulled up and passenger after passenger stepped out, the first one looked familiar, it was the thirty-three-year-old atomic physicist Jozef, he jumped nimbly down onto the tarmac and already a cluster of people was bounding up to him, "Excuse me, please—" Jacek overheard his sharp voice and now he was running up the stairs to a waiting Aeroflot TU-104A, immediately the heavy metal doors closed behind him, the TU-104A began to thunder, made its turn, and with a roar it taxied toward the runway.

"Passengers for Brno OK oh three five—" and impatiently Jacek ran toward his plane, we want to be first and get a seat by the window, he handed the stewardess his ticket and rushed up the motorized stairway to our highest beach, made of aluminum, the passengers took their seats, the bang of the door could be heard, and three men in blue-grey uniforms walked down the aisle, which of them is the captain—

The roar of the motors made the cigar-shaped cabin vibrate and outside the window the red warning lights were already flashing in the grass along the runway, signs were lit up front on the wall of the pilot's cabin, on the left PRIPOUTEJTE SE—NADET REMNI—FASTEN SAFETY BELTS and quickly Jacek threw the linen straps over his stomach and drew them tight through the aluminum safety catch, on the right a sign was lit up NEKOURIT—NE KURIT—NO SMOKING and Jacek quickly put out his last Carmen cigarette, meanwhile we've already taken off, almost without noticing it, and Jacek glanced at his fellow passengers, no one had bothered to fasten his seat belt and a man across the aisle was even smoking a big fat cigar.

Outside the window the bluest blue-blue sky and below the blindingly bright wing that land a hundred times traversed and conquered, a desk like a steamship, on the first, glassed-in deck a regular library, on the upper deck two telephones, a metal vase for a smoke-stack, and as a mast towering above it all a magnificent *Palma areca*, a morning cigarette in the colorists' lab, in front of the windows they've torn down a factory chimney which had interfered with the clarity of the hues, in a hot bath a porcelain vessel with our own creation the color of flesh, and drying on a wooden stand Spanish moss, passion auburn, and Victoria blue, the garlands, salvos, tricklings, tremblings, shocks, and caressings of light among the grey fur of the lichens on the trunks in the trampoline of wet pine needles, the forest as recluse and the forest as multitude, the yellow Parisian sky of tin over the narrow creaking bed of young hunger, ten times happy and each time in a different place, how short a distance it is to Brno, how grotesque this miniature land-scape, cars like tiny grains and that line below is the train line, are ten happinesses more or less than one, today the Balvins are beginning to repaint their whole apartment green and Petrik Hurt goes on deluding himself, but isn't a lifetime of self-delusion one of the possible ways to take life firmly in one's hands, where anyway, in this age of relativity, is the boundary between certainty and self-delusion, obligation of course deprives, but isn't freedom just the maximum degree of deprivation, certainly also the maximum number of optional paths, but in the end one can follow only one of them, the extended freedom of a run-away rabbit in other people's gardens or the contracted state of a gardener at home, and Lenka has already planted apple trees on our piece of ground, all three of us have lain together on the grass and from every side the scent of the hair of a loved one, on our own earth FROM WHICH WE COME our daughter slept her beauty sleep and on the other side of the wall we came together, our longing contained within an order, how much happiness will be left outside such an order—

Into the frosty blue space outside the window short lashes of flame from the two tubes on the wing and in his deep seat, in horror, Jacek pressed his hand to his throat, the hecatombs of the primordial ocean are buried deep in the earth under heavy pressure, locked between the Miocene and Carboniferous ages rest the masses of the detrital waters and their sands, and when hit by a bore through a seam they burst into a destructive flood which puts an end to all mining activity, in a second the wooden matchsticks and metal wires of presumptuous mining engineering are swept away, divinely, banally I love my wife with whom I live and have a child, and my picture is only in my head, an inconceivable cut-out from a family portrait, never with anyone else but you, Lenunka, my love, I must tell you WHO WE ARE, we Josts, Daddy only played for a time at being a traveler, a sailor, and a pilot, we're at Brno already, how terribly short a flight it was—

The plane was landing at the Brno airport, with a jerk Jacek unhooked his linen belt, got up, and started toward the aisle, "Are you crazy, fellow—" his neighbor snapped at him, but without ceremony Jacek stepped over his neighbor's knees and forced his way out, it was dangerous to delay, so quick, let's be the first to the exit and we'll be in time to buy a ticket for the return flight home on this very plane, everyone is hurrying home to his

Lenickas and Lenkas, I'll be the first and by the shortest route, down with the net and the rough chin on the sweet little tummy, nothing's so sweet to kiss as our little one, and hold her hand till she falls asleep with her thumb in her mouth, this very afternoon we three can go to the pond and the movies and the swings, first I'll buy both of you ice cream and we'll take the little one to the pâtisserie, Daddy knows how much you love store-bought pastry, WHERE ARE WE FLYING— but Jacek flew on alone.

With the warning signs lit up PRIPOUTEJTE SE—NADET REMNI—FASTEN SAFETY BELTS, with thirty-nine seated passengers and one standing, the plane was landing at the Brno airport and as it set down there was an insignificant retardation of the hydraulic system on the wheels, the wheels revolved only a fraction of a second late and the plane was arrested for just a fraction of a second. But Jacek flew on. The unbelted passengers jerked slightly in their seats and then the plane glided along the ground in perfect order. But Jacek flew down the aisle, the tremendous force of inertia catapulted him forward towards the metal steps, and his face traveled up them as far as the metal platform in front of the captain's cabin.

The plane slowed down, turned, stopped, and its engines fell silent. The captain turned off the warning signs and came out of his cabin. From their seats the passengers lifted themselves and their terrified voices.

✈

**Vladimír Páral** is the author of eleven novels; *Catapult* is his third. Although the novels he published in the 1960s burlesqued and criticized the contemporary world, they were sufficiently apolitical to be published, and they were extremely popular both at home and in translation. *Catapult* is the first of Páral's novels to be translated into English. It won the award presented by the Czechoslovak Youth League to the best novel of the year.

**William Harkins** is chairman of the Slavic Languages Department at Columbia University and of the American Committee of Slavists. He has translated *Three Comic Poems* by A. S. Pushkin, and *May* by the Czech poet Karel Macha. He is also the author of *Karel Čapek* and the editor of *Czech Prose: An Anthology*.

*Garrigue Books* is the imprint for Catbird's translations from the Czech and Slovak languages, as well as for its books on Czechoslovak history and culture. The name Garrigue is meant to honor the American who became most deeply involved with Czechoslovakia: Charlotte Garrigue. Born and raised in a French Huguenot family in Brooklyn, New York, Charlotte Garrigue married Thomas Masaryk, a young Moravian (Moravia was then part of Austria; it is now the central section of Czechoslovakia) whom she met while studying in Germany. During the First World War, the imprisonment of Charlotte Garrigue Masaryk and her daughter by the Austrian government led to mass protests by women's groups in the United States. When, in 1918, Thomas Masaryk became the father and first president of Czechoslovakia, Charlotte Garrigue became the nation's first first lady.

Thomas Masaryk took the name Garrigue as his middle name. Taking his wife's maiden name was at least as unusual in nineteenth-century Austria as it would be today in the United States.

✈

This book was set by Axiom Design Systems in New York City via Ventura Publisher and Postscript. The typefaces are: regular text, Palatino; titles, Avant Garde; mock typewriter, Courier. The book was designed by Robert Wechsler. It was printed and bound at R. R. Donnelley & Sons' Harrisonburg, Virginia plant. It is printed on Sebago acid-free paper.